THE BRIDGE

A NOVEL

BY JILL COX

TOWER
19
PRESS

ISBN 978-0-9982200-0-0 (print)
ISBN 978-0-9982200-1-7 (digital)

Dancing couple vector © Shutterstock
Eiffel Tower vector © Shutterstock
Arrow vector © Creative Market

Cover design by Eddie Renz | Chemist Creative
Author portrait by Mike and ReJana Krause | BluDoor Studios
Tower 19 Press logo by Tarran Turner

Printed in the United States of America

For my parents
I love you with my whole heart and half of Meredith's

one

Pythagoras believed that three is the perfect number. Maybe he was right, or maybe he was the original Jedi Master. Whatever the reason, the number three is everywhere.

Three blind mice. Three wishes. Three's a crowd.

The third time's the charm. The third degree. The third wheel.

You can't blame a girl named Mer-e-dith Fi-o-na Sul-li-van for noticing this phenomenon. We moved to Oregon from Ireland in March, three months after my third birthday. I graduated third in my high school class – all of the hard work, none of the glory.

At Highgate College, French majors have three choices if we want to study abroad. Most people choose to spend the summer before junior year at Highgate's campus in the picturesque French town of Tours. Or, if you prefer a semester in France, you can tag along with another school's program – but their credits rarely transfer, which might explain the popularity of Highgate's summer program.

But the third choice? The one every French major fights tooth and nail to get? The coveted Beckett Endowment Scholarship, which provides room, board, travel expenses, and tuition for three Highgate students at the prestigious Centre Lafayette in Paris.

The Centre Lafayette gears its yearlong program toward an elite group of students from several top American schools. Classes are taught exclusively in French, and they're so rigorous that at the end of the year, you have fifteen course credits rather than ten. Which explains why there's a qualifying exam: a three-hour, yank-out-your-teeth-with-a-monkey-wrench kind of test that I spent every free second preparing myself for last year.

And that hard work paid off. Somehow last spring, I'd scored high enough to wrangle one of the Beckett scholarships. I still had no idea whether I'd placed first, second, or third, but it didn't matter; once we made it to this level, we were no longer competitors.

This year's Highgate delegation? Marshall Freeman, Dan Thomas, *et moi*. Champions of *Liberté, Égalité,* and *Fraternité.*

But for some reason this year, Highgate decided at the last minute to send a *fourth* student. Why would they throw off the system like that? Four is not perfect. Four is a freaking trapezoid.

So as the flight attendants began closing the overhead bins on our Paris-bound plane, I stood and turned to peer over my seatback at Marshall, the only other Highgate student onboard. I smiled and waved while he shoved a handful of kale chips in his mouth. Ranch-flavored, judging by the scent wafting my way.

"So, Marshall," I asked as casually as possible. "Any idea why they're mixing things up this year with a fourth delegate?"

"Uh, no. Do you know who it is?"

"No." I tapped my finger against my lower lip. "I'm still trying to figure out what happened. It couldn't have been a tiebreaker. They would have made the bottom two students take a new version of the test. What's your theory?"

Marshall had just pushed himself to a standing position when his mouth suddenly shifted into a grin. I guess the kale leaf covering his eyetooth distracted me temporarily because it took me one beat too long to notice we were no longer alone.

"Hey, Sully." I turned to find Pete Russell and that semi-permanent smirk of his I'd grown to despise. "You guys didn't have to stand to greet me. This isn't First Class."

No way. Someone had to be pranking me right now. Pete Russell was Lucky Number Four?

If I'd majored in something noble, like environmental science, I would be on a flight to Antarctica right now, or Ushuaia. Or even the Bikini Atoll. Sure, I might have died early from radiation poisoning there, but at least I could have skipped hours of buckled-in mental torture six inches away from the ultimate frat boy.

Pete watched me for a second, then laughed. That full-throated, you're-such-an-idiot chuckle of his that made me want to suffocate him in his own simpering glibness. As he shoved his ancient-looking duffel bag into the overhead bin right next to my brand new black leather tote, I slid back down into my seat and stifled my rage. In what bizarro universe did Highgate College's best and brightest include a kale-addicted simpleton and the reigning buffoon of Sigma Phi Beta?

"Lucky you, Freeman," Pete said over the headrest as the purser called the flight attendants to order. "Looks like you've got the whole row to yourself."

JILL COX

Through the crack between the seats, I heard (and smelled) Marshall's sigh of relief. "You think?"

"I *know*. That aisle seat was assigned to Dan Thomas, but he flew over early with his parents for some conference they had to attend. Hey, man – you got something…" Pete made a scratching motion against his tooth, then glanced down at me and smirked again.

I glared at Pete as he finally turned around and settled in beside me, scrolling through his phone. What sort of loophole had qualified Pete Freaking Russell for this moment? Okay, yes – he spouted doctoral-level insight every day in French lit class. But every other time I saw him on campus, he was either cheering on a food fight or quoting random scenes from a movie only morons enjoyed.

This guy was the boorish bane of my existence. And now he was following me to Paris.

A grin began to tug at his lips as he spoke without looking up from his phone. "You know you're staring at me, right? I mean, don't get me wrong, Sully. I like this effect I'm having on you as much as the next guy, but there's no reason you can't parcel out your admiration in tiny segments throughout the flight."

I shoved in my earbuds, turning my whole body toward the window as we taxied down the runway. As I fidgeted with the silver charm bracelet on my wrist, I thought back to dinner last night at Sullivan's, the Irish pub my parents owned on the Oregon coast.

My brother Ian had driven all the way back home from Seattle on Friday so he could chauffeur me over to the Portland airport today. And last night after my dad's extra-long prayer, Ian had slid a small black velvet box toward me. Inside, tucked under a dozen twenty-euro bills, lay a silver charm bracelet with a tiny fairy attached. Not the cartoonish kind, but something he'd picked up this summer when he'd been in the Orkney Islands updating the Scotland guidebook for work.

Oh, that clever brother of mine. Anyone else might have thought I had a Tinkerbell fixation, but the two of us knew the truth. *Fée* in French meant fairy. Just close enough to my nickname to be perfect. With my mom's blue eyes brimming over, Ian clasped the bracelet around my wrist, shifting the fairy charm right to the center.

"Your job this year, Fee, is to fill this bracelet with silver charms from every place you visit. I've started you off with this one, but the rest is up to you. Italy for spring break, London for the weekend – wherever you like. All I ask is that you put this handful of euros to good use. Don't go wasting it all on coffee. Not even in Paris."

The plane had just leveled off to its cruising altitude when I felt Pete Russell's eyes boring into the side of my head. I yanked out my earbuds and jerked my head his way. "You do know you're staring at me, right? There's no reason you can't parcel out your admiration in tiny segments, you know."

He lifted his hands in mock surrender. "Touché, Sully. I'm just sitting here listening to Marshall chomping his chips behind us while I slowly decode a mystery about you."

"And what is that?"

A grin spread to his cheeks, which were surprisingly less hairy than they'd been during last spring's Rumpelstiltskin phase. He was still sporting several days' worth of growth, but the only thing really left of his once monstrous beard was a bit of a soul patch. And then, as though he'd read my mind, Pete rubbed his chin and smiled even wider.

"The mystery," he smirked, "is that I always hear Drew Sutton on his phone with someone named Fee. Now that I've seen your bracelet, I get it. *Fée,* Fee. Very cute."

"It's not cute. It's none of your business. And since when do you know Drew?"

Pete scratched his soul patch again, sneering at me like a silent movie villain. Suddenly, all the missing pieces clicked together.

Sigma Phi Freaking Beta. My childhood friend Drew and *this* chucklehead were bros.

Why did I never remember those two were in the same fraternity? Probably because Drew and every other Sigma Phi I knew were the kind of guys who'd scrape off your windshield after an ice storm or climb a tree to save your cat. The types who always show up for a first date holding a dozen roses and wearing their nicest sweater.

Not Pete Russell. Most days, he looked like he'd crawled out of a yurt in the woods, thanks to his predilection for poorly groomed facial hair and his indiscriminate fashion sense.

While the captain gave the latest flying conditions over the intercom, I scanned Pete's outfit of the day: cargo pants, a black fleece covering up what I assumed was a Sigma Phi Beta formal t-shirt, light blue as always. No shock there. But then he'd completed his international flight ensemble with flip flops and a Peruvian chullo hat.

"Man, I'm beat." Pete tugged at the braids on his hat – left, right, left, right – so that his eyes barely showed below the brim. "I stayed up half the night packing only to discover a few of my things were still in storage at the Sigma Phi house. The guys had to help me dig through the basement this morning. Your boy Sutton was there. Did he tell you?"

"No. Maybe he was too distraught over the brand new Pete-shaped hole in his life."

Pete grinned lazily. "I doubt it. But he did make me promise to deliver a message if I saw you on the plane. I had to repeat it back to him five or six times until I got the words exactly right."

"Oh, yeah?" I tried to appear cool. "What was it?"

"I'd love to tell you, Fee, but my brain does not work on zero sleep," he yawned, pulling the brim of his hat all the way over his eyes. "Ask me tomorrow. I don't want to mess this one up."

And just like that, Pete Russell was out. No matter how many times Marshall said hello on his way to and from the lavatory, no matter how many times the plane bumped and shimmied, Pete hardly shifted, his arms crossed in triumph for the entire eleven-hour stretch. He didn't even snore. He just Sleeping Beauty-ed his way across the time zones, like this was his hundredth trip.

If he hadn't looked so rosy-cheeked and childlike, I might've shoved an earbud up his nose.

But then somewhere between the arrivals gate and the baggage claim at Charles de Gaulle, Pete disappeared. Disappeared, and never returned. Which gave me a while to think as Marshall and I waited in the taxi line. So I made a decision: it was time to stop sweating this four-person twist. Someone had made Paris possible for me, and I wouldn't allow anyone to ruin this year. Not even Pete Russell.

I touched my bracelet again, rubbing the tiny fairy charm between my fingers like a talisman against everything that might go wrong. This was Paris, and I was finally here.

Team Fee forever.

two

The Centre Lafayette was on the rue Guynemer in the sixth *arrondissement*, just across the street from Luxembourg Gardens. The modern façade was rather nondescript, but once you stepped through the heavy black doors it was like stepping back in time into an eighteenth-century hunting lodge – everything from floor-to-ceiling mahogany paneling to ornate doorknobs. Light poured in from a wall of glass at the far end of the entry hallway, and the energy created by all of the students milling around in the courtyard beyond reminded me of a movie set on some Ivy League campus in the 1950s.

From the outside, the Centre Lafayette could've been any old building, but on the inside? It was a charming little beehive, and I was in love.

I followed Marshall down a small passageway lined with hunter green ivy-patterned wallpaper into a cloakroom where everyone seemed to be storing their luggage. While Marshall found space for our bags, I continued on a few more steps until I stumbled upon a large, open room where several students were already seated.

The same deep mahogany paneling I'd seen in the foyer filled this space, except on the left where a glass wall revealed a staircase and three levels of quiet study rooms beyond. Twelve long, well-worn tables were set up in three distinct rows, with four or five metal chairs at each table – just enough for all fifty of us. All of the chairs faced a central dais near the far wall where a microphone and a projection screen stood at the ready. Every single sound echoed and bounced from the beautifully polished hardwood floor to the ceiling towering thirty feet above me. This had to be the famous *Grande Salle*.

Marshall still hadn't caught up to me, so I followed my nose down a few steps to a small room beyond. Yes! The famous coffee vending machine. No lie, the Centre Lafayette online forums had entire sub-chats dedicated to the drink options of this magical device. Sampling every flavor was at the top of my First-Week-in-Paris Bucket List.

While the inner mechanism whirred to life and brewed my first selection – *un café express* – the window panes thumped softly against the sills as a light breeze swept into the small room, carrying with it the tiniest whiff of baking bread. I stared out the open window into the courtyard beyond. A handful of green benches were scattered about, as well as three tiny white buildings on the far end that appeared to be garden sheds converted into classrooms.

I wanted to fly back in time and hug my younger self. She'd pushed me to come back to Paris every second of the past three and a half years. *Thank you,* I wanted to whisper. *You were so right.*

The sound of heels clacking on hardwood jarred me back to the present. I glanced down at my watch. How was it already almost eleven? I yanked my second cup of coffee – *un café au lait* – from the machine and zoomed back to the *Grande Salle*, plopping down next to Marshall just as the program director began her spiel.

"*Bienvenue, je m'appelle Madame Beauchamp,*" she was saying as I grabbed my notebook from my messenger bag. But for the next thirty seconds while I dug frantically for a pen, all I heard was *blah blah seminars, blah blah housing*. I'd spent an hour packing my school bag with this very moment in mind. Miss something in orientation, fail at life. So why hadn't I packed a pen?

My head was practically buried inside my bag when I heard the screech of metal against hardwood from the empty seat on my left. When I looked up, I saw Pete Russell dressed in a button-down shirt and nice jeans, holding the exact brand and color of pen I use. Every trace of the soul patch was gone, his face as smooth as a Marine's.

No sign of the chullo hat, either. I'd never seen Pete once without his chestnut hair in a mess, and now, it was cut so short that I almost did not recognize him. There was no way could have cut it this morning. He'd had enough time to shave, but not to do both.

"Everything okay, Sully?" For once, Pete wasn't smiling with his mouth but with his eyes. Huh. For two years, I'd been trying to figure out who he looked like, and now… whoa. I would never tell anyone this, but Pete looked so much like Chris Pratt, the two of them could be related.

Well, not completely. I was pretty sure Chris Pratt's eyes were green and Pete's were deep brown, like a golden retriever's or something. But they both had the same twinkle.

Hold on a minute. Since when did I notice Pete Russell's eyes twinkling? Gross. I needed a nap.

three

Pete didn't even try to contain his laughter when he handed over my pen. "You okay, Fee?"

"Don't call me that," I said under my breath. "Did you steal this from me on the plane?"

"Someone hasn't had enough coffee today," he sing-songed past me over to Marshall, then slid my half-empty cup toward me. "Drink up, old chap. We've got a long meeting ahead of us."

At the front of the room, Madame Beauchamp cleared her throat. "*Pardon, monsieur? Mademoiselle? S'il vous plaît?*"

Oh, this was *so* not how I wanted to start off the school year.

For the next ninety minutes, I did my best to focus while Madame Beauchamp prepared us for the following week. On Tuesday and Wednesday, we would have ten seminars total, each one a mini-presentation of the course offerings for this year. On Thursday morning, we'd select our year-long courses, immediately followed by a long weekend in Normandy with the entire Centre Lafayette faculty. The following Monday, September 4th, would be the official start of school.

About halfway through the meeting, I realized Pete and I weren't bumping elbows as we scribbled down our notes. Which meant I also noticed, for the very first time ever, that Pete was left-handed like me. What? How had I possibly missed *that* detail? Back at Highgate, I generally sat wherever he was *not*, but spotting lefties was my thing. There were so few of us around that I couldn't help myself.

Before she dismissed us, Madame Beauchamp handed out housing assignments for those who hadn't arranged their own apartments. I would be living in the *chambre de bonne* of a woman called Marie-France de Clavéry. Those were some pretty aristocratic sounding names she had. I imagined an old biddy with purple hair and a raspy voice from too many years of smoking wearing a cardigan sweater and pencil skirt. And maybe an Hermès scarf, a Birkin bag, and a beret, because when I stereotype, I cover all my bases.

By the time I returned to the cloakroom, Marshall was nowhere to be found, and Pete was dislodging my gigantic green suitcase from the fold. The one with the tattered Republic of Ireland patch.

"Let go of that," I screeched, jumping over two duffel bags, then overshooting the telescoping handle and smacking Pete in the gut with it. Hard.

"Whoa," he chuckled, holding me at arm's length by my shoulder. "I know you hate to get on the teacher's bad side, Fee, but violence is never the answer."

"Sorry," I muttered. Even though I definitely was *not*.

Pete deftly maneuvered the suitcase off to the side, then cocked his head at me. "I didn't think this was possible, Fee, but it looks like you've reached your caffeine saturation point. How about this: let me navigate this bag out of the building for you, and I'll tell you how I ended up with your pen."

I eyed him for a long moment, then nodded. "Fine. You win, Russell. Now 'fess up."

Pete watched me warily, like he thought I might change my mind, then grinned. "Your pen was sitting right next to your notebook. All I did was pick it up off the table and hand it to you."

"But…" I blinked, then blinked again. "Ugh. You may be right about my caffeine level."

Just then, Dan Thomas appeared before us, flanked by a smiling girl with the most gorgeous dark curls I had ever seen. They both looked so normal. So *awake*.

"Hey, guys," he smiled. "How was your flight?"

"Long," I said. "You look disgustingly perfect, Danny."

"Um… thanks?" He brushed his floppy bangs away from his glasses. "Guys, this is Anne. We met this morning. She goes to Addison College."

Anne nodded first at Pete, then stuck her hand out to shake mine. "Madame Beauchamp asked me to find you," she said in French, reminding the rest of us that we had a language pledge to uphold on campus. "I got here Friday so I've already moved in, but don't worry, I left you the nicer room. And you will love Marie-France."

"Oh. So, we're living together?" I answered in French.

"Sort of. Our rooms are next door to each other. Come on. We live about half a mile north of here on rue Bonaparte."

"Great! Pete and I will come with you," Dan smiled. "That's on the way to our flat, too."

Our flat? Well, that explained the change of clothes and the clean face. Pete must have gone straight to his apartment from the airport instead of going to school. How he knew where to go was another question altogether.

I shouldn't have been surprised that Pete and Dan would live together, but I was. For whatever reason, I'd pegged Dan Thomas as the type to want local student housing, if only for the experience. But I guess it made sense. Those two had always been tight, and not just because they were in the same fraternity. I just didn't get why someone as gallant as Dan would hang out with a loon like Pete.

"After you," Dan grinned down at Anne, who turned on her riding boot heel and headed down the ivy corridor, followed by Dan, Pete and my suitcase.

four

Twelve minutes later, we arrived on the fifth floor of our apartment building. The moment Marie-France de Clavéry opened the door, I felt ashamed of myself for the stodgy, conservative matron I'd imagined. Though she was well into her forties, Marie-France seemed at least a decade younger, with black, shoulder-length hair and perfectly styled bangs. She was, in fact, wearing a cardigan-plus-pencil-skirt combo, but she looked smart, not dowdy. When I noticed her funky high heels and the crinkled laugh lines around her dark eyes, I knew we would get along. In fact, the only fault I could find with this woman was her refusal to speak English.

"*Meredith!*" Marie-France pronounced my name *May-Ray-Deet* as she kissed both my cheeks. "Here you are, and with so few bags! You and Anne are so unlike the young ladies who lived here last year. And who are these gentlemen?"

Poor Dan started off on the wrong foot by calling her "Madame de Clavéry" rather than "Marie-France," and to his extreme dismay, she spent the next five minutes explaining why he should address her by her first name while still employing the formal "you" to a guy no less than twenty-five years her junior. Hey there, *Madame de Messages Mixtes*. Way to confuse the kid.

By the end of Marie-France's giddy rant, Dan was done speaking for the day, full stop.

While Anne and Pete did their best to fill the awkward silence, I scanned the enormous living room. When Madame Beauchamp had handed out our housing assignments earlier, she'd warned us that our flat might be small in comparison to the average single family residence back home. But this apartment was bigger than my house in Lincoln City. Spacious, quirky… like something out of a magazine.

I shifted from side to side, aching to see the *chambres de bonne*. Back in the day, the uppermost floors in many Parisian buildings belonged to the domestic help. These days, they were prime real estate for students or singletons needing somewhere affordable to live.

Noticing my impatience, Marie-France asked us to follow her up the back staircase. Since I was the only one with a bag, Pete and Dan hoisted my suitcase up two flights, and when we arrived at the seventh floor landing, Marie-France opened the first door on the left. "Here you go, Meredith," she smiled. "This room is yours."

Had we been alone, I might have shed half a kilo of tears as I followed Marie-France into the narrow room. With an ease I knew I would never replicate, she freed the long casement window panes and *volet* shutters from their locked position and motioned for me to step closer. The seventh floor was just below the Mansard roof of the building, so the exterior wall pitched upward at the same diagonal as the room. I stared out of the gabled window for so long that I didn't notice when Marie-France and the rest of them left me to check out Anne's room down the hall.

After a few moments, I unzipped my suitcase to find the photos I'd stored on the inside pouch. The wall behind my desk was a bulletin board from floor to ceiling, and the room's previous occupant had left just enough thumbtacks to make things homey.

The first thing I placed on the board – right in the center – was a postcard from our restaurant. The graphic designer had gone for a mid-century vintage feel, even though our restaurant was less than two decades old. The word SULLIVAN'S looked like the Hollywood sign, hovering over the coastal highway into Lincoln City.

To the left, I placed a picture of my mother lying flat on the window seat of my bedroom, her feet propped up against the far wall, with my tiny four-year-old self perched on her lap. She was holding a book facing me, and my hands waved in the air as I recited the story back to her. But the thing I loved most about this photo was that my brother was only ten when he took it. The image was composed and lit like some national ad campaign for cotton. Or literacy.

I picked up another photo and pegged it to the right of the coaster. The Newport Big Band Society's gilded logo decorated the bottom left corner just below my dad blowing into his clarinet. Ian took this one, too, which is probably why my dad's bright green eyes are dancing at the camera instead of focused on the sheet music.

At the top of my wonky triangle, I placed a photo from high school, when I'd won the Oregon state championship in Irish dancing. The bodice of my black dress was embroidered with emerald green Celtic knots, and blinged to the max with matching emerald green rhinestones. I'd curled my normally straight auburn hair in ringlets and pulled it into a ponytail that definitely looked like a hairpiece considering the volume of those curls. The medallion hanging from my neck might as well have been Olympic gold, judging from the look of pride on my brother's face, his right arm thrown casually over my shoulder. It was his first year working full-time at *Greg's Guidebooks*, which probably explains why their logo was embroidered on his fleece.

A twinge of guilt plucked at my nerves as a Drew-shaped hole glared back at me from the wall. On the day they'd posted the Beckett scholarship winners on the French department website last spring, I hadn't believed my eyes. I hadn't *wanted* to believe them, because Drew Sutton – my oldest friend and the boy I loved most in the world – was suddenly, inexplicably single. The more time we spent together over the summer, the crazier it had felt to leave for Paris. But in all those days and hours we'd spent together working at Sullivan's or hanging out at the beach, Drew had never once asked me to stay.

He hadn't even tried.

Maybe soon, a million new pictures would fill the blank space where Drew should be. But for now, in the center of the board, I had everything that mattered from home.

The floor creaked on the far side of the room. I whirled around expecting to find Marie-France again, but found Pete instead. He sauntered across the ancient floorboards and joined me beside my desk, his eyes roaming briefly over the photo collage. Then he smiled and shoved his hands in his pockets. "Sorry, Sully. Didn't mean to scare you. I just wanted to say goodbye."

I shrugged, then stepped away from my desk, back over to the window.

Pete joined me, bending forward under the gabled ceiling to peer outside. "Whoa. How cool is this view? By December, you'll have your very own *Rooftops Under Snow* out here."

I felt my eyebrows knotting together as I watched Pete take in the view. Did he seriously just reference a painting by Caillebotte? I'd bought that exact print on my high school trip to France, and it had been on my dorm room wall the past two years. There was no way Pete could've known that. He barely knew me.

The top of his newly shorn head touched the gable above us, but Pete still craned his neck far into the corner of the sloped ceiling by the window. "Hey, come here," he said, pushing his head all the way outside. "If you stand just right, you can see the spires of Saint Sulpice. Look, just above the corner of the roof here. Do you see them?"

Without thinking, I followed his lead, stretching further out the window than I might have dared on my own. There they were, two mismatched towers that must have been recently cleaned, judging by the lack of soot visible to the naked eye. The sky above us was unreal, with perfect fluffy clouds in all the right places. I pulled the sunglasses out of my front pocket so that the biggest jokester of all time wouldn't see my eyes fill with tears.

Pete stood behind me for a long time, then suddenly ducked back under the gable and retreated across my room in three long strides. I turned to find him pausing under the doorway, hand raised. "See you, Sully. I think Dan's waiting for me downstairs."

"Hey, Pete, can I ask you something?"

He stepped back into my room. "Yeah?"

I walked to where he stood then crossed my arms, sunglasses still perched on my nose. "When you vanished at the airport, did you go to a barber or something?"

Pete laughed, but not in his usual, haughty way. For the first time, I could imagine what he had been like as a kid. He lifted an eyebrow and smiled. "You're getting better at those mind games of yours, Fee. Here I thought you were going to ask me about the farewell message Sutton gave me for you."

I took off my sunglasses and propped them on top my head. "I know you think I'm kidding around, but I'm not. Don't call me Fee, Pete. I mean it."

Pete watched me strangely for a moment, then cocked his head to the side. "Why not?"

"Listen, I've let you call me a lot of things over the years without complaining. And I admit, you've come up with some good ones: Sully, McMeredith, Ginger Red Riding Hood…"

"Don't forget Gingeraffe. That was my personal favorite."

"Yes, that one was… unique." I touched my hair self-consciously, then stood to my full height. "Look, here's the deal: only two people in the world call me Fee. One is my brother, and one is Drew Sutton. And maybe I'm reading into things, but it feels off when you say it, like you're mocking both me *and* Drew. Maybe you think that's hilarious, but it's not. He's off-limits, okay?"

For half a second, I could have sworn regret flickered in his eyes. But then he ducked under the door again and smiled. "Fair enough, Sully. Fair enough. Hey, you should ask Anne where to get your school supply fix. We both know you're craving some A4 spirals."

For the first time maybe ever, I smiled at him. "Already at the top of my to-do list for today, old chap. Guess I'd better unpack."

"Wait, you really *are* going school supply shopping?" Pete's eyes widened. "I can't believe I was right! Dan just bet me ten bucks – er, euros – that the first thing you would do was walk to the Louvre, but I said you'd go to the *papeterie* first. Oh, man. Wait 'til I tell him."

I had to laugh as I heard his feet clipping at top speed down the stairs.

A breeze blew the door-like window panes open a little wider. I walked once again to the gable and surveyed my surroundings. To my left, the rue Bonaparte ambled half a mile up to the River Seine. And to my right, even though I couldn't see them, lay the Luxembourg Gardens and the Centre Lafayette. For better or for worse, this was my little corner of the world for the next year.

I leaned out of the window and began to breathe.

five

Pete had not been wrong about my school supply addiction. Once I'd unpacked, Anne and I walked to the *papeterie* down the street to stock up on everything from proper A4 European-sized paper to pens and a million other things we didn't know we needed.

Good thing we had those supplies ready, too, because on Tuesday and Wednesday we sat scribbling for five classes each day, frantically keeping pace with professors in a language not our own. And both nights at dinner with Marie-France, Neither Anne nor I could contain ourselves. I had never been so excited about any classes in my life.

On Thursday, after our course enrollment, the entire student body of the Centre Lafayette boarded two enormous motorcoaches bound for Normandy. Because Anne and I were the first ones to board, we scored the prime seats: right in the center of the bus, there was one table with four chairs each. It was the only place a row faced backward, so I took that seat and Anne took the one opposite, saving the two free spots for her friends from Addison College, Harper Anderson and Kelly James.

As the bus hulked down the streets of Montparnasse, then over the river at Porte de Saint Cloud, the Haussmann-esque uniformity of central Paris gave way to smaller suburban homes, and my classmates settled in for the short trip to Monet's home at Giverny. In other words, everyone scrolled their smart device, taking advantage of the free Wi-Fi on the bus, searching for news from home. Completely normal, yes. Probably healthy, even. After all, we'd been in France almost a week. A little homesickness was normal at this point.

Here's a tip: when your sleep schedule's wonky and your brain is taxed from overuse, the Internet is your frenemy. "Don't look back, Fee," Ian had warned me at the airport last Sunday. "Fill up that bracelet I gave you with new memories. Your future self will thank you someday."

I rarely listened to my brother, but for once, he made sense. *Step forward*, I'd told myself. But then I'd boarded this bus full of strangers, and all of Ian's logic flew out of my brain. Now, I found myself staring at Lindsay Foster's daily duck-face selfie, heavily filtered, including the requisite view of her décolletage and its newest accessory.

Drew's Sigma Phi Beta lavaliere.

Okay, not *new* – recycled. But still officially official. Again.

Harper was sitting next to me, and after I didn't move for a full fifteen seconds she peeked over at my screen. "Friend of yours?"

I tapped the home key to erase Lindsay's image from my screen and laid the phone face down on the table before me. "Oh, you know. Just some girl back home."

"Just some girl, huh?" Harper scowled at me, her blue eyes bright in the sunlight, despite the shadow from her dark bangs. "You know, Meredith, one of the benefits of going to school with people from all different colleges is that you don't have to be diplomatic about the people back home. Tell me anything you like about Duckface there. I'm on your side by default."

I paused for a minute, then turned my phone back over. "All right," I glanced from one Addison girl to the next. "So Lindsay dates my friend Drew from home, and…"

Kelly pulled her long blond hair into a top knot as she rolled her eyes. "Stop right there. We already know the rest of the story. Blondie plus your hometown boy equals total nightmare."

"I don't know if I'd call her a *nightmare*. It's just… okay, so you know those people who are together, but then they're not, but oh wait, yes they are, and you have to hopscotch right alongside them because the on-and-off never ends?"

"Like I said, a *nightmare*," Kelly scowled. "Glad to know those people exist everywhere. I take it you and Duckface aren't besties?"

I practically snorted into my sleeve. "Hardly. But I can't exactly hate her. See, Drew's family and mine are so close that our lives are forever entangled. He and I have a standing Friday morning breakfast date, he works at my parents' restaurant every summer, and our families have shared Christmas Day every year for… well, I don't remember a year when we *weren't* together."

Anne let out a whistle, her eyes wide. "I can't even say that about my immediate family."

"Right? So yeah, maybe Lindsay's not my favorite person in the world. But considering those golden Greek letters around her neck, I need to get over it. Again."

Harper watched me from the other side of the table. "So, you and this Drew guy never…"

"Please," I laughed. "You're talking to the supreme empress of the friend zone."

"You sure?" She picked up my phone, swiped right, and within two seconds, she was scrolling my photos. "You guys look pretty cozy in all these two-headed selfies you took last month."

I felt my ears redden, because what Harper saw before her was only a fraction of the truth.

I thought back to two weeks ago, before Drew had headed back to school for fraternity recruitment. We'd spent all night hanging out on Devil's Lake, flat on our backs, shoulder-to-shoulder in his dinghy, staring at the night sky and laughing so hard I felt like my pancreas might rupture. We'd stayed awake until the sky above us shifted from midnight blue to indigo, talking our way around Paris until Drew asked the question he'd avoided all summer.

"Humor me for a minute, Fee." Drew slid his shoulder out from under my head, then pushed himself to a seated position across from me. "Explain why it has to be Paris, because I just don't understand. Why couldn't you have done the summer program in Tours like the rest of the French majors?"

"Because I won the Beckett scholarship for *Paris*, Drew." I sat up, pulling my knees to my chest. "Everyone wants that scholarship. You take art history classes looking at the actual paintings in the Musée d'Orsay. You learn history and literature by touring the actual places you're studying. You don't understand that?"

"Of course I do. But you could have done all of that on the summer program. I mean, it wouldn't have been Paris, but…"

"Exactly. It wouldn't have been Paris."

He watched me for a minute, a shadow crossing his face. "So what happens if you meet the heir to the French throne in Paris and you never come back home?"

Despite the moonlight, it was too dark to get a clear read on Drew's face, so the pleading in his voice tripped me up momentarily. Yes, he'd just set my insides fluttering, but I knew better than to take Drew seriously. Attaching meaning to his words had always been my downfall, and this time was no different. My only weapon whenever he played this game was to play along. So I smiled, plucked up my courage, and lobbed that nonsense right back his way.

"Do you even open your textbooks, Mister History Major? There's no heir to the throne. France has been a republic for ages. See, a republic is…".

"I know what constitutes a republic, thank you very much." Drew slid over next to me, our backs pressed against the starboard side. "But there's still an heir to the French throne, just in case the Windsors try to take over, right?"

"How should I know?"

"Do you even open your textbooks, *Mademoiselle French Major?*" Drew fixed his gaze on me, his eyes lingering just a second too long on my lips. "Okay, what if you're walking through the Tuileries one day, and Prince Charming is there, waiting to whisk you off your feet?"

"Hold on a second. How do *you* know about the Tuileries?"

"Former palace, burned to the ground by the Paris Commune then transformed into gardens for the public. I know things, Fee." Drew smiled slowly, then steepled his hands, tapping his fingers together like an evil mastermind. "Listen, sweetie, I don't want to hurt your feelings, but you're not the most experienced gold digger on the planet. Someone has to guide you, or you'll wind up with some creepy viscount. Hey, how do you say that word? Viz-count? Vie-count?"

"Don't call me *sweetie*. And PS – I do know how to avoid stranger danger."

"If you say so." Drew picked up a stray piece of rope from the floor of the boat and began to twirl it absentmindedly. "Now, about this mystery prince, or duke, or whatever. Before you make him any promises, be sure he owns plenty of horses."

"Why?"

"What do you mean, why?" He lifted an eyebrow. "Everyone knows the stable boy is always the lady of the manor's special friend."

"Who, you?" I frowned. "But I thought you hated horses."

"I do. They scare the crap out of me, but sacrifices must be made." Drew moved his right hand in my direction. "Now, be a pal and shake on this with me. The second you find a nice, *preferably dowdy* aristocrat, give me a call, and I'll hop on the next flight. Deal?"

I watched his face for a minute, just in case this was some sort of trick. When I took his hand, I gripped it playfully, pumping it up and down like a politician. But Drew didn't return my silly gesture. He closed his hand around mine and brought it toward him, holding it so securely against his chest that I could feel his heart pounding.

"Our future depends on you, Fee," he said softly, eyes back on my lips. "It's up to you to get the best pre-nup possible, because I have my heart set on retiring in Maui before I'm thirty. Or the Maldives. Or Madeira. I'm not picky."

"You'd have to learn Portuguese if you move to Madeira," I said quietly, hyper aware of Drew's fingers against mine.

"See why I need you in my life? Without you, I'd be speaking the wrong language, and then how would I survive?"

Drew's eyes softened, then his lips curled into the flirtiest grin he'd ever given me. And even though I knew better than to play his game, my insides fluttered more than ever. "It's a good thing you've got that beach blond surfer vibe going on these days," I quipped. "Someone with your looks should always make the most of his youth. Botox will only get you so far in life, you know."

"So true, so true." Drew slid his thumb slowly along my wrist. "Maybe after I dump you, I can find some cougar who's still a couple of decades older than me. Someone whose millions will make your royal divorce settlement look like Monopoly money."

"Have you learned nothing, Drew Sutton?" I scowled. "Cougars are so early 2000s. You can do better than that."

Drew looked up at the sky for a minute, then back at me. "A reality star?"

"Now you're on the right track. Dream big, Sutton. There's someone for everyone, even for you. I have faith."

He squeezed my hand tighter against his chest, smiling sadly. "What will I do without you this year, Fee? You're the only person who knows how to insult and flatter me in the same breath."

The banter. The *butterflies*. Sitting there with him in the boat that night, I'd wished upon every star in the galaxy that nine time zones would be enough to set me free from this boy who'd held my heart prisoner for far too long. So when on-again-off-again Lindsay made her reappearance in the Drew-verse three days later, I took it as a sign.

The two-headed selfies, the nights on the lake, the wistful glances? Nothing but Lindsay bait. The second I realized that, I stopped questioning my move to Paris.

And now, here I was, with three new friends studying my face for the truth. And not a single one of them looked like they believed me anymore than I believed myself.

"You okay, Meredith?" Anne asked. "You look like you might be sick."

"Never better," I breathed in deeply. "Hey, does someone have a deck of cards? Seems silly to waste time on our phones when we've got this table between us just waiting to be used."

Kelly dug in her bag, produced a deck of cards, and the four of us poker-faced one another the rest of the drive to Giverny. Of course, I did not win a single round, but that wasn't the point. Today was the day I would finally see Monet's home in person, and no one got to ruin that. Right?

Wrong. For the rest of my life, whenever I looked back on this weekend, my brain would draw a blank on the manor's salmon-colored exterior and the splendor of the gardens thanks to that stupid lavaliere. The only image I'd recall was the koi in the lily pad pond.

Madame Beauchamp explained that the Japanese word for that particular species of carp is also a homonym with the word for friendship and love. As she waxed on and on about the famous bridge over the lily pad ponds, I fought the urge to raise my fists in defiance.

Time to re-evaluate this lesson plan, Madame, I thought. *Sure, love and friendship might* seem *all noble, but in the end, they're nothing but scavengers, sucking scum from the murky waters of life.*

Yeah, that's right. Try painting *that* symbolism, Monet.

six

It was Seventies Karaoke Night at *Le Somnambuliste*, the gritty, cave-like establishment we found after dinner just down the street from our hotel in Rouen. Take my advice: never enter a bar called "The Sleepwalker." At ten o'clock on the dot, the flashing lights began to polka-dot the walls behind us, and the world's worst ABBA impersonators took to the stage, decked out in neon satin jumpsuits and platform heels.

By the second verse of *Waterloo*, I noticed Pete Russell hovering to my left behind Anne, whispering something in her ear. Then, just as suddenly, he cheered and whooped so loudly for the satin sisters on stage that I was momentarily distracted and didn't notice Anne slip away. The next instant, there sat Pete in Anne's chair, the usual Russell smirk plastered across his face, his eyes fixed on mine.

"Hey," he bellowed above the music. "Why so glum tonight, Sully?"

"What?"

Pete slid his arm along my seat back, bending his face toward my ear. "I said, why so glum? Wait, let me guess. You are morally opposed to anything resembling fun."

I rolled my eyes. "You can't be *morally* opposed to fun. That makes no sense."

Pete watched me for a minute, then grinned. "Don't tell me you'd rather be studying?"

"Whatever you say, Pete." I sighed, turned my head back to the stage, and for a split second, I thought he was leaving. But then he bent so close that I could feel the warmth of his breath on my cheek, his lips brushing against my ear as he spoke.

"Here's the deal, Sully," Pete said softly. "For the past half-hour, your negative vibe has flooded this entire table. So I ask again, why so gloomy tonight? Did you forget your favorite notebook back in Paris? Or did someone steal your favorite pen again?"

I'd spent the better part of the last two years battling Pete Russell's wit. Every day since I'd known him, I'd always been able to match him, barb for barb. But tonight was different, and not just because I'd lost my pluck somewhere between Giverny and Rouen. Tonight, despite his tone, Pete's words didn't feel like a weapon. And as I lifted my eyes to meet his, I realized he was actually concerned.

"I have an idea," he said as the Swedish wannabes finally left the stage. "How about a karaoke duel?"

I blinked, then blinked again. "A what?"

"A contest. I pick a song for Dan and me, you pick one for the ladies, and we let the audience decide who wins. This is Rouen. We've got ourselves a room full of unbiased judges."

"A contest, huh?" I let my forehead crinkle as I tried to read between the lines. "What are the stakes? You losers buy us a round of Lafayette machine coffee on Monday?"

"Better," he smiled. "The loser, whoever he *or she* may be, must perform Sugarhill Gang's *Apache*, complete with *Ultimate Dance Dubs 3* choreography."

Freshman year in the dorms, the resident advisors had organized a monthly *Ultimate Dance Dubs* competition in the lobby game room. The *Apache* dance was always in one of the semi-final rounds, and I'd made it to the championship round at least once that year. So had both guys, but I wasn't afraid. There was no way we would lose.

I fixed Pete with a smug grin, then nodded. "Not a bad idea, Russell. But just so you know, *Apache* came out in the eighties, and tonight they're featuring seventies music. Not that you care about following protocol."

"Wow, Sully. You really do hate breaking the rules. So we have a deal?"

"We have a deal." I shoved my hand in Pete's direction. "You'd better start practicing that tricky lasso hop, kid, because *we* are going to win this battle, fair and square."

"Yeah?" Pete took my outstretched hand, pumped it once, then smirked. "We'll see about that. Hey, thanks for winning me some more euros, by the way. Dan bet me twenty that I couldn't cheer you up in three minutes or less, and we've just made it under the wire, with twelve seconds to spare. Monday, your first cup of coffee's on me."

And with that, Pete Russell zoomed back to his side of the table, oblivious to the fact that he'd just pissed me off so badly I was going to take him down, no matter the cost.

For the sake of fairness, Pete and Dan headed to a remote location across the bar to decide their karaoke selection, which gave me just the right amount of privacy to organize my troops. After I explained the bet, Kelly immediately hopped on board.

"You know what we should do?" Her blue eyes brightened. "*Copacabana.* It's like, the quintessential seventies song. Who *wouldn't* love it?"

"Me," Harper groaned. "Seriously, Kelly, if I hear that song one more time, I will walk out of here, find Joan of Arc's stake, and burn *myself.*"

"Ever since freshman year, we've had this thing," Anne explained, turning to me. "Whenever one of us has drama, the other two show up in that person's room with *Copacabana* already cued up. Kelly forces us to do this crazy choreography until every person laughs. It's ridiculous, but it works."

I found myself grinning, then aching, because I hadn't had that sort of girlfriend solidarity in... well, ever. Between dancing, studying, working, and Drew, girlfriends had been a luxury I couldn't afford. Watching the Addison girls these last few days had shifted something deep inside me that I hadn't known was missing. Secretly, I hoped they'd adopt me for a year.

Turns out four's not such a bad number after all.

After a full thirty seconds of protest, Harper sighed. "Fine. Considering how many times Kelly's forced it down our throats, it's probably the only seventies song we all know by heart."

As Kelly walked me through her homespun choreography, my eyes kept straying to the guys' corner on the opposite end of the bar. Pete and Dan were rehearsing like a squadron of cadets getting ready for a drill. I had to hand it to Pete Russell. No matter the outcome, he'd just managed to unite a group of virtual strangers in the sole pursuit of cheering me up. Or humiliating me.

Minutes later, Pete returned, a euro coin in hand. "Heads, you're first. Tails, we're second."

I took the coin and investigated both sides. "Hold on. There's no heads or tails on a euro."

"Picky, picky," Pete scowled. "Come on, Ginger Rogers. Quit stalling. The numbered side is heads, country side is tails. You flip."

So I did, and it was only when the coin was mid-air that I realized I'd fallen prey to the oldest trick in the book. No matter which side turned up, Pete and Dan won the second spot. He grabbed the coin on its descent, slammed it onto the table, then lifted his hand for the reveal.

"Tails," he grinned. "Aw, thanks, Sully. You just won me ten more euros. Dan thought he could get back what he lost by betting you wouldn't fall for that coin trick. Lucky for me, I know you better."

"That's what you think." I grabbed the coin off the table and walked away, chiding myself for falling into his trap. That coin trick was for suckers. I made a mental note to search his backpack on Monday for Sun Tzu's *Art of War* or whichever strategic playbook Pete was studying these days. The Snark-And-Nicknames Russell I'd always known was so much easier to combat than Nice-And-Friendly Pete.

seven

Because there were only a handful of performers tonight, there was no formal sign-up for karaoke. Harper, Anne, and I simply followed Kelly to the bartender, who cued up *Copacabana* and waited for us to take the stage. There were already six mic stands on the makeshift stage, so Kelly stood at the one in the center, then nodded to Jean-François-Whatever-The-Bartender to begin our song.

As the percussion intro bled through the monitors, I could see Pete and Dan laughing their heads off back in our far corner of the bar, and I might have taken it as a compliment had I not also noticed that these uppity girls from our program – Meg Green and her minions – were sitting two tables away from the stage. All five of them were glaring at us. Wait, not glaring – *judging*. Something about their nose-in-the-air disdain combined with the hysterical high-fiving going on in the back corner rattled me, and I missed my first cue.

Scratch that. I missed every cue.

You know when you're watching a children's dance recital, and there's always one kid half a measure behind, relying on classmates for the right steps? That was me. It might not have been so noticeable if my teammates hadn't kept glancing back at me in horror. Kelly, Anne, and Harper did their best to keep the audience engaged, but when my shoe flew offstage, the crowd erupted in laughter. And then again when I tripped over the monitor wires.

Dear Oregon State Irish Dance Association: please strip that gingeraffe of her medal.

"Nice one, Sully," Pete smirked, crossing my path as I stumbled off the stage. "Thanks for throwing that victory for us. You're a peach."

I was about to retort back but Anne grabbed me by both elbows from behind and propelled me back to our table at the far end of the bar. None of my new friends dared to look at me. We just slumped into our seats, all four heads down, eyes closed.

Then the jaunty opening bars of Wild Cherry's *Play That Funky Music* came over the loudspeaker, and I saw Kelly's face crumple just as I groaned. I should have known Pete and Dan would pick this song. The Sigma Phi Beta pledge class performed this on the quad during initiation our first year at Highgate. People talked about it for weeks afterward. Drew sang all the verses while Pete, Dan, and the rest of their pledge class made total fools out of themselves wearing outlandish accessories, like feather boas, crazy glasses, and enormous cowboy hats.

Even though there were no props (and no Drew) tonight, those guys had schooled us before the chorus began. Dan had been tasked with the first two verses – further proof of Pete's tactical genius. Not only did Dan have an unexpectedly gorgeous voice, he strutted around like Mick Jagger so convincingly that even I believed he spent every weekend on stage.

By the second verse, I knew we'd lost. Dan's floppy bangs were drenched in sweat, like streams of brown molasses running down his forehead and into his eyes. And every single female in the bar was screaming at the top of her lungs. Especially the Italians.

At some point, Pete jumped off the stage to help Dan get the whole crowd on their feet. That nitwit Meg Green was standing on top of her chair, bouncing to the music like she was the only person in the universe who mattered. While I held my breath for the impending twerk train wreck, Pete Russell suddenly appeared before me, out of breath and sweating like a fool.

"How you feeling now, Sully?" The smugness in his tone was unbearable. "Hope your recall on *Apache* is a little stronger than your last performance, because…"

Pete pinched his nose together like he'd just gotten downwind of Marshall Freeman after his kale chips, then winked at me and ran back to the stage area. Only he stopped short. With little to no effort, he joined that Meg girl on top of her chair, wrapped his arm around her waist and produced a microphone from his pocket as he began the third verse. Totally off-key.

Well, hallelujah. At least he was bad at *something*.

But did anyone in the bar notice? No way. At the last minute, Pete jumped back on stage and directed different sections of the bar to sing the final echo-repeat section of the song. The Addison girls and I stood in awe. No way could two Oregon frat boys create spontaneous magic like that. One hundred percent impossible.

As the crowd cheered them off the stage, I saw Pete chatting up the bartender, presumably to order up *Apache* on our behalf. But some

Frenchman had already taken center stage, butchering The Eagles' *Desperado* in an operatic voice and terrible diction. *Senses*, I urged telepathically. *You can't come to your 'sentence,' bro. English isn't even your language. Read what is on the screen.*

After two painful minutes, I finally stood and faced the Addison girls. "Listen, I'm really sorry, guys, but we have to go onstage now."

Anne's eyes widened. "I knew it. There was a loser's clause?"

"Oh, come on." Kelly waved her hand dismissively. "It can't be that bad."

"Right." I rested my hands on my hips. "You're right, it's not that bad. Pete never said all four of us have to dance. He just said 'you,' which technically means me. Meredith Sullivan. The one who brought mortal disgrace upon the motherland. So, I'll dance. It'll be fine, really."

Harper's eyes narrowed. "Dance to what, exactly?"

I tried not to wince as I answered. "Sugarhill Gang's *Apache*. The *Ultimate Dance Dubs 3* choreography. Do you know it?"

"Yes, and no way," Harper steamed. "I refuse to do any of that whooping."

"Technically, the track will do that part." Kelly pulled her blond hair into a ponytail, readying for battle. "Okay, Meredith, you do the dance, I'll take care of the rap. Harper and Anne can back me up on the chorus."

The other two started to protest, but just then, the bartender announced *Ah-pah-shay* over the loudspeaker, and time was up. When the four of us took the stage again, there were actual boos coming from every corner of the room. Luckily for me, that sort of negative feedback only served to rally my inner competitor. No way would Pete Russell see me fail twice in one night.

When the music began, I started the up-and-down arm and leg pumps, executing every move like a boss. By the time Kelly started to rap, the crowd was actually cheering. But midway through my rotation, I discovered why. Pete and Dan had joined us onstage, and bookish, elegant Anne had grabbed Kelly's mic to perform the second verse.

Every single word, straight from memory.

In my shock, I stopped dancing. But then Pete caught my eye, lifting his hand above his head and rotating his finger in a circle. *Lasso*, he mouthed. For once, I didn't roll my eyes. I just did as I was told, and did it with a smile. A real one.

Within twenty seconds, the whole bar had joined us – French, Italian, Monegasque, Meg Green Minion… whatever. Later, as the six of us tromped down the medieval streets of Rouen back to the hotel, I had to admit: I'd never had that much fun in my entire life. Never.

Pete Russell had conned me right out of my misery.

eight

The sky was so unusually bright and the air so crisp the next morning as we boarded the bus that I had to pull a sweater out of my bag before the bus driver loaded it in the undercarriage. But despite the dazzling sunshine outside, a somber mood crept like a fog among us on the drive to the American Cemetery at Colleville-Sur-Mer. No one spoke. No one slept. Everyone watched the Norman landscape slide past and prepared ourselves for what was to come.

At your average student bus tour stop, you would see clusters of friends walking along, their laughter floating on the wind, but today was different. I stood for a long time by the northern reflecting pool, near the memorial, and watched my classmates tread carefully among the rows of grave markers. Without exception, each person explored alone. Not a cloud hung in the sky, and the grassy hill below me was so brilliantly green that if it weren't for the thousands of crosses and

Stars of David sloping down to the sea, you might never know what happened here.

Madame Beauchamp had dedicated two hours of our day to explore this place from our shared history. After a while, I meandered down to the memorial chapel at the midpoint of the cemetery, then kept walking along the path. The chapel's location at the crossroads of four gravel walkways made a visual barrier, so most people turned back after they toured the inside. But there were still four full sections of graves beyond, so I walked another hundred meters or so, reaching into my messenger bag to pull out the camera my brother had given me last Christmas, then trained the lens up the nearest row to my right. At the far end near the sea, I spotted Pete Russell through the viewfinder, tugging his hood over his head, crouching down in front of one specific cross.

I watched for a few moments as he slid two tiny flags from the sleeve of his fleece – one American, one French – rolling them back and forth in his fingers as he took in the white cross before him. Then he pushed both flags gently into the ground at the base of the headstone and lifted his hand to where the name was engraved, trailing his fingers along the words.

I should have headed elsewhere. I should have respected whatever moment he was having in this of all places. But instead I walked down the row of graves to stand beside him.

"Hey, Sully," he nodded his head toward the cross as I approached. "Come see this."

Without a word, I stepped closer. The headstone read:

JILL COX

****

Peter S. Beckett
First Lieutenant, U. S. Army
Independence, Missouri
June 6, 1944

****

"That's my great-grandfather on my mom's side," Pete said quietly, shifting slightly to make room for me beside him. "He made it off the beach but died coming up the hill, just over there."

The hairs on my arms stood on end. I had never met anyone who could say such a thing about a relative. "Wait, is that how you got your name? You're named after *this* Peter?"

"Sort of." Pete bent over to straighten the flags he'd just prodded into the ground. "My mom named me after her dad, Peter Beckett, Junior. He was born in August 1944."

"Wow. So, your granddad…"

"Never knew his father." Pete stood upright again, and the two of us stayed motionless for a while, listening to the wind whistling past. I bent forward to run my fingers along the lettering of Pete's great-grandfather's name, trying to imagine how this must feel. None of my relatives had ever fought in a war. Even if you'd never met the person who died, this was still huge. A real-life hero was buried here, and Pete shared his name and his blood.

I turned to face him, pushing my sunglasses back up my nose. "You brought those flags all the way from home just for this visit?"

Pete laughed a little. "My grandmother asked me to bring these two with me and leave them here. That's the real reason I ran back to the Sigma Phi house last Sunday morning – to find these flags in my storage bins. It's sort of a miracle that I made it to the airport at all."

"But how did you know where to find his grave? Did you look it up online or something?"

Pete looked down the row toward the sea for a few seconds, then turned back to me. "I've been here before. I used to come with my family twice a year when we lived in Paris."

Oh hey – welcome back, Sneaky Pete. There was no way he was telling the truth. This guy's favorite pastime had always been making me question my sanity. Good thing I knew how to return the favor.

"Parisian childhood, huh? That's cool." I opened my messenger bag to put my camera away and took my time disassembling the lens from the body. "Let me guess – you were here from age three to six?"

"Four to eight." Even through his dark lenses, I could see Pete blinking at me in disbelief. "Hey, how'd you guess that?"

"Oh, you know – the native-level accent, the easy recall of the most arcane grammar rule. Oh, and the annoyingly accurate cadence of your speech. You can't pick those things up in a high school classroom, my friend. They can only be acquired during prime language learning years."

"Well, that's true. Guess I'm lucky that way."

"Exactly. So is your mom a Romanov?"

Pete blinked again. "Sorry?"

"You heard me, Pyotr. There must be some reason your family had to move to France when you were a child. So what happened? Did the Bolsheviks finally track you down?"

Pete pulled my sunglasses off my face, turning them over and over in his hand. "Have you got a hidden camera in these glasses?"

I snatched my sunglasses out of his hand and shoved them back onto my nose. "Don't be glib, Pyotr Petrovich Romanov Russell, rightful Grand Duke of St. Petersburg. Just tell me the truth."

Pete stood motionless for a moment, a shadow crossing his face. But then he took off his aviators and started polishing them on the pouch of his hoodie, over and over and over again. Then, before he lifted them back onto his face, he fixed his gaze on me in a way that made me feel like a kid in the principal's office.

"I am telling the truth, Meredith. For four years, I lived with my parents in a flat on rue Guénégaud. My grandparents bought it in the eighties before real estate went berserk here. That's where Dan and I live now. You and Anne should come visit soon. I'd like that."

The Pete standing before me was someone I'd never seen before. The swagger had disappeared, and as he slid the glasses back on his face, he seemed slighter somehow. And much, *much* older, like some ancient soul walking among us, who had finally shed the post-adolescent body he'd shanghaied so he could disappear among the masses.

"So, wait." My mouth went dry. "You guys really did just pack up and move to France? Isn't that a little unusual?"

"Says an Irish girl whose family just picked up and moved to Oregon," he grinned. "But yeah, that's what happened. We moved here so my mom could earn a couple of master's degrees."

"Huh. I guess that explains why you deconstruct Balzac and Dumas like a boss."

"So many inappropriate jokes I could make right there." The smile on Pete's lips widened. "My mom's plan was to get a doctorate when we got back to the States, but instead, she decided she loved teaching high school. She always told me she preferred building the foundation than trying to repair all the cracks on the other end of the spectrum."

My mind could not keep track of all the pieces of this puzzle. "Was she *your* teacher?"

"She was." He pointed at the grave below. "Those two flags were from my mom's classroom, which is why my grandmother wanted me to leave them here. I think First Lieutenant Beckett would've loved it. Don't you?"

I studied Pete for a few seconds as he bent over again, fiddling again with the flags like he was buying time, waiting for a wormhole to open up and let him out of this dimension. When he looked back up at me, I asked the next obvious question.

"So what did your dad do while your mom was studying? Was he your manny?"

"Manny, photojournalist." Pete stood, kicking at a clump of dirt. "Depended on the day."

Pete's dad is a photojournalist? If my brother Ian knew, he would be knocking down the Russells' front door without half a second of hesitation.

Was there actually a wormhole around here? Because this was nuts. If you'd told me two weeks ago that Pete Russell and I would have one single thing in common besides our major, I would have told you to lay off the whiskey bottle. I'd learned more about him in the last hour than I had in the two years before. And I felt a little sick as I realized how badly I'd misjudged him.

"Well, sir, you have lived quite a life," I said, propping my hands on my hips. "So, I guess your parents are retired now, huh?"

The color drained from his face. "Why would you ask me that?"

"What do you mean, *why*? You keep talking about their jobs in the past tense, and..."

Pete smiled again – a sort of sickly half-smile – and in the mirrored shades of his aviator sunglasses, I watched the panic bloom across my own face. Had I paid attention like a normal, compassionate person, I would have noticed the signs of his discomfort ten minutes earlier.

Pete Russell's parents were dead.

He'd just confirmed it without a word. The grief was right there, rolling off him in waves and into the silence around us. As I stood there watching him watching me, I wished with my whole soul that I had turned left instead of right earlier at the memorial chapel up the hill. I could keep wishing that for the rest of my life, but it wouldn't make any difference. Some things you can't take back. So when gigantic tears spilled down my cheeks, I let them fall. Not only for Pete's loss, but for the words I'd just wielded like a broadsword.

nine

Maybe Pete was used to people acting crazy around him, because when he saw me crying, he clasped his left hand around my shoulder and squeezed gently. Even though I could see years' worth of grief bubbling just below his calm expression, I could also tell that at that moment, he was more concerned about *me*. How had I misjudged him for so long?

Because that's what I did best. Within thirty seconds of our first meeting, I'd locked Pete in a dolt-sized box and never set him free. In my mind, the messy goatee and oversized clothing were signs of sloth. The need to out-snark everyone reeked of Mommy issues. Or Daddy issues. Or both. And obviously, his penchant for nicknaming me was proof of a warped brain.

One time, I'd even mocked Pete's tattoo – the Mandarin characters for *grace* or *peace* or something noble like that – right to his face. I still couldn't tell you why I did it. I'd never mocked Drew,

and his tattoo was actually cringeworthy: his name backwards –
WERD – in block letters on his forearm so that it would always show
up as 'DREW' in pictures (which, of course, it doesn't). He wasn't
even drunk at the time. Just moronic enough to execute one of Ian's
dares.

I opened my mouth to speak, but only managed two syllables.
"Pete, I'm…"

What? Sorry? Ashamed of myself? The worst person on all
seven continents? All of these words and more flew through my mind
but refused to leave. So I just stood there, stammering until Pete's
expression morphed from concern to something between horror and
pity. But then he smiled and lowered his hand from my shoulder,
waving it like he wanted to Jedi-mind-trick me right out of this
moment and into the next.

"We'd better go, Sully," he said, bending to pick up my bag from
the ground. "The bus leaves in fifteen minutes."

And because I was a lunatic, I simply cleared my throat, took the
strap of my messenger bag from his outstretched hand, then gestured
for him to lead the way. Neither of us said another word as our feet
walked in unison, first on the soft grass carpeting the gravesites, then
on the gravel walkway leading back to the exit.

Crunch. Crunch. Awkward silence. Crunch.

Just past the chapel, Pete finally spoke. "Hey, Sully? I have a
question. Weren't you and Lindsay Foster roommates?"

It took a few seconds for Normal Meredith to emerge, what with
the half ton of contrition weighing her down. "Um… I'm sorry,
what?"

"You lived with Lindsay freshman year, right?" He repeated.
"I've been thinking all morning about those *Ultimate Dance Dubs*

competitions we used to have at Highgate, and that got me thinking how you and Lindsay were sort of inseparable back in the day. Or did I dream that?"

"No," I said without looking his way. "We lived together. Just freshman year, though."

Pete cast me a sidelong glance. "You didn't want to live with her again last year?"

"No. Last year, I got a single. I had to study for the Beckett qualifying exam."

"Right," Pete said, shoving his hands in his pockets. "So, is that how you know Sutton? Lindsay introduced you guys?"

I actually snorted. I couldn't help myself. "No, Drew and I have been friends since kindergarten. See how I'm alphabetically cursed?"

"Russell, Sullivan, Sutton." Pete's face softened. "Good one, Sully. So what was our Andrew like as a kid?"

"Whip smart. He was salutatorian in high school, you know."

"No way."

"Don't let the surfer vibe fool you. Life-of-the-party Drew never existed until college. The kid I grew up with spent every minute of his pre-college life either playing sports, working at my parents' restaurant, or studying. He's at Highgate on a full ride."

"Are you serious?" Pete's eyes went wide. "I would not have guessed that. So, what? Did bespectacled baby Sutton give you his favorite pencil one day at school and the rest was history?"

"You're hilarious," I rolled my eyes. "No, Drew and his mom moved to Oregon from this small town in East Texas right before kindergarten. He had such a twang; none of the other kids had ever heard someone speaking English with a different accent than their own, so you can imagine how that went. I don't think he said more than one word a day for the entire first month of school. I hated it."

"I can see that. Did you Riverdance your way across their faces?"

"No doubt I thought about it," I grinned. "But my younger self was a little more whimsical than the Meredith you know today. So instead of violence, I wrote him a story one day in class and gave it to him at recess. After that, we were sidekicks forevermore."

"Rewind one second. Did you say you write stories?"

"I used to."

"Maybe you should start up again. That colorful imagination of yours should be put to better use," he smirked. "But wait, didn't Sutton live with his grandparents growing up?"

"Yeah." The breeze from the ocean chilled me so quickly that I actually shivered. "Drew's dad left before he was old enough to remember, so that's why they moved to Oregon – to live with his mom's parents. When she died, he took the Suttons' last name. We were ten."

"Oh. Well, that's… I'm sorry. I had no idea. Was… I mean, did she get sick, or…?"

I tugged my sweater closer to me and shook my head. "Her heart just stopped one night while she was sleeping. They did an autopsy and everything, but there was no medical explanation. My mom thinks she just really loved Drew's dad, so she died of a broken heart."

Pete nodded, his eyes fixed on the ground. "I've heard that happens."

"Me, too." We walked on in silence for a hundred feet or so, and as we ambled, I considered asking Pete why he and Drew weren't better friends. The more we talked, the more I realized those two might understand each other in a way none of the rest of us could.

As we neared the gates, Pete took his sunglasses off his face and stopped walking. "Can I ask you something else, Sully?"

"Sure, go ahead."

"What would it take for *us* to be friends? You and me, I mean," he added quietly. "It feels like things have been easier between us since we got to Paris, so maybe you should tell me what I did wrong back home. I don't want to screw it up on this side of the world, too."

"You really don't know?" Pete shook his head. So I took a deep breath and continued. "Do you remember meeting me on the first day at Highgate?"

Pete eyed me strangely. "Yeah. Why?"

"Well, this may sound dumb, but I'd spent most of the summer fretting about that first French class. First impressions are crucial at a new school, and people are creatures of habit. Where you sit matters. Especially when it's your major."

"No, I get that. Too close to the front and you're too eager. Too far back? Slacker city."

"Exactly. Except that when I walked into Room 207 of Hatley Hall, I found a very intimidating beast in that optimal middle seat, perusing his textbook like he could not care less."

The color drained from Pete's face. "Oh. Wait, Sully, I can explain…"

I held up my hand to silence him. "You gave the impression of being the type of person to speak only French in class. So I asked you very politely, 'Um, *pardon. C'est le cours de Composition 3301?*' But you didn't look up from your book. You just nodded. So I sat down behind you and wished I could disappear."

Pete's eyebrows knotted together. "Hold on a second. That's not entirely true. I know I talked to you that day."

"Oh, you talked to me. After what felt like an eternity, you swiveled around in your seat, turned your snapback around, eyed my t-shirt and said, 'You've got to be kidding me, man. *Lincoln City*? I *hate* that dump.'"

A brief flash of something crossed Pete's face. "You were wearing a Sullivan's Restaurant t-shirt. Kelly green."

"You remember?"

"Of course I do." His smile drew into a thin line as he crossed his arms over his chest. "So, wait – that's it? We've spent the last two years at odds with each other over a t-shirt?"

"Pete, you insulted my parents' livelihood *and* my hometown in less than ten words. How did you expect me to respond?"

He grew quiet again, and for a moment, he looked at me so strangely that I wondered if I'd missed something. But then he shoved his hands in his pockets again and shrugged. "It doesn't matter. The only thing that matters is that I hurt your feelings, and for that, I'm sorry."

I walked ahead, listening to our feet fall together on the gravel again. But ten steps away from the bus, Pete wrapped his fingers gently around my elbow.

"Nothing below a marquis," he said as I turned toward him. "That was the message."

"What are you talking about?"

"Last week as I was leaving the Sigma Phi house, Drew Sutton asked me if I knew you. When I said yes, he asked me to remind you not to settle for anything less than a marquis. What did he mean?"

"Nothing really." Every capillary in my body lit up in flames. "I mean, this will sound so ridiculous out of context, but Drew and I have this inside joke about my meeting an aristocrat while I'm here."

I shook my head as I laughed under my breath. "Like that would ever happen."

"Huh," Pete muttered, nodding hello to some girl as she passed by. "Nothing lower than a marquis. So that means no barons, no counts…"

"Right?" I laughed again hollowly. "What else is there? A prince? Anyway, it's just a stupid joke. I'm not sure why he even brought it up."

A grin spread slowly across his face. "You might not meet a prince, but you might cross paths with a Grand Duke someday. Like, say… maybe one from St. Petersburg?"

He stood still, looking down at me while my brain caught up. *Pyotr Petrovich Romanov Russell, rightful Grand Duke of St. Petersburg.* Either Pete was messing with my head again, or…

"Watch out, ladies and gentlemen. The lightbulb just flickered." He jumped over to the bus door, bowed deeply, then held out his hand for me to climb aboard. "*Dasvidaniya*, Tsarina Fiona Sullyevna. I'll make sure to let Sutton know you're holding up your end of the bargain."

ten

My schedule every Monday started with *La Francophonie*, a general French culture class, followed by three hours of nineteenth-century lit. Friday was a walking tour class known as *Promenade Parisienne*. Art history met every Tuesday and Thursday at the Musée d'Orsay. But my favorite class was History of France.

History major Drew would be so proud of me. That is, if we were communicating in any way more significant than messaging funny memes to each another.

Our professor, Monsieur Ludovic, was so extraordinary that the Centre Lafayette provided him with round-trip transport on the high-speed TGV train every week from Tours, where he lived. At one-thirty every Wednesday, Monsieur Ludovic breezed into the *Conservatoire*, his lecture already pouring from his lips like we'd missed something important and might never get it back.

Guillaume Ludovic was an odd bird, to be sure. His wild hair was salt-and-peppery, and he wore it bushy and unkempt, like Einstein's. And he wore the exact same outfit every week.

Black pants and shoes. A black sweater. A crisp, white Oxford cloth button-down with a white ascot at his neck.

Maybe it was a uniform.

Whenever Monsieur Ludovic stepped through the door, I expected him to be wearing a cape for some reason. I guess something in his stride made me think of the Three Musketeers. Or maybe more accurately, Professor Snape.

Of course, there's always one person who doesn't appreciate even the most amazing teacher. Every week, without fail, my boy Marshall Freeman would pull out a gigantic, seventy percent dark chocolate bar at some crucial moment in Monsieur Ludovic's address. Crinkling the wrapper unabashedly, he gnawed off chunk after chunk from the chocolate brick he held in both hands like a baby bottle, with zero awareness that he'd sidetracked the lecture.

The Wednesday evening after our second history class, Anne and I found Marie-France waiting on the sidewalk outside her apartment. Forget television. Her new source of entertainment was the Lafayette Channel. Which is why the following week, she widened our circle to include Dan, Harper, Kelly, and Pete.

The Lost Generation may have had Gertrude Stein, but we had Marie-France. Wednesday night dinners on the rue Bonaparte were just the sort of thing you dream about when you imagine living in Paris. She pushed our language boundaries and taught us her culture, but she made us think outside the box about our own culture, too.

During dessert on our third Wednesday night together, Marie-France leaned back in her chair at the head of the table and spread her arms wide at us. "*Ah, mes amis,*" she sighed. "*Vous êtes les flèches dans mon carquois.*"

Aw. We were 'the arrows in her quiver.'

With just seven words, Marie-France had galvanized our posse. Kelly even found these vintage-looking arrow stickers in all shapes and sizes at the flea market near their apartment, and the following Monday before class, she doled them out to each of us by the coffee machine.

By the end of the day, there were arrow stickers popping up all over the Centre Lafayette, some with a motto: "That's so *flèche.*" I even heard that girl Meg Green say she'd spotted one on the Métro.

Anne and I rarely saw the inside of our *chambres de bonnes* except to sleep, but despite the flurry of activity, I was getting the best grades of my life. So when my laptop started chirping at me in the middle of the last Saturday night in September, I was surprised when I opened my chat window to find a very angry older brother staring back at me.

"Hey, look. You *do* exist," Ian chided. "Are you trying to put me in the hospital?"

"What are you whining about? I talk to Mom and Dad all the time. Is it my problem that they don't pass my news along to you?"

"You are so missing the point, Fee. How am I supposed to know you are healthy and alive? Me? Your needy brother who has no life?"

"Oh, listen to the humblebrag king feeling sorry for himself. By the extra gel in your spiky black hair and the fancy hotel bedding behind you, I'm guessing Greg's latest guidebook update has you five-star suffering in what, Oslo? Helsinki? Some new hotspot in Greenland, maybe?"

"Portland," he smirked. "And stop changing the subject. You know I rely heavily on your social media presence to keep my big brotherly nerves under control. I didn't buy you that fancy camera for Christmas last year so you could use it as a paperweight."

"Ian, come on. I'm half-asleep. Do you know what time it is?"

"It's time for you to start acting like my school nerd sister instead of her extroverted clone. Be honest, Fee: are you drinking too much?"

"Are you?" I growled. "Seriously, Ian, why are you freaking out? I'm just doing what you told me. *Don't look back, Fee*," I mimicked his hybrid Irish-American accent. "*Fill up that bracelet with new memories*. Those were your words."

I watched Ian's shoulders slacken a bit, then he relaxed against the pillows behind him. "I know they were. And I meant them, but I sort of expected you to document every street sign, lamppost, and doorknob within a ten-foot radius of you so I would know you are okay. At least for the first couple of weeks until you got settled. Instead, I find myself stalking total strangers' feeds for some sign of life, and I've got to say, Fee, you and your new friends are either really busy studying or you're busy coupling off. I just can't decide if I want to know which."

I laughed so hard that I was worried I would wake Anne next door. "Now I know you're drunk. No one's coupling off, Ian. Why would you even say that?"

Ian picked up his phone, and within a few seconds, my own phone buzzed. I opened the message to find a black-and-white photo of my history notes Pete had posted on Facebook earlier that week, followed by a screen shot of the accompanying caption:

Save me a seat in class tomorrow, Sully. You've got a real cliffhanger going on with this cartoon of yours, and I don't want to miss an installment. What will become of Edith of Nantes, the buxom waitress with the winning smile? Will she stay with Henri IV, or fly off to St. Barth's with that handsome Hugh Guennot? I have to know. Hey, maybe you could introduce a Grand Duke? #PlotTwist

I didn't want to laugh. I really didn't. But between Ian's crimson scowl and the words of Pete's message, I couldn't stop myself.

"I can't believe you, Meredith," Ian squealed. "First, you make no attempts to hide your outrageous flirting with some frat boy named Pete on the most public forum in the world, and now you're laughing about it? What has gotten into you?"

"Ian, you are completely overreacting. Trust me."

"I might have believed you a month ago, but now Andrew Sutton texts me – and this is not an exaggeration – *hourly* about this Pete Russell guy. I have no choice but to overreact."

"Whoa, whoa, whoa, rewind," I said, tossing my cell phone over to my bed. "First of all, let's talk about the Facebook post. Obviously, you've forgotten French history, or else your real concern would be my academic standing. Do you know how it felt to discover I'd misunderstood an entire lecture on the Edict of Nantes, the Huguenots, and the St. Bartholomew's Day Massacre? What if I fail, Ian? These classes count toward my major."

"Fascinating." Ian's eyes widened, and he leaned in toward the camera. "Defensive about her grades, not defensive about the fella. Maybe it's a good thing I'm meeting our friend Andrew for breakfast tomorrow morning. For once, he's only ten percent as nervous as he *should* be."

"Wait. You drove to Portland to see Drew?"

Ian laughed, that full-throated, high pitched childlike laugh that I loved so much it almost made my eyes fill up. "No, you dork. Greg sent me here to handle a couple of meetings earlier today. I head back to Seattle tomorrow."

"Oh. Right, of course. But you *are* going to see Drew?"

"Yes." Ian's smile was halfway between pity and irritation. "We spoke right before I called you. He spent about three seconds telling me Lindsay dumped him, *again*, and then thirty minutes on this Pete person. Is this guy new to Highgate? How come I've never heard of him before?"

"Drew and Lindsay broke up again? Are you sure?"

"You didn't know?" Ian watched me for a few seconds, then frowned. "Wow. When Drew told me you guys didn't talk much, I assumed he was pulling my leg. Now I feel kind of bad."

"For what?"

He looked at me strangely for a minute, then lifted an eyebrow. "Well, I might have mentioned that your new friend Pete appears dashing and debonair. You know, like Hemingway. In fact, you know that black-and-white photo you posted of you and your friends at La Rotonde? I may have screenshotted it over to Drew and labeled you *The Not-So-Lost Generation: Hadley + Tatie + Zelda + Scott.*"

Oh, fantastic. "Why do you taunt him, Ian? Drew won't catch your reference. Not everyone spends their life researching the American expat community in 1920s Paris. The only reason you know about it is because you work for a guidebook company."

"It's cool, Fee. He took it well. Here's the text he sent me."

My phone buzzed again – a blurry shot of what must have been Drew's middle finger. "Classy, Ian. Come on, don't mess with Drew. I mean it. You know he takes you seriously."

"I know, I know. But he makes it so easy," he smiled. "Now, listen, cut your brother some slack and tell me how the charm bracelet's filling up."

"Pretty well so far. I've gotten a couple of obvious ones for Paris and I picked up one in Rouen and another in the shape of Normandy."

"Not too shabby, young lady. And how many have you gotten outside of France?"

"I've only been here five weeks! Don't I get time to adjust?"

Ian smiled again, his eyes softening. "Sounds like you're doing just fine. Hey, grab that old-school paper planner I see by your bed and block off the weekend after my birthday, okay? I'm coming to Europe for a few days."

"Shut up!" I nearly hugged the screen. "Already?"

"Yeah, Greg is sending me to Prague that weekend to update some shots for the guidebook, and he said it's cool if you tag along. I fly into Charles de Gaulle on the first, and we can hop a flight east the next day. Unless you already have plans that weekend."

"No. In fact, I was just wondering yesterday what to do, because the Centre Lafayette observes All Saints' Day from Wednesday to Friday this year."

"*Merci beaucoup*, Napoleonic Code. I knew that guy was useful for something."

"I don't think Napoleon determined religious holidays, Ian."

"Oh, what do you know? You can't tell the difference between an Edith and an Edict."

"Clever. Hey, I'll check with Marie-France to see if you can stay in one of the empty *chambres de bonnes* down the hall. Unless Greg is springing for a suite at the Ritz or something."

"I wish." Ian cocked his head to the side, then moved the screen closer to his face. "You know I expect to meet your friends, right? That includes Mister History Notes."

"Hey, I've got nothing to hide. But let's keep your Internet stalking our little secret, okay? I don't want my friends to get the wrong idea about you."

Ian's eyes narrowed. "So much deflection in so few words. You realize you haven't asked me a single thing about the Lindsay breakup, right? Are you just trying to make me feel guilty for suggesting that you stop fretting over our mutual friend Andrew, or do you actually not care?"

I peered into the camera. "What's it like to sit behind that screen and judge everyone else's lives? Hold on, where did you say you were again? Back in Mum and Dad's basement?"

"You're cute, Fee," Ian waved at the camera. "I miss you."

"Miss you back, troll. Make sure you leave the basement tomorrow to get some Vitamin D. I don't want you getting rickets. Or do I mean scurvy?"

And with that, Ian clicked off the screen. I was scribbling *Prague* in my planner when my phone buzzed again from Ian. Then again. And over and over until my phone memory was filled with memes he'd created using photos he'd skimmed online from Drew, Lindsay, and even Pete.

So I pulled a Sharpie off my desk and scribbled *#ByeFelicia* on my own middle finger. Then sent that image on its way.

eleven

La Nuit Blanche is this epic event that comes around every October in Paris. All over the city, artists and musicians from around the globe display their work or perform at various monuments and key locations. A *nuit blanche* literally means a "white night," but it's what we English speakers call an "all-nighter." For one night, all of Paris stays up until dawn, walking the town and observing one another while they soak up the culture of the moment.

Usually *La Nuit Blanche* takes place on a Friday evening, but this year, because Friday was some random bank holiday, they moved it forward a day. Before the sun had gone down on Thursday evening, Anne was ready to go.

"What do you think?" She twirled around in my narrow room. "I'm going for cute but comfortable while not obviously either one."

Anne looked almost regal standing there, half of her hair pulled up, her dark natural curls falling around her shoulders in perfect ringlets. My hair would never do that in a million years. I fought the urge to channel Ramona Quimby when she yanked Susan Kushner's curls. BOING.

"Love the boots, love the sweater, love your hair. Why are you even asking me this? You always look perfect. I, on the other hand, look like a matron."

She stood next to me in the mirror, scrutinizing herself while she fiddled with her curls again for the millionth time, and I had to wonder why. If she was primping for someone in particular, I didn't know who. A couple of weeks ago at Wednesday night dinner, she'd practically morphed into the heart-eyed emoji, but I couldn't tell yet who'd inspired the shift.

Since the day Monsieur Ludovic first mentioned *La Nuit Blanche* in class, Anne and Pete had been strategizing our itinerary for the evening. At any given break between classes, you could find them in the courtyard with their heads bent together, reading up on the venues, plotting the fastest route there from the other locations, and then entering their research on Anne's spreadsheet. Their obsession bordered on psychotic, which made it hard to imagine anything romantic afoot.

But whenever we hung out in Luxembourg Gardens or after school at a café, Anne *always* sat next to Dan. And really, who could blame her? Besides the floppy hair and the general knowledge about interesting things, Dan Thomas was steadfast and loyal – the kind of guy you could count on in a pinch. Like the time my raven-haired next-door neighbor forgot her keys at school one Friday afternoon. Guess who volunteered to scale the outside wall of the Centre Lafayette and climb through the second story classroom window on her behalf?

Dan Thomas from Eugene, Oregon, ladies and gentleman. Which is why I secretly hoped Anne's primp session was for him.

"Are you sure I shouldn't change to the cardigan?" She asked, twisting from side to side. "The weather's so weird right now. They say it'll be cold tonight, but what if it's not?"

"You know you think too much, right?" I bumped her hip with mine. "Go direct these questions at your own mirror. Mine has its own disaster to solve."

"Here." Anne opened my closet, dug around for maybe twelve seconds, then handed me the perfect jeans + sweater + boots combo. I dressed quickly and pulled my hair into a high ponytail. Then I waited for Anne while she switched tops three more times.

And then waited some more while she switched her boots.

Pete's family's flat was on a whimsical little street less than ten minutes north of Marie-France's place, just a few steps from the Seine. So many streets in Paris had been widened during the Haussmann period, but not the rue Guénégaud. You could almost hear the people sing, you know? Minus the barricades and the blood and Gavroche sprinting down the street, of course.

Pete and Dan lived just above the red awning entrance to their building on the *deuxième étage* (or second floor, even though we'd call it the third floor in the States). The entire west-facing wall of their flat looked out over the street, thanks to a floor-to-ceiling, glass-enclosed balcony that must have been added sometime during the last century, judging by the Art Nouveau-ish metal scrolling along the edges. And while there were surely other Parisian apartments that had added this feature over the years, theirs was the only one like it that I'd seen. It was definitely the only one on this street. Add in the exposed brick walls in the living room and the fifty-year-old hardwood floors, and it seemed pretty obvious how Pete's grandmother had kept the place at full occupancy all these years. It was the best apartment ever.

The second Harper and Kelly arrived at the rue Guénégaud, Anne pulled her homemade quiche from the oven, and from that point forward, she made certain the entire process clipped along with military precision. Eat your quiche, hear half the itinerary. Eat your salad, hear the second half. Have one last sip of wine, and don't dawdle on your way out the door.

As we walked the short distance from the apartment to Notre Dame Cathedral, I watched Anne and Pete chatting easily at the head of the group. Both of them spoke French so flawlessly that people regularly believed they were native speakers. They were both extraordinarily bright. But Pete was a goofball, whereas Anne was the most sophisticated person I knew. Maybe that explained why I found it so difficult to imagine them together.

I felt Dan fall in beside me on the crosswalk near the St. Michel Fountain. He brushed that floppy brown hair away from his glasses, then shot me a look. "Okay, I'm going to say something awful right now, and I'm only going to say it to you because everyone else thinks Pete Russell is swell. It's not their fault. They've only known him three and a half seconds. But I have to live with the guy, and you know as well as I do that he's not perfect, right?"

I examined Dan, whose face was pale in the moonlight. "What's on your mind, Danny?"

"I don't know, it's just… well, like right now." He lifted his right hand toward the front of the group. "Is he running for mayor or something? The guy talks to *everyone*. Have you noticed? The baker flirts outrageously with him every morning when we pass her shop.

And heaven forbid we go to the normal grocery store to buy vegetables because Pete 'knows a guy' half a mile away that he doesn't want to put out of business by convenience shopping from some chain store closer to home."

I stifled a smile. "Helping the local economy isn't a bad thing, you know."

Dan shot me a sideways look. "Oh, great. He's gotten to you, too, hasn't he?"

"Hey, relax." I looped my arm through his. "I'm Switzerland, my friend. No, wait. I'm better than Switzerland. I'm the Vatican. You can confess all your dirty laundry to me, and I'll hear you out every time, but only if you tell the absolute truth. Like how your bad mood tonight has very little to do with Pete, and a whole lot to do with the girl he's babbling at right now."

"It's that obvious, huh?" Dan groaned. "Oh, man. Anne's so gorgeous that I can hardly form a complete thought around her, but not Pete. He's all *blah dee blah blah* for an entire ten minutes without even taking a breath."

"I'm fairly certain *blah dee blah blah* is all she's hearing," I said, squeezing Dan's arm in solidarity. "What do you think he's rambling on about? The overuse of the subjunctive in literary analysis?"

"What?" He pretended to gasp. "Why would anyone dare overuse the subjunctive? The horror."

"Right, right. Hmm. Maybe he's explaining why Proust is superior to Hugo in every way, if people could just get on board with all the extra words."

"The words, or the madeleines?" Dan chuckled, his glasses glinting in the lamplight. "Thanks. I knew you would understand."

"Of course I understand. I'm highly intuitive, you know."

"Sure you are," he smiled. "Listen, I'm not an idiot, okay? Anne could have any guy she wanted, including the holy grail of junior year abroad: a real-life Parisian local, preferably not named Jacques or Pierre."

"Don't be glib. The Franco-American thing happens. A lot, apparently. When I asked Marshall Freeman yesterday where he zooms off to every day after class, you know what he said?"

"What?"

"'*Elle s'appelle Élodie.*' That was it. Then he flew out the door."

"Élodie, his *concierge's* daughter?" Dan started laughing so hard I was worried he might burst a blood vessel. "No way. They're dating? Well played, Marshall. That girl is cute."

"Is she? Here I've been imagining a tiny waif with chocolate brown hair and kale green eyes," I sighed. "You know, Dan, if Marshall won over Élodie, why can't you date Anne?"

Dan slowed his pace a bit and shrugged. "Seems kind of pointless. At the end of the year, we'll all go back to our own schools. She's from Boston. I'm a backwoods bumpkin from Oregon."

"Come on. Eugene is hardly backwoods. And aren't your parents professors?"

"Okay, fine. So it wouldn't be the weirdest match in history." Dan looked again to the front of the group, then stopped walking, full stop. "But what about Pete?"

"What about him?"

Dan gave me a funny look. "He's my best friend, Meredith."

Ignoring the unexpected pang in my gut at his implication, I took Dan's elbow again, steering him forward. "I heard tonight's moon would be the brightest it will ever be for the next four hundred years. Surely that's a good sign, right?"

He looked up at the sky. "No pressure, moon."

I lifted my hand to my eyes and peered up. "You hear that, bro? Don't let our boy down!"

When Dan laughed he sounded like a little kid. "You've been hanging out with Pete too much, *bro.* If you start calling me every nickname under the sun, I'll have to find a new route to school because I can't handle two of you."

"Suit yourself, Clark Kent. Get it? *Suit* yourself?"

"Meredith…"

"It's cool, Quasimodo. I got your back."

Dan snorted, and within two seconds I was laughing so hard I couldn't breathe. By the time we finally stumbled up to the sound-and-light show at Notre Dame, the rest of our group had disappeared into the masses. Lasers trailed across the Gothic façade. Different spotlights jumped and illuminated the cathedral to the sounds of Mozart's *Magic Flute.* But I couldn't stop staring at the moon. If something that beautiful could overpower the beauty of somewhere like Paris, then surely Anne could see adorable Dan for the gem that he was. Otherwise, everything I'd ever believed about life and love was a total sham.

Come on, moon. Don't fail us now.

twelve

The Notre Dame installation only lasted a few minutes. A couple of the spotlights died, which turned the whole scene sort of wonky. So we headed over to the modern dance performance at the Hotel de Ville, which was interesting… mostly because three of the dancers ran screaming offstage after their headpieces caught on fire. Acrobats filled the courtyard of the Centre Pompidou, twirling ribbons and tubes that burped out confetti, which might have been fun if it hadn't been for the countdown clock inside my brain. The Tuileries Big Band concert started at midnight, and it was the one and only event on the itinerary I actually wanted to see.

When we reached the Arc de Triomphe du Carrousel fifteen minutes before show time, Anne checked her notes again and gestured for us to circle up. "Okay," she said, teeth chattering. "We have two choices at this venue: American Bandstand outside here at the

Tuileries, or the film inside the Louvre, where it will be comfy and warm."

"Not American Bandstand, Annie," I corrected. "*Big Band*. We talked about this."

"Oh, right," she said, glancing back down at the paper in her hand. "So, the film showing here at the Louvre won the *Palme d'Or* at Cannes last spring. But to be honest, it could be about matchsticks and I'd still go, because plush seats plus no wind is a good enough reason for me. Who wants to join me?"

Dan was the first to move over to Team Anne, which made me beam a little bit. But then, as if on cue, a blustery wind blew in off the river and sent everyone into a frenzy. When I looked up again, three people huddled around Anne.

And one stood by me.

"Didn't you two hear me?" Anne shot Pete a withering look. "You're headed to a band concert in this cold."

"It's *Big Band*, Annie," Pete imitated me perfectly, scorn and all. "Look, Meredith has her reasons for going to this concert. Is it her fault you guys didn't dress warmly enough?"

Anne's eyes shifted from Pete to me several times, a crooked grin tugging at her mouth. "No worries," she said coolly. "We'll just meet you back here. What time?"

Pete kicked his foot a little on the gravel. "I dunno. Three? On the Pont des Arts?"

"Can we *go*?" Tiny Harper bounced up and down in place. "I'm turning into a popsicle out here."

And just like that, the rest of our friends zoomed away down the secret staircase to the Louvre Carrousel. Pete and I watched them until the last head disappeared, and then, just like at the Normandy cemetery, our feet fell into step together down the gravel path.

"Go ahead and say it, Sully," Pete put up his hands in mock surrender as we left the shadow of the Arc du Carrousel. "You're no fragile snowflake. We both know you're capable of navigating this town just fine without me. But please don't make me watch that film. I don't care if it did win the *Palme d'Or*. It will put me to sleep."

"Okay, but just so you know, I'm staying for the long haul. So if you get cold or bored…"

Pete shook his head and laughed. "Look, don't go spreading this information far and wide, but I have been known to listen to Big Band with my grandmother from time to time. And by that, I mean every night while we cook dinner."

That stopped me mid-stride. "Are you serious?"

"What? You had me pegged for the I-hate-everything-but-indie station?"

"Maybe. Didn't I hear you were a roadie right after high school?"

Pete laughed so hard his cheeks went red. "Who in the world told you that?"

"Who knows," I muttered as we started walking again. "I've heard all kinds of rumors why you're a year older than the rest of us."

"Really?" Pete shook his head, still laughing under his breath. "Like what?"

"Well, there's the roadie rumor. Then I heard you did a stint in white-collar prison for hacking. But I choose to believe that you were a greenhorn on some crab boat in Alaska."

"I had no idea my life was so fascinating," Pete said quietly, casting a glance my way. "So how about you? Are you some sort of USO groupie? Is that why we're here tonight?"

"No," I laughed. "My dad plays clarinet. That's how my parents met, at one of his gigs. He still plays in a little quintet down the coast in Newport. Do you know it?"

"Of course I know Newport." Pete's face lit all the way up, like I'd just admitted my dad was secretly Santa Claus, or the President of the United States. "Wow, Sully. Any favorite songs?"

"Well, my dad's favorite is *Green Dolphin Street*, but no one's ever heard of it."

Pete smiled again, shoving his hands in his pockets. "Not only do I know it, I've seen that movie about fifteen times. It's one of my grandmother's favorites."

My stomach flipped. He could have said he actually *was* a Romanov, and I would've been less shocked. "All right. Which version is better: the one by Miles Davis or Bill Evans?"

"What kind of question is that?" Pete lifted an eyebrow. "Bill Evans for the win."

Impressive. Everyone knew Miles Davis. Only real fans knew Bill Evans.

"What about your favorite song, Sully? Something by Ella Fitzgerald?"

"Good guess, but no. I love Ella, of course, but my favorite song is *Caravan*. The original version, not the Nat King Cole cover."

"Duke Ellington," Pete smiled approvingly. "You're two for two. Not too shabby for a girl from a small coastal town."

I couldn't help but beam at the compliment. "Okay, now it's your turn. No wait, don't tell me. Your favorite song is some obscure B-side from the underground scene in war-torn Sarajevo."

"Was there an underground scene in Sarajevo?" Pete's eyes searched mine, like I knew something he didn't. "No, mine's a pretty standard choice. Do you know *Begin the Beguine*?"

"Are you kidding me right now? I love that song. My parents danced to it at their wedding. Did you know that Cole Porter wrote it here in Paris at the Ritz?"

Every muscle in Pete's face twitched into a smile. "Wow, Sully. I owe you an apology. One of us hasn't given the other enough credit the past two years."

No lie, Russell. Make that two of us.

thirteen

We reached the concert area just north of the first reflecting pool as the pianist trilled the intro to *Take the A Train*. Every tree in that particular section of the gardens had been lit with a million tiny lights, as though all the fairies in the world had flocked to these trees for the evening. Each member of the band was dressed to the nines in tailored tuxedos and black shoes so shiny I swear I could see the moon's reflection from a hundred yards away.

Fifteen or sixteen round tables filled the space before us, with a handful of wooden chairs at each one. The organizers had laid a temporary parquet-like floor in front of the bandstand, and several people were already flocking up the center aisle to dance. Without hesitation, Pete grabbed my hand and pulled me toward the other dancers. But the second we reached the dance floor, my wits took hold of me and I froze in place.

"What are you doing?" I squealed loudly enough that several people spun around to see what was the matter. Pete must have thought I was kidding at first, but when he saw my horror, he took my elbow and led me over to the side of the stage, under the trees.

I'd never realized how tall Pete was until he was looming over me beneath the fairy lights.

"What's up, Sully?" He asked, so softly that only I could have heard him. "I thought you were some sort of Irish dance champion back home. Or did the Highgate rumor mill get that one wrong, too?"

Until this year, I'd always believed Pete Russell was the vilest creature on the planet, and because I was a crazy person – a crazy, *lonely* person – I was unable to think past his kind, dark eyes and the surprisingly nice smell of his breath so close to my face.

Hold on. Why was I thinking about Pete's *breath*? Had someone given me drugs tonight?

"Pete, *please*," I begged. "I haven't danced in ages. Can't we just sit down and enjoy the music? You have no idea how embarrassing this will be. For both of us."

Pete peered over my left shoulder, then over my right. "Is someone here grading you?"

"Of course not. You're missing my point."

Pete lowered his face so that we were looking directly into each other's eyes. His nose was almost touching mine, and his lips were... well, they were too close. "Look, Sully, you seem to be having difficulty with your English comprehension right now, which is understandable since we spend most of our days speaking French. I'll spell this out for you: no one else is with us. It's just you and me and the band, okay? Besides, how many times in your life will you get the chance to dance to a live orchestra in the middle of the Tuileries on a night like tonight?"

I didn't move. I just stared back at him, blinking. How could I argue with Pete's logic? This was one of those moments you didn't skip in life. So when the lines along his eyes creased upward, I couldn't help it. My mouth tugged into a smile.

"There's my girl," Pete grinned. Then he led me by the hand back to the dance floor just as the band started a new song.

Begin the Beguine.

Dazed by the coincidence, it took a moment before I registered movement in my feet as well as the not-so-unpleasant sensation of Pete's arms guiding me deftly around the dance floor. The other dancers whirled around us, some laughing, some taking themselves very seriously (especially one couple dressed in forties garb). I couldn't quite believe how easy it felt, thanks to Pete's strength and confidence. How did a jokester like him know how to dance like this? There was no awkwardness between us. Just a guy leading a girl, one step at a time.

When I was a little kid, I watched all the old movies with my parents. My favorite part was always the sweet ingénue floating around the dance floor in the arms of her male lead. Tonight, under the canopy of twinkling lights, I was that ingénue. And when the music ended, Pete was still holding me, his expression somewhere between surprise and anticipation. And warmth.

I willed my lungs to breathe normally, which I might have attributed to the dancing if Pete's gaze hadn't just traveled from my eyes to my lips. But just then, the percussion section began the opening riff of *Sing, Sing, Sing*, and Pete's face lit all the way up.

"Yes!" He looked up at the band, then back at me, wrapping a hand around my waist. "Tell me you know how to Lindy Hop."

"Maybe a little bit," I lied. Those concerts of my dad's down in Newport? There was always a Lindy Hop and Jitterbug class whenever the band took a break, taught by yours truly and a local dance teacher. But the thing about dances like the Lindy Hop is that they can go very wrong, *very* quickly. It was challenging enough with the Newport dance teacher, and I trusted that guy completely. During those lessons, whenever we switched partners, it was a complete nightmare. Inexperience plus unfamiliarity do not make for great dancing. It took practice. *Lots* of practice.

"No," I stammered, pulling away. "Seriously, Pete, it has been years. I don't think I even remember the basics. What if I bump into someone or punch them in the face?"

"Sully, please." Pete took my hand in his again, sliding his thumb along mine. "All you have to do is let me lead, just like last time. If you're not having fun by the time this song is over, I promise we'll sit down. Just trust me, okay?"

And with that, he pulled me onto the dance floor, twirled me once, and never let me go.

I couldn't believe how different it felt dancing with Pete. His confidence made me forget every single fear that normally plagued me. The way he held my hand was tender but secure, and when he spun me on the dance floor, I knew I could count on his arms to hold me in place. There was no way I could have made a mistake because we were connected, mind reading mind, anticipating one another's next move like we'd been dancing together for years.

Soon enough I was channeling my inner USO girl, determined to upstage that overzealous couple showing off in their wide-legged trousers and doo-wop shoes. I even let Pete flip me.

When the song ended, the people at the tables just beyond the dance floor stood and cheered for us. I looked at Pete and laughed, and when he nodded, I understood. We bowed together. Then he flipped me one more time, and the whole place erupted again. Even the band was clapping.

"You… are… such a … liar," Pete said between heaving breaths as we left the dance floor. "You have *so* done that before."

"Maybe," I grinned. "But it's never been like *that*."

"Of course not," he grinned back. "You weren't dancing with me."

fourteen

After he bought us a couple of water bottles from a nearby concession stand, Pete motioned for me to follow him over to the reflecting pool, away from the music and the dancing. I wasn't going to tell him this, but I'd loved this quieter part of the Tuileries ever since the first time I'd come to Paris. The number of times I'd imagined myself sitting here over the years must be in the thousands by now. There was something about sitting right on the axis of so much history that always made me a little starry-eyed.

With the Louvre behind us, the Seine to our left, and the Place de la Concorde beyond, we were the King and Queen of France.

As we each plopped into our own green metal chair, I gave Pete the stink eye. "So, do you DVR *Dancing with the Stars* and practice down in your grandmother's basement every night or something?"

Pete took a sip from his water bottle, eyeing me back, then turned his whole body toward me. "Look, I will tell you, but this needs to stay between us, okay? I can't have you blurting out my secrets in the middle of Wednesday night dinner."

I lifted my hand to my heart. "You have my word."

"Okay. So in the eighth grade, my soccer coach forced our entire team to take Lindy Hop lessons with the girls' team."

"What? Why would he do that?"

Pete rolled his eyes. "The girls' coach at my school heard about some other team using that technique to improve footwork, and she convinced my coach that we should all go in on it together. For weeks, it was Lindy Hop Central on the soccer field. I want you to imagine that for a second: a bunch of gangly boys matched up with girls who were a hundred times cooler than we were, all dancing to music from the middle of the last century."

I had to laugh at the image. "Wait, you've remembered it that well for all these years?"

"Oh, I'm not finished with my confession yet." He lifted an eyebrow, then continued. "Now, this next part is actually Code Red security clearance, okay? You have to swear to me you won't tell your buddy Sutton what I'm about to tell you next, because while I know everyone finds him hilarious, charming, and totally adorable, even you have to admit that he's not quite as enlightened a person as he should be."

I pushed down the urge to defend Drew and nodded. "You can trust me, Pete."

Pete's eyes searched mine for a moment longer. "You sure? Because if Drew Sutton were to find out, for example, that I was the captain of my high school's competitive swing dance team, it might undermine years' worth of hard-earned street cred among my so-called brothers."

My eyes grew as wide as that bright moon in the sky because... whoa. I had not seen that one coming. And to my shock, Pete's face flushed bright crimson in response.

"Oh, don't look at me like that. Sully. It's not *that* weird."

I sat up straight in my chair. "I'm sorry, competitive swing dancing? Are you kidding me right now, Pete Russell? Wait a minute. Is this about a girl?"

"See, I knew you caught on quicker than the average person." He tapped the side of his nose. "Her name was Brooks Darby. She was a senior, I was a freshman. Her family lived down the street from us, so she drove me home from school every day."

"Aw. Did little Pete have a crush on his babysitter?"

"Laugh it up, Sully. The heart wants what it wants." Pete lifted his eyes to the sky and his hands to his heart, mocking his younger self. "But see, I haven't always been the specimen of masculine grace and swagger that you know and admire today. For weeks and weeks, Brooks and I drove to and from school without a single word. Until one morning, when she mentioned that I would need to find another ride home that afternoon because she was in charge of auditions for – wait for it – the Ducky Shincrackers."

That time, I laughed so hard I actually snorted. "You're making this up."

"Oh, I wish I were," he sighed. "A 'ducky shincracker' is forties slang for a good dancer, so when swing dance came back on the scene in the nineties, some teacher at St. Francis Prep started a competitive team. By the time I got to high school, it had become sort of a big deal. We even performed at pep rallies and football games."

"Really? That's kind of fun, actually."

The muscles in Pete's jaw relaxed a bit and he smiled. "I thought so, too. So when Brooks told me about the auditions, I figured I'd impress her by showing up."

"And did you?"

"Please," he huffed. "You should know me well enough by now to realize I'm at my best whenever I've got an audience. Were you not at *Le Somnambuliste* in Rouen?"

"Oh, I was there. Who do you think booed you from the back of the room?"

"Well, we can't all be experts at everything like you are, champ," Pete grinned, dangling his fingers to mock my Irish step-dancing days. "I impressed Brooks enough to make the team that day, but sadly that was as far as it went. She had a boyfriend. Some senior soccer player who felt it his job to ruin my life when I made the varsity soccer team a couple of months later."

"Aw. Poor little Petey Russell. And you didn't bail after all that?"

"Are you kidding me?" He beamed. "I'm no idiot. Half the girls in school wanted to be a Ducky Shincracker. I figured the odds were in my favor that someday I'd win *someone* over with my mad skills."

Someday indeed.

fifteen

As we exited the gardens near the Pont Royal sometime after 2:30 a.m., I instinctively began to walk a little faster. Three hours ago I was just here to hear some Big Band music, and now, I was trying to rid myself of this crazy attraction to Pete Freaking Russell. Was there some sort of rip in the space-time continuum?

And what about Anne? If Dan's fears were warranted and she had a thing for Pete, he was off-limits. I'd never broken girl code before, and I wasn't about to start now.

But I couldn't stop thinking about what Drew had said that night at Devil's Lake this summer. *You could be walking through the Tuileries one day and there Prince Charming will be, waiting to whisk you off your feet.* All Romanov jokes aside, I could almost believe those words had been prophetic.

Wait a minute, *what*? This was Pete Russell. The king of the offensive nickname. The ruiner of every single French class at

Highgate College. How many U-turns had I made the last two years just so I wouldn't have to speak to him? One bazillion, at least.

I looked up at the moon and scowled. *I thought we made a deal. You're supposed to help my boy Dan. Why are you still hanging around here?*

"So, what have you got planned this weekend, Sully?" Pete asked as we reached the sidewalk along the river Seine. "Besides Dan and Kelly's birthday party on Saturday, of course."

I'd almost forgotten about that. "I don't know," I said quietly. "My brother's been hassling me about filling up my bracelet with more charms, so I thought I might head down to Versailles."

"Yeah, you could do that." Pete was silent for a minute, then stopped. "Or you could come with me to the Gare du Nord early Sunday morning and we could hop the first train."

I stood there, stunned. "Just like that? No matter where it's headed?"

Pete stepped a little closer. "Can you give me a good reason why not?"

A tiny laugh escaped me, and I'm not sure why, but I laid my hand across my heart. "Um, I can give you about fifty. What if it goes all the way to Belgium? Or the Netherlands?"

"What if it does?" In Pete's dark eyes, I could see the reflection of the lamplight behind me. "We'll hop off the train, find a charm for your bracelet, then take the next train back to Paris. You don't have to see every museum or historical site for a visit to count, Sully."

My brain felt like it might jump out of my skull. Pete Russell and I were standing under some Parisian street lamp, meters away from the Seine, and he was asking me, what? On a date? To escape with him to Gretna Green like Lydia Bennet and Mr. Wickham?

But before I could figure out what anything meant, we were suddenly surrounded by loud American voices, rambling on and on about their evening, pushing us forward on the sidewalk toward the Pont des Arts.

"You guys missed out," Kelly was saying, her long blond hair swooshing from side to side as she looped one arm through mine and the other through Pete's. "The director was completely drunk. Do you know how ridiculous it sounds to slur in French?"

"Yeah, you guys missed it!" Dan said over his shoulder. "The whole cast came on stage, but the director was so hammered he couldn't hold his microphone. Then the lead actress walked off the stage, and it was so awkward and quiet that Kelly started *church giggling*."

"Rewind and tell the truth, Dan Thomas," Kelly shouted. "You guys, Dan was laughing so hard that an usher told him to be quiet."

"Okay, well, that's true," Dan said over his shoulder as he turned to walk normally. "But the lead actor – you know, the one who's supposed to win the *César*? He was so fidgety he couldn't sit still. If I had to guess, he'd been lining mirrors with the white stuff backstage. And when the lead actress left, he ran over to the director, and punched the guy square on the jaw!"

By the time we reached the wooden stairs to the Pont des Arts, everyone was so engrossed in their own tales that they failed to notice the young couple fifty feet away. With my friends flanking me on both sides of the nearest double-sided bench, I sat facing south, watching the pair leaning against the Plexiglas-lined balustrade, their foreheads resting against each other's.

My friends chattered on, oblivious, as the guy wrote something on an object only he and his companion could see. For a handful of years, millions of people had come to this bridge to declare their love for one another by attaching a padlock to the chain link fence of the balustrade, then throwing the keys into the River Seine below.

Total schmaltz, I know. But ever since my first visit to Paris in high school, I'd been obsessed with this tradition. The moment two people clicked that lock into place, they were hitching their wagons to the same glorious star for all eternity.

If anyone knew how many times I'd imagined myself on this bridge with my one true love, they would've pushed me over the railing for my own good.

But a couple of years ago, the City of Paris had declared war on romance and cut every last padlock off the bridge, replacing the railing's chain link with an impenetrable wall of Plexiglas.

Rude.

Kelly and Dan were still rambling on – something about champagne bottles getting smashed on the floor of the Louvre – when the guy moved behind his girl, wrapping his arms around her as she leaned slightly over the railing. Panic rose in my throat. Had she lost something? Did she see a body floating below? Then she looked back at him over her shoulder and nodded. He dropped the small metallic object in her hand, and together, they bent over the railing and dropped it into the water.

Then he lifted a chain over her head and around her neck, and I suddenly understood.

Very clever. They'd reversed the tradition, dropping their padlock into the river and keeping the keys.

When they started kissing, I finally looked away, and that's when I caught Pete staring at me. *Really* staring, with the strangest grin on his face. What in the world? I was beginning to wonder if this bright moon business could cause the earth to spin backwards on its axis, because nothing about tonight actually felt real.

"Meredith?" Harper waved her tiny hand in my face. "Did you hear me? How was the concert?"

I looked back at Pete, and there wasn't even a trace of the smile from before. He shrugged nonchalantly, then stood and stretched his arms to the sky. "Snooze fest," he said, bending one elbow over his head, then the other. "Sully put me to sleep rambling on and on about the underground jazz scene in Sarajevo back in the seventies."

"The *forties*," I corrected, then rolled my eyes at Harper, hoping Pete meant for me to play along. "Would you believe Pete didn't hear three words before he conked out? You guys should be glad he wasn't at the film with you. Pete snores so loudly, that drug-fueled actor might have punched *him* instead of the director."

Maybe that was all they needed to hear, because then they started talking about some blogger who accused the writers of plagiarism during the post-film Q&A. Certainly no one noticed Pete's eyes locking with mine again, a smile spreading so imperceptibly across his face that I later wondered if I'd imagined it. Pete and I had a secret. Several, actually – each one so irrelevant that it would sound nonsensical to anyone else, but each one belonged to us.

Something about that meant more to me than I could understand.

The Eiffel Tower stood proudly in the distance, floodlit in blue, white, and red to commemorate yet another *Nuit Blanche*. Sometime in the past few moments, while the six of us sat together on the northernmost bench, the sky had changed from ebony to cobalt to a deep violet blue. None of us spoke. We just breathed in the beauty of Paris at dawn.

After coffee and croissants at Dan and Pete's apartment, we all trekked down to school. But as we rounded the corner across from the Luxembourg Gardens, my friends' chatter grew dim against the sound of a taxi idling a hundred yards away at the door of the Centre Lafayette. The driver and passenger argued so loudly I could decipher their words. And even with his back turned, I would have recognized the passenger's voice in any city, on any continent in the world.

It was Drew.

sixteen

I sprinted down the sidewalk and across the busy rue de Vaugirard to the taxi, begging the driver in French to wait just a minute.

"Fee!" Drew shouted, grabbing and hugging me so abruptly that he nearly knocked the wind out of me. "You have to help me, okay? This guy is trying to rip me off. The meter only said forty euros but he says I owe forty-five."

The driver, who clearly understood English, turned to me and began explaining in French what I already understood. "Drew, there's a five euro charge for your duffel bag. He's not trying to rip you off. It's right there on the window."

He glanced at the sign on the cab. "Well, I can't read that," he said defiantly. "It's in *French*."

Without hesitation, I grabbed Drew's wallet out of his hands and gave the driver his forty euros plus an additional ten – five for the extra bag and five for his trouble. The taxi pulled away from the curb just as my friends arrived on the scene.

"Sutton." Though Pete's voice was low, surprise was written all over his face. "What in the world are you doing here?"

Drew's eyes narrowed as he glanced first at Pete, then at me, then back again at Pete. "Oh. Hey, Russell. I forgot you were here."

"Sure you did." Pete shot me a look, then narrowed his eyes at Drew. "You've got mad ninja timing, bro. I'll give you that much."

As they stood across from each other, posturing like a couple of rams, I was fascinated by how slight Drew looked in comparison to Pete, and Drew was not a small guy. The two of them were the same height, but Drew's lean physique suddenly seemed ... well, juvenile. Pete completely overshadowed him. Maybe it was just home court advantage.

"What's up, Sutton?" Dan stepped forward to intervene, grabbing Drew's hand in a series of clasps that I assumed was some fraternity handshake. "Man, that flight here is brutal. Hey, Meredith, maybe we could put Drew's bag in the storeroom for him?"

"Good idea," I mumbled, grateful for the help. Dan grabbed Drew's duffel bag and carried it inside past the *gardienne's* lair while Pete answered a call on his cell phone and walked away. I sort of wondered if he'd faked it. It was the middle of the night back home.

Somehow I corralled the rest of us inside to the entry hall, and there we stood – Drew, me, and three girls he'd never seen before in his life – an awkward silence sucking the air out of the room until Kelly saved the day.

"Hi, Drew," she said in her best future teacher voice. "I'm Kelly, and this is Harper and Anne." They both raised their hands without a word. "Thanks for letting us borrow Meredith this year. Things wouldn't be the same without her around."

"I get that," he said softly, shooting a glance my way that lasted several seconds longer than it should have. What in the world was going on? And how had Drew found enough extra cash in his account for a round-trip ticket to Paris?

"Coffee," Kelly blurted, grabbing Drew by the shoulders. "You must need coffee after such a long flight. We'll go get you a cup. How do you take it?"

Drew's face contorted as he turned to me. "Um... what should...? I've never had French coffee before."

"Black, with extra sugar," I instructed Kelly, handing her a few euro coins. "Would you bring me one, too? But just black on that second one."

She nodded her head, winked, then zoomed through the glass doors into the courtyard, with Harper and Anne scuffling behind her without a word, like she was Miss Clavel or something.

And just like that, we were alone. I motioned for Drew to follow me to a faculty conference room just across from the *gardienne's* office where I'd never thought to enter before now because it's restricted. But I closed the long double doors behind us for privacy, then turned back to Drew.

Somehow, in the handful of weeks I'd been gone, the planes of Drew's face had grown more defined. The sun-washed freckles on his nose were still there, but the streaks of platinum and gold were fading back into his normal tawny color. And he'd clipped it short for once in his life.

But it was his eyes that I knew to avoid if I wanted to stay safe. My whole life, one look into their dark blueness and the left side of my brain stopped working. And today was no different.

Drew Sutton had flown five thousand miles to see me. *Only* me.

He pulled me slowly toward him, wrapping his arms around me in a way he never had before, his hands cradling me against his chest. "Don't move," he whispered, his lips brushing against my hair. "Just give me a minute. I've missed you so, so much."

For longer than I would ever admit, I let myself cling to him while he held me so tight. Drew was *here*. He was in Paris. And something about the combination of those two things felt … off. So when he turned his head a little and his lips were suddenly against my temple, I pushed myself back. And then I stepped back again two more paces just so I could breathe. "Why are you here, Drew?"

"What do you mean, *why*?" He sort of half-laughed, half-scoffed. "It's Friday morning, Fee. We have a breakfast tradition, remember?"

"I remember. But why today? It's not even your fall break."

Drew leaned against the conference table behind him, then crossed his arms against his chest. "Did I break a rule or something? Because you're definitely freaking me out right now."

"The feeling is mutual."

"Okay, okay." He pushed himself upright, then stepped toward me again, the lines at the corner of his eyes twitching in amusement. "Maybe I should have told you I was coming, but the truth is, I'm here to get a status report on Operation: Sugar Daddy. Do you know how disappointed I am, Fee? You promised me an inheritance, and all you've actually done is go to school and hang out with your new friends. If you ask me, you've only got yourself to blame for this unannounced visit. France needs an heir, you need a pre-nup, and I need that stable boy gig."

Two months ago, that would have been all it took for Drew to win me over. The flattery, the swoony eyes, the swagger for days... all of it had been my personal Kryptonite. But this? Something about Drew's timing felt shady. And *how* had he paid for that flight?

So when his expression softened and he threaded his thumb through the belt loop at my waist, I wasn't sure how to decipher the haze that fell over my vision. The anger I'd felt just a moment before shifted to confusion. And maybe that all-nighter had taken a greater toll than I'd realized because it felt... well, it really, *really* felt like Drew Sutton was about to kiss me.

"*Mademoiselle?*" A female voice said from the doorway behind me. It was the *gardienne*. And even though he didn't know a single word of French, the change in Drew's expression indicated he understood the reprimand that followed.

Absolutely no students allowed in this room. Ever.

Especially not those whose fickle hearts swayed to and fro like Foucault's pendulum.

Just like Drew Sutton.

Or me.

seventeen

The *gardienne* held the door wide until Drew and I had both reached the entry hallway. "Whoa," he leaned over to whisper just above my ear. "Is there a cat around or something? Or does all of Paris smell like this?"

But I didn't answer him. I couldn't answer him, because after the rollercoaster of the past ten minutes, I was having a hard enough time putting one foot in front of the other. As we walked down the corridor to meet up with my crew, Drew's gaze passed from the ivy wallpaper to the half-timbered ceiling above, and then as we passed the *Grande Salle*, he stood silent in the doorway for a full minute. I had described the Centre Lafayette, room by room, in the one and only letter I'd written Drew during our first week here. I'd hardly expected him to care, but now, as he walked alongside me, it occurred to me that this was Drew's version of *Promenade Parisienne*. In the same way my class explored the city through the eyes of the authors we studied,

Drew appeared to be exploring *my* Paris, and in that moment, I felt my resolve begin to crack.

Just then, I saw Monsieur Salinger beginning his lecture out in the courtyard, and I grabbed Drew's arm with one hand while I dug through my bag for my notebook and pen with the other. We tagged on to the back of the group and marched along behind them all the way out the front door like we'd been there all along. Drew blended into the crowd, head held high, so naturally that Monsieur Salinger probably never noticed the intrusion. He just prattled on, pointing out every nook and cranny on today's route and its significance in the general literary canon.

Because Salinger had the reputation for putting even the tiniest details on each test, we were all scribbling away. I did my best to stay on task, but having Drew around was too distracting to stay focused for long. Kelly had handed him both our cups of coffee fairly early on in the walk, but he was struggling, staring hard at Monsieur Salinger, like if he tried hard enough, he might understand something, *anything*. Every couple of minutes, he yawned adorably, which in turn made my classmates yawn, and each time, Drew's face blazed crimson. Against my better judgment, I found myself grinning like an idiot at all the cute.

At the steps of Oscar Wilde's place on Notre Dame des Champs, my phone buzzed over and over in my pocket. It was text upon text from Kelly, who was standing directly in front of me, typing like she always did into her phone without once dropping her gaze away from the professor. One line at a time, she sent the following message:

what if you + drew = movie love?
major swoon avec sigh
fyi, anne's staying with us this weekend
NO PROTESTS or drew sees COPACABANA footage
you have been warned
<3 <3 <3

One by one, my friends dispersed at the end of the walking tour, each one vanishing without so much as a quick goodbye to the others. By the time we got back to school, Drew and I were alone again.

My favorite part of the Centre Lafayette had always been the wall of glass that lined the hallway near the entrance. So much light, so much beauty in the courtyard just behind its panes. As Drew shuffled the contents of his bag around right in the middle of the hallway, trying to find space for the jacket and sweater he'd already peeled off, I stood at the glass wall and waited.

Two guys from one of the other colleges walked past Drew and me, ignoring the grunts and the cursing, and headed out the glass door into the courtyard. Because I'd gotten in the bad habit of being nosy, my eyes drifted along with them. As they walked past a bench at the far end of the courtyard, I saw Pete Russell, still talking on the phone, his fingers shoved into his hair in a way that made my stomach clench.

Something was wrong.

The bustle of people walking past must have drawn his attention upward, because at that moment, his eyes connected with mine. And I suddenly realized Pete had been absent from class all morning.

It's strange. All Pete did was lift the fingers of his free hand a couple of inches, and I knew it was more than a wave. He was answering a question I hadn't asked. He nodded once in Drew's direction, then smiled. When I turned, I saw why. Drew's butt was pushed up against the glass as he struggled to lengthen the strap on his duffel bag.

I zoomed over to Drew and took the strap from his hand. "Here, let me try. Those things can be persnickety."

"Persnickety?" Drew laughed. "Are you using word-of-the-day toilet paper again, Fee?"

"Don't mock," I scowled, twisting and untwisting the strap as I spoke. "You know that toilet paper helped me score fifty points higher than you on the SAT, right, Mister Salutatorian?"

"Exactly, because you're... hey, do you mind? I'm trying not to take this personally, Fee, but you can't blame me for feeling slighted when your eyes keep wandering from me to an empty courtyard."

I followed Drew's gaze outside. Not one soul remained.

eighteen

Drew insisted that we follow my normal Friday lunch tradition instead of heading straight to the apartment. So we grabbed a couple of sandwiches and headed over to the central pond of the Luxembourg Gardens. The topaz sky felt huge over the park, but the air felt oddly thin, like it might evaporate and take me with it.

Every quarter hour or so, I'd beg Drew to let me take him sightseeing, but he refused, happy for the moment to fill up this corner of my world. The afternoon sun lit each goldenrod streak in his hair while he rattled on about Highgate and the changing leaves on campus, about Lincoln City and our families. He spent thirty-seven minutes describing the latest Sigma Phi Beta pledge class and how many different shenanigans they'd pulled already.

Thirty-seven minutes. I know, because I timed him. He never once mentioned Lindsay or any other girl. And that was the weirdest thing of all.

In the fifteen years we'd been friends, Drew and I had spent countless hours together under every condition. Working every free hour after school at Sullivan's. Camping with our families. Laughing in the school library until someone kicked us out. Hanging out in his boat on Devil's Lake late into the night, plotting what object to swipe from Ian's old bedroom so he'd freak out the next time he came home.

A few weeks ago, if you'd asked me who knew me best in the world, my answer without hesitation would've been Drew Sutton. Before I came to Paris, I would have believed that 'til my dying day.

But as I watched him, the realization that Drew had never cared about this part of my life hit me with the force of a grenade. I couldn't begin to count the number of times we'd argued about my studying French. When I'd come home from my trip to Paris in high school, Drew had thwarted every anecdote and ignored every photo. And this past summer, my moving here had hung in the air between us, though he'd done his best to distract me with sarcasm and outrageous flirting.

Which is why, as his beautiful blue eyes prowled over every inch of my new world, my instinct was to march him and his bags to the nearest taxi stand, destination: Charles de Gaulle Airport. Because something did *not* add up here. Not one bit.

"So this is where you live," Drew said as he hoisted his duffel bag into Marie-France's apartment that evening, eyes wide as they took in the room. "No offense, Fee, but this is a little fancier than I imagined from the pictures you posted online."

"That's because Anne and I live two floors up in rooms the size of the Highgate dorm closets. At least, that's how they'll appear to you since you're only a Muggle."

"That I am," he grinned. "But wait – where's the famous Marie-France? Still at work?"

"She's in Venice." I crossed the room and threw open the windows with ease, smiling to myself that I'd finally gotten the hang of things. "She flies there once a month to visit this Scottish guy she's seeing. He lives on some island nearby. It's called Burano, I think?"

"Scottish? Wait, she flies all the way to Venice just for the weekend? That's nuts."

Says the guy who just flew across North America *and* the Atlantic for unspecified reasons. Just for the weekend.

I walked into the kitchen and filled the tea kettle. Drew puttered around the apartment for a few minutes, peeking into every room like it was a museum. The light outside had faded, and surely Drew was fading, too. There was no way he had slept five minutes on his flight here. So I poured us both some tea and headed back to the living room, where Drew stood at the window.

"I hate to tell you this, Fee, but one of your neighbors on the third floor over there is swanning around in his tighty-whities. Is he… wait, is he dancing?"

"Don't be a creeper," I sighed, placing the mug in his hand. A smile spread across Drew's face, then he started to laugh in his way that always sounded like singing – the same laugh he had as a kid. Everything between us suddenly felt so normal we could have been back in my room at home. Everything, that is, except the way Drew's eyes kept searching mine.

"That's Saint Sulpice," I said, nodding toward the church across the square. "I like seeing it at this time of day, with the lights, and the sky just this shade of blue."

"Meredith." Drew took both our mugs and placed them on the coffee table behind him, then wrapped one hand gently around my elbow. "Tell me the truth: are you angry that I'm here?"

"Why would you ask that?"

"I don't know. When I got to your school this morning, I felt like I was intruding on your life or something."

The Drew standing in front of me was the old Drew – the one who'd listened to millions of my stories on the playground and helped me with math homework every night. The boy I knew before the boomerang girlfriend and the mercurial game-playing. And now he seemed so bewildered that I could feel it creep through his fingers up my elbow and all the way into my heart.

"You're not intruding," I said quietly. "But you still haven't told me why you're here."

Drew let go of my elbow, crossed his arms and turned to look outside. "I had this whole thing planned. I was going to take you to dinner tonight, and we would walk past Notre Dame, and then over that little bridge over to that Saint-Louis island. I even made reservations for us in some *crêperie*, and I've been practicing how to order just the right thing in French."

"Wait… how'd you know we should do all of those things?"

"I have my ways." Drew turned to me, lifting his thumb to my cheek. "I'm so tired, Fee. Aren't you tired?"

"Sure," I laughed nervously. "I didn't sleep a wink last night, and you must be jet-lagged."

"No." Drew slid his fingers into my hair, and then kissed me – just once, and then once more. "I'm so tired of fighting *this*."

And just like that, he was kissing me like I'd always imagined he would, like there was nowhere in the world he would rather be.

nineteen

The number one thing about Drew that no one ever believes is that he is a morning person. I don't mean like the I-wake-up-at-dawn-to-practice-yoga-and-eat-kefir sort of way. No, no.

Once he's up, everyone's up. Whether the moon is still out or not.

Which is how I found myself sitting in Marie-France's kitchen at half past five on a Saturday morning, my hands wrapped around an enormous cup of coffee and my eyes propped open with imaginary toothpicks while Drew prattled on about his plans for the day. Turns out he'd bought *Greg's Guidebook* to Paris a few weeks ago – the latest edition, with a couple dozen photos courtesy of the one and only Ian Sullivan – because he refused to see Paris from the beaten path.

"Any idiot can find his way to oversized radio towers and flying buttresses, Fee," he chided through a mouthful of *pain au chocolat*.

"Today, we visit the places you won't find on the hop-on-hop-off bus tours. Today, we're going somewhere I bet even you haven't been."

Ever since the ninth grade, Drew had been obsessed with the Roman Empire. It was the reason he'd picked history as his major. So when we arrived at the Musée de Cluny later that morning, I had to laugh. He was right. Drew had found someplace in Paris I had yet to explore.

How the Cluny guys had decided to construct their abbey above Roman ruins six hundred years ago, I had no clue. But one look at Drew's face as we entered the courtyard of the gothic castle-like structure, and I knew this was a better choice for us today than, say, the Louvre, with its thousands of visitors and security lines out the door. After he bought our tickets, Drew slipped his hand in mine and guided me toward the Roman *frigidarium*.

I'm not going to lie: something about the way he was taking charge today had me imagining Drew as some towheaded knight, sporting chain mail with a sword in his free hand, ready to defend his lady if some Huns leapt out from the emergency exit.

"What?" Sir Drew the Fair whispered, a smile spreading across his whole face. "Don't tell me you're surprised I found this place on my own? I did learn how to *read*, you know."

I wanted to quip back. I wanted to tease him, or make him laugh, but I couldn't. All I could really do was let myself feel what I'd spent two months trying to escape. A voice inside my head begged me not to let my guard down, that the timing was too weird considering… well, considering who else I'd let inside my head recently. But I didn't listen.

Today, Drew deserved a chance to prove me wrong.

Half an hour later, we entered the dimly lit room of the *Lady and the Unicorn* tapestries. I had to suppress a laugh as Drew tugged me along behind him from one image to the next, because I already knew what he had not yet realized. Everyone under the age of forty had seen these tapestries a hundred times. When we paused before the sixth and final tapestry – the one with the dark blue tent – Drew's eyes widened.

"These are in the Gryffindor Common Room," he said reverently. "Well, at least in the movie version, right? Did you know these tapestries existed in real life?"

"*Greg's Guidebook* doesn't say anything about them?"

"I didn't read past the Roman section," Drew laughed under his breath. Then he pointed at the banner above the young lady's head. "What does that say?"

"*À mon seul désir.*"

"Well, I can read that much for myself." A crooked smile formed on Drew's lips as he pulled me close. "What does it mean?"

"I'm not really sure what it means in this case, because… well, if you read it literally, it says something like 'to my only desire.' But if you take it in the context of the other five tapestries, which represent the five senses, maybe it means she's renouncing her humanity to serve a greater purpose? Or that she's exerting her free will? Or, wait… she might be giving her heart to the man who gave her that necklace she's holding. What do you think?"

He lowered his face to mine. "Why have I never taken you to a museum before now? This nerdy side of you is hot, Fee."

Drew's lips were suddenly on mine and he was pushing me breathlessly up against a wall in the nearest dark corner. Good thing the only other person in the room was a docent who had fallen asleep at the other end, because this kiss was different from last night's. Today, as if he knew my resistance had finally broken down, Drew seemed to be making up for lost time.

And maybe I was too, because when Drew paused for a split second, I took a lesson from the tapestry lady and exerted my own free will, maneuvering us around so that Drew was against the wall instead. Neither of us breathed for long stretches of time, but that didn't stop us from kissing harder, faster. Drew cradled his fingers around the back of my head, pulling me closer as his lips searched mine, our bodies nestled against each other.

Drew pulled away first, breathing heavily. Then he held me tight like he had yesterday when he first arrived. "I'm sorry," he said softly into my hair. "I should never have waited so long. I just... I didn't want to mess up what we have, and now..."

As we stood there in the dark, holding onto each other like the world might explode into tiny little pieces if we shifted even one millimeter, I knew exactly how he felt. For every ounce of happiness this brought me, there were at least two ounces of regret. If only he'd told me sooner how he felt – would it have been worth giving up Paris?

Drew had barely been here twenty-four hours, and already I missed him.

twenty

It was weird enough that Drew knew Pete from their fraternity. But yesterday, just as we got back from our class walk, I'd heard Dan Thomas inviting Drew to his shared birthday party with Kelly tonight up in Montmartre. It made sense, after all – Dan was a Sigma Phi Beta too. But for whatever reason, my stomach had flipped, and as the hours ticked down to the party, those stomach flips earned themselves Olympic gold in both the individual event and the all-around.

Okay, okay, not just any old reason. It rhymed with Pete Russell.

At lunch, Drew had suggested that we walk from my apartment up to the party in Montmartre, and I'd agreed, because seeing Paris through Drew's eyes was making me swoony all over again. So we'd left my apartment at three, crossing over to the Right Bank of the Seine just at the Place de la Concorde. A decision I quickly regretted as we passed the Tuileries' entrance.

"Hold on a minute, Fee," he said, tugging back against my hand as I tried to speed forward. "Is this… isn't this the Tuileries?"

I looked over at the gilded gate to our right, which so obviously marked this as a place of importance. Of royalty. "Yep," I said as flatly as I could, scowling. "Wow, look at the crowds. This place is always crawling with tourists."

"I'm a tourist," he said. "Can't we take a short detour? You know, just in case your future boyfriend's waiting? A promise is still a promise, after all."

Drew's eyes were laughing, but I felt the air fleeing my lungs as I soldiered forward onto the gravel walkway, feeling like the biggest turncoat on two whole continents, unsure which Sigma Phi Beta brother I was betraying most by being here. But I knew it was past time to tell Drew about Thursday night. Even if I kept some secrets locked far, far away.

"So, they had this Big Band concert here on Thursday night," I blurted, just as we reached the second reflecting pool – the one where Pete and I had hung out after dancing. I noticed our two chairs sitting almost exactly where we'd left them, and nearly lost my breath again. Drew, who had been vaguely listening to me prattle on up to that point, followed my gaze to the chairs, and then stopped in his place.

"Yeah? Were they as good as Jamie's band?"

"Not even close." I slid my fingers in between Drew's. Hearing him call my dad Jamie always made me smile a little bit. All the rest of my friends called him Mr. Sullivan, but Drew and my dad were tight. Like on a scale of one to hero-of-the-century, my dad was off the recordable scale as far as Drew was concerned.

The leaves on the Tuileries trees had exploded in such bright orange and yellow since Thursday night that I felt like we were walking in a Dr. Seuss book. Or maybe it was just the strangeness of marking time in a place that had once been a joke with Drew, and then a dream with Pete. The wind had picked up again, just like it had on Thursday night, and as though my friends' voices were still echoing inside the garden walls, Drew asked the most obvious question of all.

"Did anyone go with you? To the concert, I mean?"

"Well, sort of." I felt my face flush, and hoped he thought it was the wind. "I mean, there was this all-night festival happening, and it was super cold. We'd planned for all six of us to see the concert, but then there was some movie inside the Louvre, so…"

"You went by yourself? Fee, that's…"

"I didn't go by myself." Dropping my fingers away from Drew's, I pulled a scarf from my purse and wrapped it high around my neck. "Pete came, too. He didn't want to see the film."

Drew walked along in silence for a few seconds, and with each crunch of the gravel, I could almost see the thought bubbles forming over his head, growing bigger and louder and uglier by the moment. But he never said a word. Instead, he took my hand again, tucked it under his elbow, then gestured toward the Orangerie. "What's this building on the left? It looks grim. Tell me it used to be a prison. Or a torture chamber. Seriously, Fee, there has to be something ugly about this town. I get the feeling Paris wants me to believe she's the place you belong."

The expression on his face made my heart ache in all the worst ways. "That's a museum," I said, wrapping my free hand around his arm and squeezing it tight. "Lots of Impressionists. They've got two whole rooms dedicated to Monet's water lilies."

"So *that's* where the real ones are?" Drew laughed ruefully. "I hope you didn't move nine time zones just for Monet, Fee. That would be a real waste. They sell fifty versions of that print at the Highgate bookstore. Half the girls at school have those water lilies hanging in their dorm rooms."

Had I not just dodged a Pete Russell-sized bullet, I might have asked Drew how he knew so much about the girls' dorms. Instead, I started back into tour guide mode, explaining the importance of the Egyptian obelisk rising before us in the Place de la Concorde, thanking my lucky stars that Monsieur Salinger had gone into such explicit detail during our class visit the week before. Within two minutes, Drew was so distracted by all the history on every corner that I had to wonder how different things might have been if he'd flown here last weekend instead.

Or worse, how different they might have been *next* weekend.

twenty-one

Even though the sun had already begun to set, the cobblestone streets at the Place du Tertre still bustled with frenetic energy. Artists bartered with tourists, caricaturists mobbed teenagers entering the square, and accordionists jostled in and out of the crowd, hoping to recreate that quintessential Gene Kelly ambiance for anyone expecting real life to mirror *An American in Paris.*

As the light faded and the artists and musicians began to leave the square, Drew and I wandered back the short distance to the Sacré Coeur Basilica, the last moments of the sunset bathing Paris in a rosy glow. We sat on the steps just down from the church, and I slid my arm again into Drew's, resting my head on his shoulder.

About thirty steps below us, a very slight, very drunk Edith Piaf impersonator wearing an enormous black feather boa began to sing *Hymne à l'Amour*. Ah, the "Ode to Love." Her voice wasn't perfect, but she crooned each word with her whole heart and half of Celine Dion's. I was so transfixed I didn't feel Drew nudging me.

"Hey, Fee." He squeezed my arm against his side. "Sit up. I want to ask you something."

"Just a minute," I whispered back, patting his thigh. "This is my favorite part."

"Come on, Meredith. I really need to talk to you before the birthday party."

I shifted my gaze lazily away from Edith to find Drew digging in his jacket pocket. When he produced a flat black box the size of an old-school cell phone and flipped it open, I sat up at attention. There, staring back at me, was the very necklace that I had seen prominently displayed between Lindsay Foster's two best assets the day we drove to Normandy only six weeks before.

Sigma. Phi. Freaking. Beta.

"This is a lavaliere," Drew explained, as if I'd been living in a convent for the last two years. "It's a stupid tradition, I know. But I was hoping that, you know, maybe you'd wear mine?"

I felt my chest tighten as I met his gaze. "You're serious."

"Um… that's sort of the point. Giving someone your letters means you're ready to tell the world you're exclusive. I flew five thousand miles to see you, Meredith. Is that not romantic enough for you? Should I have scheduled our names to flash on the Eiffel Tower instead?"

"Oh, don't worry, your gesture was plenty grand," I said snidely as my cheeks began to burn. "I am curious, though. Was I supposed to magically forget that this seriously symbolic necklace was draped around Lindsay Foster's neck until five minutes ago?"

"Not five minutes ago," he scowled. "A month."

Below us, Edith belted out the bridge to *Hymne à l'Amour*. Those lyrics were some of the most beautiful words I'd ever heard, but in that moment? It was all wrong. Not only had Edith shifted to the wrong key, the specter of Lindsay Foster filled the space between us; her perfect blond hair, her perfect smile, and her perfect everything else taunted me with all the times Drew had been hers and never mine.

Under normal circumstances, the panic crossing Drew's face at the exact second Edith's voice went pitchy might have made me laugh. Instead, tears filled my eyes and rolled down my cheeks without even a second's warning. What was the matter with me? All I'd ever wanted for *years* was to be with this guy, and now, I was ruining it for both of us.

Drew shoved the box back into his pocket then cupped my face in his hands, his thumbs brushing desperately at my tears like he could rewind the last three minutes with his touch. "Tell me what to do, Fee," he begged. "I don't understand where I've screwed this up. Everything I planned, everything I imagined would win you over has been wrong. So, just tell me what you want from me and I promise to make it happen."

While the caterwauling continued below us, I took Drew's hands away from my cheeks and held them in mine. "See, you zoomed in here yesterday without any warning and started setting up all these new parameters with symbolic jewelry and off-the-beaten-path itineraries and…"

"The kissing?" He smiled. "Tell me you haven't hated that part."

"No," I laughed softly. "But see, my brain is still standing in front of the Centre Lafayette with the cab driver, trying to process the fact that you're here. I don't know how long you've been planning this trip, Drew, but I haven't caught up to you yet. And for the record, it has *not* been a month since you broke up with Lindsay. It's been a handful of hours and eighteen days. Maybe nineteen. I'm not really good with time-change math. In any case, it hasn't been long."

"Okay then, eighteen days, give or take a time zone." He lifted my chin so our eyes met. "I don't know what I was thinking. I shouldn't have... I'm just... Meredith, I'm *sorry*."

I didn't answer. I just looked down the steps at Edith, who was now serenading a bunch of Italian teenagers with the jaunty *Mon Manège à Moi*. When I looked back over at Drew, he was taking the little black box out of his pocket again. He slid the lavaliere onto his palm, then smashed the box under his foot. After the tiniest fraction of a pause, he jogged down the steps and laid the lavaliere inside Edith's tip jar where she'd see it, and then bowed to her before he jogged back up the stairs to pull me up to my feet.

When he wrapped his arms around me, I understood: Drew finally got it. The two of us had no reason for golden letters or any other symbol. We had each other. That was all that mattered.

twenty-two

The café known as *Plus Ça Change* was not far from the Sacré Coeur, and as Drew and I ambled down the serpentine streets of Montmartre, I realized we must look like those credit card commercials I'd been known to mock. You know the type: two people gaze lovingly into each other's eyes as they tarry along the cobblestones, filtered within an inch of their lives in lilac and coral hues? Yeah, I hated those ads. But tonight, I wasn't fighting my mushy side anymore.

Bring on the *fromage,* Paris. My hometown boy was here, and I was finally happy.

But even after all that extra time I gave us, Drew and I still arrived at Dan and Kelly's party a quarter-hour later than we should have. There were five other groups celebrating inside the tiny bistro, which was hardly surprising. This place was famous among college kids the world over for serving wine in baby bottles. When Drew and

I arrived at the table, Dan jumped up from the center of the left side, his face flushed from either the wine or the not-so-festive mood.

"Hey," he said, kissing me briefly on the cheek before fist-bumping Drew. "Thank you guys for coming. Did you have a hard time finding this place?"

"No," Drew grinned, glancing nervously around. "Are we the last ones here?"

"Apparently so," Anne snarled. "Tell me, do all people in Oregon value spur-of-the-moment adventures over someone's once-in-a-lifetime birthday? Because where I'm from, that's just rude."

Dan winced, then gestured for me to sit down in the seat to his right and for Drew to sit beside me at the head of the table. I looked around the rest of the group. Everything appeared normal enough. At the opposite end of the table from Drew sat Anne, tapping furiously away on her phone. To her left, across from Dan and me, were Harper and Kelly, both smiling so uncomfortably that I finally realized why.

Pete Russell was missing in action.

As Harper and Kelly re-introduced themselves to Drew, I watched Dan shredding the end of his napkin between his thumb and forefinger while taking huge gulps from his baby bottle. When he noticed me watching him, he set the bottle back on the table, a watery smile on his lips.

"Sorry," he shrugged. "I should probably slow down."

"You want to tell me what's going on?" I said softly so that Drew wouldn't hear.

"Not especially," Dan muttered. His whole demeanor reminded me of the Degas painting we'd been studying in art history earlier in the week of the lady drinking absinthe. Face forward, eyes downcast, nose slightly red, sad expression. Poor Dan looked helpless, forlorn, and in desperate need of his bed.

The waiter delivered a new round of baby bottles to the group while Drew jabbered on to Kelly about his first impressions of Paris. So I took the opportunity and bent closer to Dan. "Why isn't your flatmate here?"

"Officially?" He half-chuckled, half-sighed. "Pete doesn't drink. You know that, right?"

I did know that. I'd noticed it first in Rouen, then every Wednesday night at Marie-France's dinners. There hadn't been a single time we'd gone out as a group that I'd seen him drink anything harder than coffee, but I'd never asked him about it. "What are you saying, Dan? That Pete left town so he wouldn't be tempted? That's a little extreme."

He shook his head. "I think that's what he wants everyone else to believe. But here's the truth: Pete's grandmother called yesterday morning to let him know her cancer isn't responding to treatment. They're going to get her into some experimental trials, but it's risky."

"*Cancer*?" I remembered Pete's face yesterday in the courtyard. "Did Pete know she was sick?"

"Yeah. She got diagnosed sometime early this summer. Stage four breast cancer. I thought for sure he would've told you by now."

I thought back on Pete's arrival that day we flew to Paris. Disheveled, harried… and now I knew he had a good reason. I felt a little bit sick remembering how ugly I'd behaved.

"Dan, if Pete's grandmother is sick, why is he in Paris with us? He should be at home."

"That's what he thinks too, but Gigi didn't give him that option. She made him promise to spend at least a semester with us, and once he got here, she put restrictions on all his credit cards and airline miles so he couldn't book a flight home without her permission. He was on the phone all morning while we were in class yesterday trying to convince someone *somewhere* to lift her rules. No dice. Not in the era of identity theft."

"That's… I don't know what to say. He must be devastated."

"Listen, don't fret about Pete," Dan said quietly. "This is sort of his shtick – he freaks out, he bails on all his plans, and then he comes back like nothing ever happened. I should have known he'd leave town to blow off steam after he spent most of yesterday locked up in his room. I'm just thankful he left a note this time."

"What did it say?"

"That he was sorry he would miss my birthday, but he was headed to Gare de Lyon to take the first available train this morning. He promised to be back by the time class starts on Monday."

I turned to look at Drew, who had his phone turned toward my friends, showing them old YouTube videos of my Irish dance competitions. *Merci*, free Wi-Fi. I turned back to Dan, who was mid-swig on a fresh bottle. "Dan, I need you to focus for just a minute. How can you be so certain Pete's okay? Have you checked in with him or something?"

Dan's eyes narrowed behind his glasses, and then he smiled. "Oh, I'm certain alright. And you would be too if you'd taken a look at your Facebook feed today. I guess Sutton's kept you occupied."

While Drew cracked himself and the rest of the table up with Mini-Meredith and her championship flailing legs, I jumped on Facebook to send Pete a message about his grandmother. But as soon as I did, I finally caught Dan's meaning.

My news feed was full of pictures featuring Pete Russell on a train, flanked by some classmates I recognized but barely knew. In another post, he was standing with those same guys beside a cogwheel train, then again on top of a mountain. In the last tagged picture, Pete was by himself, bending out from a covered bridge that I recognized from the thousand and one pictures my brother had taken at this same spot: the medieval Chapel Bridge in Lucerne, Switzerland.

Photo credit: Megan Elizabeth Green. Manhattan, New York.

I couldn't believe it. From the second I'd seen the two of them dancing on top of that chair in Rouen, I'd wondered if Meg was into Pete, but I'd really never wondered the reverse. It was an impossible pairing. They didn't have one thing in common.

At least, that's what I'd told myself.

Meg and her little coterie of Upper East Side pals left town every weekend on a whim for some mind-blowing destination. The Addison girls and I took bets every Thursday on where they'd go.

Night skiing in Chamonix!

The Montenegro Film Festival!

The ice hotel in Reykjavik!

Cocktails in Capri!

Wherever their destination, Meg and her minions would arrive back at school every Monday, cackling over photographic evidence of all-nighters hanging out with the fabulous crowd, like some outcast from a British boy band or an up-and-coming YouTube star. And always, at the vortex of fabulous and famous, Queen Meg ruled.

Numbness crept over me. When Pete had asked me to hop a train with him this weekend, is this what he'd had in mind? Hanging out with a bunch of jetsetters in *Switzerland*? No way. I couldn't believe it. Pete Russell had more depth in his toenail than Meg Green had in her entire soul.

And yet, in this photo, he looked serene. Contented. Like he was right where he belonged.

I stared at his face for so long that I forgot to send him a message. And when I finally looked up again, I found Drew's eyes on my screen, his lips drawn in a thin line. Then he lifted his eyes to mine, and the look he gave me filled my veins with ice.

For the next hour, Drew laid on the charm. When Harper asked him to tell them all something about me no one else knew, he told them about the stories I'd written as a kid, recounting with cringeworthy accuracy my masterpiece about two pebbles on either side of the Atlantic Ocean that passed messages to each another on the fins of a whale. When I got up to go to the restroom and came back, Drew was sitting in my seat, his arm draped lazily across Dan's shoulder. For the next quarter hour, the two of them belted every song in the Sigma Phi Beta pledge book.

Everyone declared Drew the wine-sodden winner of Dan and Kelly's birthday party. I was the only one who noticed that, in fact, the liquid level in his bottle hadn't even dropped by one milliliter.

When the check came and the rest of the group decided to take the party to some bar near Kelly and Harper's place, Drew flashed his brightest smile and punched Dan's shoulder playfully. "Thanks for including me, Danny boy. Sorry I'm no substitute for your buddy Russell. You really have no idea how sorry."

"'Z'okay," Dan slurred back. "I love you guyzz. And you love each other, right?"

Drew's eyes met mine, then he patted Dan chummily on top of his head. "You're a good man, Daniel. Promise you'll keep my girl honest for me once I'm gone."

After more hugs and promises to be best friends forever and ever times infinity, Dan and the Addison girls headed off on foot while Drew and I caught the Métro home. Everything about us pulsated fatigue. I didn't want to entertain any other explanation for the total and absolute silence between us.

That silence followed us through Marie-France's apartment and up the back stairs to the *chambres de bonne* floor. I opened my mouth to speak as I unlocked my bedroom, but Drew slid past me through the doorway, his eyes avoiding mine.

"Good night," he mumbled miserably. And without another word, he closed my bedroom door behind him, locking the deadbolt so viciously that the door twanged in protest.

twenty-three

I did not sleep one minute that night. Well, maybe I did, but by five o'clock my eyes refused to stay closed for more than thirty seconds at a time. So I got up, got dressed, locked the door to Anne's room and crept quietly down the stairs to Marie-France's apartment.

Sitting there in the kitchen stillness, I breathed in the smoky haze of the coffee rising from my mug while I replayed the night before in my mind with digitally-enhanced closed captioning. None of the scenarios ahead of me today were good. So I waited. I drank my coffee. And I prayed for the best.

I had just brewed a second pot when Drew pushed open the back door to Marie-France's apartment at six. He looked wretched – damp hair and puffy eyes behind his adorable glasses. "Hi," he muttered, sliding into the chair at the far end of the table. "Add jet lag to the list of things I've failed at this weekend."

I poured him a cup of coffee, set it down on the table in front of him, and slid my fingers into his hair. "You look pretty good to me."

"Meredith, come on," he sighed. "Don't play around with me this morning."

"Who says I'm playing? Those glasses are my Kryptonite and you know it, Sutton."

Drew eyed me strangely for a minute, then shook his head. Then he took the coffee cup from my left hand, placed on the table next to his and lowered me onto his lap, pulling me toward him like I was the only person in the world. "You asked me Friday why I came to Paris? Here's the truth: I am legitimately terrified right now that I might lose you."

I pulled back slightly and pushed his glasses up his nose. "What makes you say that?"

Drew tightened his grip around my waist. "Do you even know how much I've missed you since August? My heart actually ached, Fee. And I can't stop thinking that once I get on that plane tomorrow, that's it. Your life here will continue on without me. You'll go your way, I'll go mine, and I'll spend the rest of my life wondering how exactly you slipped through my fingers."

"Look at me." I lifted his chin with both my hands. "You have created some storyline inside that Drew brain of yours, scripting every single moment based on how *you* thought this weekend was supposed to look. The problem is, you never accounted for my side of the equation. I'm not some girl you met in a bar last night, Drew. You helped me pull my first loose tooth. When I got my driver's license, you were the first person I drove up and down Highway 101."

"Yeah, and you were barefoot. That's illegal some places, you know."

"Don't change the subject."

Drew ran his fingers through his hair, then nudged me off his lap and motioned for me follow him to the living room. We sat on Marie-France's sofa for a long time without speaking, both of us staring at his fingers tangled in mine. I counted almost to a hundred before he looked me in the eyes again.

"I know you're not some girl I met in a bar," he said gently. "You and your family are my world, Meredith. That means every decision I make about you has bigger consequences. I never wanted to risk taking this step before now."

"So what changed?"

"You tell me. Because we both know that wasn't *my* picture you kept staring at on your phone last night."

When you've known each other as long as Drew and I have, you know the truth without saying it out loud. I had seen it in his eyes at the restaurant – whatever he'd suspected about my feelings for Pete before he got here, the truth was far worse. And now Drew had proof.

But what he also knew, much to my humiliation, was that the object of my affection was probably cozied up by a fire in some Swiss chalet next to a gorgeous snow bunny who couldn't have been more my opposite if she'd tried.

I felt my cheeks flushing and looked down, tugging at a loose string on my t-shirt. I was nearly twenty-one years old, and I still had no clue how to understand the male mind.

"Hey." Drew reached over and brushed a strand of hair behind my ear, then cupped his hand under my chin. "How about we make a truce? Just you, just me. Let's promise each other that no one will ever come between us ever again."

I leaned into his touch, relieved. "No one? Not even my new boyfriend, Count Halitosis von Wartburg?"

Drew laughed. "Not even him."

I pretended to think for a minute. "Okay. You've got yourself a truce. And as a symbol of our new truce, I'll let you pick what we do this morning."

He tapped his lip, then turned to me, beaming. "Versailles?"

"Look at you with your double entendre! Picking a truce symbol for our truce symbol."

"Yeah?" Drew grinned. "Wait, what do you mean?"

I tucked a bit of his hair behind his ear, then sighed. "It's a good thing you're pretty."

twenty-four

What a glorious autumn day – cool, crisp, and sunny. We toured the *château* and the gardens at Versailles, documenting ourselves with Drew's phone all along the way. He insisted that we paddle a boat around on the Grand Canal, although he nearly tipped us over when he shifted over to my side for a quick selfie. After lunch, we hung out for most of the afternoon exploring Marie-Antoinette's hamlet of little cottages. Drew posted a whole series of snaps as we roamed, each with one line from the 'to be or not to be' speech he remembered from high school.

I'm only ninety percent certain he knew *this* hamlet had nothing to do with *that* Hamlet.

On the train back to Paris, I convinced Drew that Ian might kill him for missing out on so much of Paris, so he let me buy us tickets for a hop-on-hop-off bus tour. Only we never hopped off. We just rode around and around on the top of the double-decker bus, seeing the sights, kissing our way through the City of Love.

It was maybe the best idea I'd ever had.

After a late dinner on the Champs-Élysées – Drew's idea – he asked if we could walk our way back across the city to Notre Dame. When I told him that might take hours, he smiled sweetly. "Yeah, I know," he said, kissing me on the cheek. "That's all the time I need."

So, back down the Champs-Élysées we strolled, toward the Place de la Concorde. But as we approached the Seine, Drew asked me the way down to the river bank. It was already past two in the morning, and I'd heard some sketchy things about the Quai des Tuileries after dark. But he insisted, so we trotted down the stairs and ambled along the river bank until the Île de la Cité split the river Seine in two.

Somehow, we made it safely back up to the street level, and before I knew it, we were walking past Notre Dame and over the tiny bridge to Île Saint-Louis. The island was silent in the darkness, and while this should have creeped me out, I was too thrilled to show Drew the apartment where I wanted to live and write someday, two stories up and halfway down the rue Saint-Louis-en-L'Île, the island's main artery. I was all prepared to head back to Marie-France's apartment afterward when Drew suddenly turned me back in the direction of Notre Dame.

"Come with me," he said, his blond hair glowing in the moonlight. "There one thing left I wanted to do."

When we got halfway over the tiny bridge between Île Saint-Louis and Île de la Cite, Drew stopped. It was just the two of us, Drew leaning forward against the railing with me standing in front of him, Notre Dame looming large to our right as the river flowed all around.

"This is Pont Saint-Louis, where I was going to bring you on Friday," he whispered quietly into my ear, sliding his arms around my waist. "You like it?"

"Of course." I pulled his arms tighter around me and leaned back against his chest. "But why here?"

His lips brushed against the skin just below my ear. "Because it sounds like this part of Paris is where you come to dream up your future. And I want you to remember me whenever you're here."

"You do?"

"Well, yeah. I flew across the world to tell you I love you, Meredith. I'm *in* love with you."

I shifted to face Drew, looping a finger between the buttons on his shirt. "Good to know. Because I'm sort of in love with you, too."

He smiled goofily down at me. "Are you sure? Because you don't have to say…"

Before he could finish, I closed the space between us, and mid-kiss, FLASH! I'd swiped the phone from his shirt pocket and recorded the moment for all eternity.

"Didn't anyone warn you about the pickpockets here?" I whispered against his lips. "They'll steal things you didn't know you had. Right out from under your nose."

"I'll never let it happen again," he whispered back, and then Drew kissed me like the wind, pushing us closer and closer until I couldn't tell where he began and I ended.

twenty-five

My life had become a really bad reality show. Choose the guy? You're living in the wrong century, sister. Choose Paris? Hope you're ready to share your future with a lot of cats.

I recalculated my options fifteen hundred different ways while Drew took forever to pack his bag. Neither of us touched our breakfast, nor did we talk much. We chose to put our lips to better use instead.

At six thirty, after the car service buzzed from downstairs, the rickety elevator clanged its way down five flights while my heart thumped so loudly I thought it might knock the elevator off its pulley. Drew was leaving, and just like that, I wanted to leave, too.

The moment the driver took Drew's bag, tears began to fall down my cheeks. Drew pulled me close and kissed me again, like this was the last time ever. "I love you," he whispered.

But I couldn't answer him back this time. I just sobbed into his shoulder until the driver revved his engine, and before I could form a sentence, the car was halfway up the rue Bonaparte with Drew inside. I stood there for ten whole minutes, tears still streaming down my face, wondering whose dumb idea it was to run away to Paris anyway.

It was still too early to head to school, so I clomped up all seven flights of the back staircase to return Anne's room back to its perfect order, fresh linens and all. But even after her room looked magazine-perfect again, I still had another hour before class. So I headed to my room and stripped my own linens, picking up my pillow first.

When I pressed my nose against the fabric to breathe in Drew's scent one last time, I felt something flat inside. So I shook it upside down, and a gigantic, thick envelope with my name on it fell out onto the mattress.

You know those oversized cards you see at the drugstore that have a pink teddy bear saying: *Roses are red, violets are blue/No one loves you as much as I do?*

They're ridiculous.

Every time we'd seen cards like that over the years, Drew and I had mocked any poor sap who wasted their money on such nonsense. Sitting down on my bed, I imagined Drew cracking up in the store when he bought it. And that made finding this silly card for me and hauling it all the way from America the most romantic thing he'd done all weekend.

Inside, there were a dozen old photos of us, and a letter, written in Drew's scrawly print.

Dear Meredith,

This has been the best weekend of my life, and before you say it, YES, that includes the weird moments. I've loved every second of being here with you. I wish I could stay. Why didn't I listen to you in the eighth grade when you told me that speaking French would make me a chick magnet? WHY WAS YOUR YOUNGER SELF ALWAYS SO MUCH WISER THAN MINE?

If you decide when I leave that the distance is too much, I get it. But if you still want to see where this goes, I'll do whatever it takes to make you happy. So, if you're ready, just change your relationship status on Facebook. It's your call.

I love you,
Drew

PS- Look up at your bulletin board. You forgot someone important. Ahem.
PSS- I made a MereDrew playlist. (Well, I tried. Your music's lame.)
PSSS- I thought you might want the pictures I took this weekend, so I downloaded them onto your laptop. I may or may not have made you an embarrassing slideshow. And a screensaver. (Don't judge, man. I had to do something to fill my time while you spent a whole hour primping before Versailles yesterday morning.)
PSSSS- Seriously, why are you still reading?!?!? LOOK UP, FEE.

I obeyed and looked up at my bulletin board. My wonky little triangle of pictures was now shaped like a plus sign, with the four most important people from my past placed around the Sullivan's postcard – north, south, east, and west.

Drew had tacked his photo down at the bottom: a black-and-white image Ian had taken this summer on the Fourth of July. Drew was wearing his glasses and grinning at the camera like a fool, his arm draped lazily around my shoulder. And despite the sparklers I held in each hand, I was looking away from the camera, smiling at Drew.

Just like always.

I stood up and walked to my computer, then pulled up the photos Drew had downloaded from the weekend. He really did make a slideshow, and set it to some screamo band cover of Rihanna's *Umbrella*. I was half-laughing, half-teary-eyed as a million two-headed selfies flashed before my eyes. And yeah, the number of kissing shots was humiliating, but each and every one was adorable.

As the images slid past on the screen, I made a decision. No more doubts. I logged in to Facebook and changed my status to "in a relationship." Immediately, I had a notification.

Drew Sutton likes your relationship status change.

Somewhere on the outskirts of Paris, my official new boyfriend was sitting in early morning rush hour traffic, using up the last of his international data plan to stalk my feed. Sad, pathetic, and exactly what I needed to know.

twenty-six

The moment I'd changed my relationship status, everything had solidified with Drew. I will spare you the sappy text I got seconds later, but let's just say that if he'd said those things before he left, I would have gone back to America with him. By the end of the day, I had about five hundred notifications from high school and college friends, with every variation of *it's about time.*

Talk about your own worst nightmare. My love-drunkness with Drew Sutton fueled a new obsession with social media, video chat, and texting. We talked more now than we had back in our Lincoln City days when we'd been inseparable. October sped by so fast that if Ian hadn't called me from SeaTac Airport on Halloween, I would have forgotten his impending visit completely.

Pictures never quite did Ian justice because his features leaned toward the quirky side of asymmetrical. But his jet-black hair and piercing green eyes were striking, and when he spoke, the entire room crackled with energy. So I made sure every member of Marie-France's quiver knew he'd be in attendance at Wednesday night dinner that week. Then I sat back and observed the pandemonium.

Marie-France was so mesmerized by my brother all evening that she spoke English with us for the first time *ever*. The. Entire. Night.

My family didn't leave Ireland until Ian was six, which left him with a slight accent on certain words and a faintly European mindset. When he'd graduated from high school, my crafty big brother convinced my parents to let him take a gap year on his own dime. By Labor Day, he'd reached his savings goal and hopped the next flight to Phnom Penh.

Somehow, Ian stretched his savings for nine months while he circled the globe. Rumor has it he visited thirty-five countries on six continents, and the images he captured earned him a photojournalism scholarship to a small fine arts college in Seattle.

Vagabonding had made my brother fearless. When Ian told me he wanted to get an internship with Greg the Guidebook Guru – the one-man European travel conglomerate with shows on public television – I told him he was crazy. No one got those internships. They were the professional equivalent of Ed McMahon showing up on your front door with a six-foot-long paycheck. Not even *The* Ian Sullivan could land a job like that.

I was wrong. The internship turned full-time once Ian graduated, and now, four years later, he's got a fancy title and more frequent flier miles than anyone could imagine. Which is how I found myself in Prague for All Saints' Day weekend.

During his Tour du Monde, Ian had managed to make all sorts of friends, so it made sense that he spent half of his professional life catching up with people from the past. When we got to Prague on

Friday morning, Ian introduced me to Pavel and Anika Nemcek, an early-thirtysomething couple he'd befriended during his month-long stay in Laos. All day, while Ian scampered from meeting to meeting with Pavel in tow as his interpreter, Anika ferried me around town on her scooter with the sole task of collecting as many silver charms for my bracelet as we could find.

Later that evening, Ian and I were settling into the guest room of their modest yet charming flat in the suburbs when he flopped back on his twin bed and sighed. "Okay, mate, we've put this off long enough. You want to tell me what's going on between you and our mutual friend Andrew?"

"No, I do not," I laughed, stacking my dirty clothes on the left side of my backpack. "Gross, Ian. You're my *brother*. Like I would fill you in on the details of my personal life."

Ian pushed himself to a seated position and watched while I zipped up my bag. "I'm not asking for details. But you haven't even said the kid's name since I arrived, and I'm not going to lie, Fee. I'm starting to get concerned."

"I've said his name."

"No. You haven't. Are you… I mean, is everything okay with you two?"

"Ian, please," I laughed, crossing the room to set my backpack near the door. "Everything is fine. What could possibly be wrong?"

"Fine?" Ian's expression went dark. "Everything is *fine*? Stop messing around, Fee. You never say something's fine unless it isn't. Sit down this instant and talk to me."

Something in the way Ian was looking at me made my stomach drop. I walked back to my bed and sat down, mirroring my brother's posture until he relaxed himself against the wall behind him. Then I waited. I waited so long that I counted him breathe in and out seventeen times.

"Your whole life," he finally said, "I've stayed out of your business. You're smart, and definitely a little too cautious, but I trust you. You know that, right?"

"Yes. Except I hear a *but* coming."

"There are no *buts*. I just want to be…" Ian rubbed his eyes. "Listen, Fee, when I took Drew to breakfast in Portland last month, he looked awful. Like, wild-eyed. I haven't seen him like that since his mom died. I thought the little dude was going to sob into his scrambled eggs."

"Don't say *little dude*, Ian. Drew's just as much a man as you are now."

"Maybe so. But when I asked him what was wrong, he said he'd finally screwed everything up. He said he was going to lose you, and he had no one but himself to blame. It was a little pathetic, actually. So pathetic that I got a little misty myself."

"What are you trying to tell me?"

"I'm the one who sent Drew to Paris," Ian smiled weakly. "Hey, don't give me that look. What good are all those air miles anyway if you can't help one of your oldest mates?"

My throat began to ache. "But why would you do that? Did he ask you for help?"

"What? No way, Meredith. He was furious that I even offered. It's not as romantic to surprise your girl in Paris if her brother pays for the tickets. So I'd appreciate it if you'd keep this secret to yourself."

"I'm not going to tell him. I'm just trying to understand why you got involved, especially since you're the one who told me to move on with my life."

"Because, Meredith. Drew told me he was in love with you. And I thought you deserved to know."

Even though our window was closed, I could hear a police car klaxon wailing in the distance. *Deee doooo, deee doooo, deee doooo,* volleying from one side of my heart to the other, like the echo of all the red flags I'd chosen to ignore. The timing. The urgency to make it all official. The complete omission of my brother's involvement.

Suddenly, Drew's grand romantic gesture felt as hollow as a chocolate Easter bunny.

For a long time, Ian watched me from across the room, every question he wasn't asking written right there on his face. I wanted to run across the room and hug him for his kind heart. I wanted to deck him for butting into my life. But mostly, I wanted a do-over of the last several months, because the worst part was knowing how blindly I'd navigated the whole thing.

"Tell me I did the right thing, Fee," Ian said after the silence had gone on too long. "Tell me I haven't messed up your year in Paris by sticking my nose in where it didn't belong."

I paused, then plastered my little sister smile onto my face. "All you ever do is look out for me, Ian. I'm sorry I'm acting weird. You just surprised me, that's all."

Ian eyed me strangely for a minute. "I don't think you understand what I'm asking you. Be honest, Fee – by sending Drew here last month, did I force you to pick him over someone else? Because I got the impression the other night at Marie-France's that you and that Pete guy had some unfinished business."

Hearing my brother say his name like that sent an unexpected pang through my chest. Ever since Drew left, Pete had stopped coming to Wednesday night dinner and started arriving to class late, which he'd never done back at Highgate. Then, at the end of every class, he would flee without a word, tapping away on his phone or wrangling things into his backpack.

Not one person even mentioned the change in his behavior, and on Wednesdays, every eye avoided that empty chair at Marie-France's table, like it had been empty all along.

So when Pete had shown up for dinner this week, chatting and laughing like it was his job, I'd spent the whole evening like a repelled magnet, orbiting the outlier from as far as possible, wary of his re-entry on the scene.

If anyone could read between the lines of my weirdness, it was my big brother. So I hopped up from the bed, crossed the room, and clicked off the light with a rueful laugh. "Dude, I always suspected you were a liar. And now I have proof."

"A liar?" I could feel Ian's eyes follow me in the darkness. "About what?"

I slipped into my twin bed, yanking the duvet up to my chin. "Do you have any idea how many times you've bragged that you can sleep like a boss anytime, anywhere?"

"I have never bragged about something that ridiculous."

"Oh, but you have, my friend," I retorted. "Except now I've got proof that you suffer from jet lag like the rest of us. You're experiencing visual hallucinations on par with unicorn sightings if you think I've got drama with a frat boy player like Pete Russell."

"I didn't say you had drama. I only meant…"

"Too late, mate. The next time you start crowing about your superhuman travel skills, I'm bringing up that one night in Prague when I witnessed the time zone delirium warp *your* brain just like it does to everybody else. Don't say I didn't warn you."

Ian laughed, quietly at first, and then full-blown guffaws. Even after he'd buried himself under his own covers, I could hear him snickering, like a little kid who'd just farted in church.

I was half a second away from drifting off when I heard his muffled voice. "Hey, Fee?"

"Yeah?"

"You're my favorite. You know that, right?"

"Ah, delirium," I sighed. "You're the gift that keeps on giving."

twenty-seven

After Ian flew back to Seattle the following Monday, I finally hit the homesick wall. The Paris skies were permanently gray, the air bone-chillingly damp, and the constant spitting rain was miserable, even for a girl from Oregon. The melancholy inside made me queasy, like I was on a constant blood sugar low. When your boyfriend *and* your family live nine time zones away, it's impossible to ignore that distance forever.

Which might explain why none of us were prepared for the full-scale frenemy assault I later dubbed Operation: Pumpkin Spice.

Pete's new friend Meg Green was that strange sort of beautiful – not gorgeous in the traditional sense, but something about her bewitched every person in her wake. Like an actress, or a supermodel.

No, wait: like a *vampire*. And she totally used it to her advantage.

So when she invited herself to Wednesday night dinner during the last week of November, the dam of my self-restraint finally burst.

"I never thought of myself as clique-ish before," I huffed, plopping down between Harper and Kelly on the sofa after Meg followed Dan and Pete out for the evening. "But doesn't she know you can't invite yourself to someone else's dinner party?"

Marie-France slipped into the armchair across from us. "You know, *les filles,* every time I think I've figured out the human race, someone like Meg proves me wrong. She had absolutely no idea that she'd offended me tonight by showing up without an invitation. Maybe she just assumed she belonged here with the rest of you?"

Kelly groaned. "Did you see the boys stand up every time she ran to the restroom? Why would they do that? She isn't royalty."

"Exactly!" Anne piped in from the kitchen. "I cannot figure out what is so fascinating about that girl."

"It's her eyes," Marie-France said matter-of-factly, taking a long sip from her wine glass. "Are they violet or indigo? I can't decide. And those lashes! Is this an American thing?"

"They're lash *extensions,*" Harper rolled her blue eyes. "You gotta admire her, though. I've never met anyone so gifted in mystique. Watch next time someone asks her a question. She offers just enough information to answer, but it's never more than vague nonsense."

Kelly stretched her long legs out before her, then slumped back against the sofa. "I always wonder if those girls she runs around with even like each other. To me, they're more like a squadron of fembots, scouring Europe for clues to a game we're too uncool to understand."

"Yes!" Anne agreed from the doorway. "But at least Meg *tries* to be nice. She actually texted me about our translation homework last night. I just wish I knew what her angle was."

"I think I know the answer to that." Harper readjusted her scarf, then leaned forward and gave Kelly a look. "We have to tell them."

My stomach knotted. "Tell us what?"

"Last weekend, we saw Meg and Pete at the movies."

An uneasy silence spread among the five of us during which two things happened. First, Anne stepped fully into the living room and shot daggers at her two best friends. Then, Marie-France looked at me so wistfully that I wondered just how intuitive she really was.

"Why haven't you told us before now?" Anne demanded.

Kelly lifted her hands in defense. "Hey, it was none of our business. Especially since it looked like a double date – Dan was there, too, with Meg's French friend. What's her name again?"

"Corinne? The one who looks like she might break in half?" Anne squeaked, then grabbed our empty glasses and stomped into the kitchen, with Marie-France right on her heels to protect her stemware.

Well, at least *that* had made me smile. Well played, Dan Thomas.

The following evening, the entire population of the Centre Lafayette celebrated Thanksgiving *à la française* at a little restaurant along the Seine called *Cocorico*. It was the cutest space you've ever seen: canary yellow walls, bookcases filled to the brim with tchotchkes, old-fashioned postcards from all over the globe decoupaged onto every surface imaginable, and planter boxes in all the windows. Even the lamps were eclectic. Feathered sconces hung on the walls, and tiny chandeliers dotted the ceiling, strung together across the room by fairy lights and hanging beads.

Because I'd taken a call from Drew just outside the door to the restaurant, I missed out on what Anne later described as the most convoluted game of musical chairs ever. Somehow, my friends were splintered among all the other groups, and when I walked in, only one seat remained: next to Madame Beauchamp's assistant, Michelle. Directly across from Pete and Meg.

Which might have been a disaster, except this was Thanksgiving in a country where Thanksgiving had no place. And mercifully, for once, Meg was not the center of attention.

It was the food.

The turkey was cut into perfectly symmetrical one-inch cubes of meat, painstakingly piled into a tiny pyramid on each of our plates. Because nothing says America like a well-balanced turkey pyramid. Didn't you know that's what you see on the back of the dollar bill?

The mashed potatoes were of the boxed variety, which should have been fine. But somewhere between the metric conversion and the chef's unfamiliarity with factory-processed food, the faux-tatoes congealed in the middle of the serving pan like a lump of clay.

And then there was the cranberry sauce. As far as I could tell, cranberries aren't a staple of the French diet. In fact, I had yet to see one all year. Not to be deterred by this small detail, the clever French chef improvised, creating what he saw as an improvement to America's favorite bitter berry. In the middle of the table where the cranberry sauce should be sat a gorgeous strawberry purée, blended to the consistency of baby food. Deeeeee-licious.

Finally, in lieu of the traditional pumpkin, apple, or pecan pie, the chef at *Cocorico* had prepared the tiniest, most beautifully plated kumquat tarts, eight to a plate. And if bite-sized tropical fruit tarts weren't bizarre enough, he'd placed tiny marzipan pilgrims on top of each tartlet, like an octet of creepy garden gnomes, including pointy red hats.

For two hours, we all laughed so hard that none of us could breathe, let alone eat. At first, poor Michelle was offended. Not that I blamed her; she'd probably been organizing this meal for at least three months. But with tears streaming down his face and the kindest words possible, Pete Russell explained it all away. Thanks to his deft command of the language, Michelle eventually joined in on the joke, running over to Madame Beauchamp's table to explain the insanity.

That was when I saw it: the look. Pete shot Meg a furtive, almost imperceptible mini-glance that I might not have even noticed had I not experienced the same thing weeks before on the Pont des Arts. The two of them had a secret no one else knew. What it was, I had no idea. But I thought back to that night in Rouen, when Pete had jumped on top of that chair with Meg. Had she been his real target all along?

Wow. Same game, different girl. Maybe Sigma Phi Beta taught *all* their pledges how to use ginger bait.

twenty-eight

December 13th. Happy twenty-one years to me.

Early in life, I'd learned to keep my birthday expectations low. Between holiday parties and school vacations, December was one big time crunch. Why should this year be any different?

And then there was the city-wide shutdown that started the day after Thanksgiving. Transportation employees had gone on strike to protest another year without a cost-of-living raise, and one by one, the rest of the municipal services had followed suit.

All of them except school. (And, mercifully, waste collection.)

For the rest of Paris, today was nothing more than Day Sixteen of a new revolution. Or so I believed until Anne burst through my door while I was video-chatting with Drew.

"*Joyeux anniversaire!*" She unhinged the *volet* shutters, then stepped in front of the monitor. "See ya, Drew!" She waved to the screen. "The sky's celebrating, so your girl has to go!"

THE BRIDGE

Though it was still dark at seven a.m., I followed Anne to the window, pushing wide the outside shutters. Quarter-sized snowflakes spiraled lazily through the air, landing softly in the courtyard below. "This is like that painting from art history," Anne whispered, wide-eyed, ignoring the flakes landing in her hair. "The one with the rooftops. Who was that by again?"

"Caillebotte," I smiled, thinking back to what Pete had said our first day here. *By December, you'll have your very own* Rooftops Under Snow *out here.* Yep. Right on time.

We zoomed through our normal morning rituals, then clambered downstairs, where Marie-France was preparing my favorite breakfast: scrambled eggs, bacon (the Irish kind), and toast. *All I Want for Christmas Is You* streamed through the whole apartment, and the three of us danced around the kitchen like a bunch of elfin lunatics while we set the table. Marie-France boogied so vigorously that she split her pencil skirt right up the back.

The French educational calendar was divided into trimesters, so while this wasn't finals week, it certainly felt like it. Monsieur Ludovic had warned us today's history test would cover both the seventeenth and eighteenth centuries, and for a week Pete had been hassling us all to come early this morning for a last-minute review.

So when Anne and I walked into the *Grande Salle*, I wasn't surprised to see so many people. Pete Russell was a tyrant. Snow and the lack of public transport were insufficient reasons to provoke his wrath. Except some of these people weren't in our history class.

Just then, everyone began to sing "Happy Birthday" to me in French. Never, not once in my whole life, had so many people gathered to celebrate me. And before I knew it, I was ugly crying in the best way possible.

Harper handed me a daintily wrapped bouquet of multi-colored tulips, and Kelly handed me two dozen red roses.

"Drew slipped me fifty euros the night of Dan's party," she bubbled. "Major swoon *avec* sigh, my friend. No guy I know plans that far ahead."

"Yeah, we know, hashtag Movie Love," Harper smirked. "Come on, Meredith. Time to get the birthday girl caffeinated. You've got a big day ahead."

Dan and Pete were at a table at the far end of the *Grande Salle* setting out chocolate croissants and pouring coffee from what I assumed were the faculty break room carafes. When I reached them, Dan handed me the largest cup on the table.

"December birthdays always get shafted, but yours fell on a particularly bad week this year," he said apologetically. "Everyone deserves to be celebrated, strike or no strike."

"Yes, yes, isn't December tragic? Now drink up, Sully." A grin spread across Pete's face as he handed me a second cup of coffee. "Test review starts in thirty minutes."

As I watched his grin spread sideways, a sickening ache crept into my chest. Until this year, I'd never known you could miss someone you saw all day, every day. But I did. I missed Pete. Not just because his attention felt like sunlight shining through the window on the coldest day of the year. It was worse than that. I missed the person who saw things about me that most people missed. The person most likely to challenge me to try harder, even without saying a word.

I missed Pete Russell. Even when he was standing right in front of me.

twenty-nine

Monsieur Ludovic allowed us four hours to complete the history test that afternoon, but my brain gave out after three and my hand quickly followed. So I turned in my blue exam booklet, grabbed my bag, and sauntered outside.

As though it was its own microcosm, hidden away from the Parisian din just over the wall, the Centre Lafayette courtyard was so silent that I could actually hear the snowflakes as they pirouetted to the ground. I walked to the far end of the space, lowered myself gently onto an ancient green bench, closed my eyes, and breathed in Paris on my twenty-first birthday.

The crunch of boots on the frosty ground behind me stirred my attention. Pete plunked down beside me on the bench, the famous chullo hat perched lackadaisically onto his head.

"If you have to take a test on your birthday, that one wasn't so bad." From his gloved hand, he offered me a cup of vending machine coffee, steam swirling and dancing among the snowflakes. I took it in both hands, and lifted it to my face, breathing in the warmth.

"Easy for you to say. Judging by that study session you led earlier, I'm going to guess you've taken six hundred pages of notes since September."

"Well, those of us who lack your doodling talents have to learn this information the old-fashioned way."

Snowflakes collected on Pete's hat and on the curls that peeked out from underneath it. I'd always noticed that when Pete was quiet, his face seemed much older than his twenty-two years. But today I could see what he must have looked like before his parents died. There was something boyish in the way he was looking out at me from under that hat. It made me want to tug the braids of the chullo hat down, then run cackling across the courtyard in triumph.

"So what are you up to the rest of the day?" I asked instead, acutely aware that even in hushed tones, my voice was bouncing off every surface. "Auditioning for some folk band?"

Pete laughed a little, tugging his hat down by both braids. "Maybe. But first, I should probably tackle that review we have to complete for *Promenade Parisienne*. Want to come with me to *La Rotonde*? Two minds are better than one."

He said it so nonchalantly that at first my brain didn't register the invitation. But once it did, even my ears turned crimson. In the days before Drew's visit, Anne and I had spent most every afternoon with Dan and Pete at *Café de la Rotonde*. Pete and I always sat in left-handed solidarity on the same side because it's a pain to knock elbows all the time with your right-handed friends. At least, that's what I'd told myself. Even though I'd secretly hoped it meant something more.

THE BRIDGE

Every time, I'd imagined us as Hemingway and Hadley, F. Scott Fitzgerald and Zelda. I was dorky like that, but something about the *Rotonde* had made life magical those first few weeks.

Sitting here in the snow, I had to admit that the magic probably had less to do with the Lost Generation than it did with the dark brown eyes holding my gaze right now.

"Listen, Pete." I sat up a little straighter, sipping my coffee slowly. "The *Rotonde* sounds fun and all, but I'm not sure what Anne has planned this afternoon. Can I check in with her first?"

"Well, you could. But she just walked out the front door with Dan a minute ago," Pete grinned slyly. "Come on, Sully. I don't want to go by myself. Just come with me for a couple of hours. I promise to get you home before dinner."

When we got to the café, I followed Pete to our usual seats by the window, where he ordered us a pot of tea to share. I had to laugh. From the first time we'd come here in September, Pete had always insisted I share a pot of tea with him. Dan had mocked him: "Who drinks tea in France?"

Pete had ignored him completely, until one day, the week of *La Nuit Blanche*. "Dude," he'd said. "Meredith's *Irish*. If she doesn't have tea on the regular, she'll turn into a fairy. Do you want to be the victim of her first spell?"

"Fairies don't cast spells," I smirked. "They just trick fools into doing their bidding."

Pete's eyes had gone playfully wide. "Fools, huh?" He'd poured the rest of the tea into my cup. "Drink up, Sully. Let's keep you on the juice so I can sleep tonight."

I'd taken a slow sip of my tea, then lowered my cup a little, grinning. "If you insist. But I should warn you: fairies work their most dangerous magic while you're sleeping."

And now, more than two months later, I couldn't help smiling as I thought about the impish look in his eye as he'd turned back to our friends, his knee suddenly pressed against mine, where it had stayed the rest of that afternoon. Watching him now as he poured my cup of Irish breakfast tea, I couldn't help but wonder if he remembered that day, too. It felt like a thousand years ago.

"Let me see your notes, Russell," I said, pointing to his messenger bag. "I spent half your study session this morning trying to decide if you're having an illicit affair with some history professor at the Sorbonne or if you are, in fact, one of *them.*"

Pete tilted his head slightly. "One of who?"

"The *academics*." I unwrapped my scarf from my neck. "Every professor on both continents worships your brain. Just promise me this: if they invite you back to that faculty lounge, you'll teach me the secret handshake."

Another smile spread across Pete's face as he began cleaning sugar crystals from the table with his index finger. "For all you know, I'm paying them a weekly stipend."

"Stop that."

Pete brushed the sugar from his finger onto the floor, then lifted his eyes to mine. "Okay, confession: I know it's not the most lucrative career, but yeah, teaching's always been my goal. Well, teaching, then grad school. Then some more teaching. And maybe by then I'll have enough saved to spend a couple of months in the tropics, right before I keel over from exhaustion."

"Sounds about right. I hear the Maldives are a nice place to spend your final days."

"Thanks for the tip." He took a sip of his tea. "What about you, Sully? When do you start prepping your audition for the Former Irish Step Dance Champion World Tour?"

"Very funny," I pretended to scowl. "To be honest, I have no clue what I'll do after college. I usually say grad school when people ask, but actually, I think I might copy Ian and travel for a while."

"By yourself? Or will Sutton join you?"

My chest tightened. I'd never even considered that scenario. In fact, until recently, I'd never imagined Drew going anywhere outside the States, except maybe Rome. The fact that I hadn't woven him into my future plans by now made my chest constrict further.

"It's not as hard as you might think, getting around the world on a dime," Pete continued, his eyes following a couple of kids chasing each other down the sidewalk on roller skates. "I traveled around for almost nine months after high school myself."

"What? No, you didn't." I laughed so hard I nearly snorted. But then I took one look at Pete's befuddled face, and I wanted to smack myself. What was wrong with me? Pete's parents were dead. His family hadn't stopped him from circling the globe because they weren't... oh, man. Now I felt like a kangaroo was using my chest as target practice for its freaky powerful kicks.

"Oh," I finally sputtered, tugging my hair behind my ears. "Well, I guess that explains why you and my brother had so much to talk about when he was here last month."

"I guess so," Pete grinned, and sort of shook his head. "Although, I have to tell you that your brother's thirty-five-countries-on-a-shoestring made me feel a little... I don't know..."

"Silly? Juvenile? Insignificant?"

"For starters." Pete shook his head again, then looked back outside. I watched quietly while that clever mind whirred inside. I might have given anything to know where it was taking him.

"So, where'd you go?" I finally asked, interrupting his thoughts. "Please don't say Phuket."

"No, actually…" he paused, still looking outside. "I came here first. This friend of mine was headed here to study, so Gigi sent me over the first part of January to get the place ready for her."

Her? My stomach clenched. "Well, that was chivalrous of you."

The right side of Pete's mouth curled up as he glanced my way. "Don't be too impressed. I had other motivations. It was Brooks. She was the girl down the street who used to –"

"– drive you to school. I remember." My skin crawled as my mind filled in blanks I hadn't realized were there. "Wow. Paris with the famous Brooks. How long were you here?"

"Long enough to be in the way." Pete's dark eyes danced in the table's candlelight. "Good thing I had a job waiting for me in China."

"Okay, now you really *are* making things up."

"I promise it's true." Pete laid his right hand over his heart. "My parents' best friends from college have a son named James, and he runs this non-profit in Shanghai. I stayed there from February until several work teams arrived in early June."

"Don't tell me you're also fluent in Mandarin."

"Hardly." He tugged his hat from his head, then ran his fingers through his curls. "Looking back, I should have stayed through the summer. But instead, I headed to New Zealand for their winter. I worked in a ski resort outside Queenstown. That's where I got this hat, actually."

"Really? I would have guessed Peru."

Pete laughed under his breath. "Peru might have been a better choice. New Zealand was sort of a bust."

By the look on his face, I figured there was a girl involved in that story, too.

I picked up his hat from the table and tugged it onto my head. "No wonder you were so weird freshman year, Russell. If I'd known you'd been living upside down *and* in the wrong season, I might have cut you a little more slack that first day."

Pete laughed and wiggled the hat further down my forehead by the braids. Then he reached into his pocket and pulled out a tiny package wrapped in Christmas paper. "Listen, I hope this isn't weird, but I got you something. Just think of it as a hybrid birthday gift and peace offering. You know, for the years when we weren't so friendly."

I picked up the package and opened it cautiously. Inside was a gently tarnished silver charm of the Pont des Arts. It must have been at least half a century old, and it was absolutely beautiful.

"Where did you find this? I've been looking all over Paris for one of these charms."

Pete smiled widely. "I've had it a while, actually. I saw it one day this fall in a bookstall near the apartment. You know, the ones by the Seine? Some lady there sells vintage Paris charms. You should check it out and see what else she has. I can go with you if you want."

I stared at the charm, then lifted my eyes to him. "Thank you, Pete. It's perfect."

Pete watched me just like he had in the early morning hours of *La Nuit Blanche*. Between Drew and Meg and the passage of time, I'd explained away that night's enchantment as nothing more than a lonely, lovesick girl projecting her imagination onto the chivalry of a well-mannered friend.

But now, sitting next to Pete as the snow fell on the darkening cityscape outside, I saw a parallel path to the one I'd taken that weekend. And for the first time in two months, I let my heart wonder where Pete and I would be… if only.

thirty

Pete was blithe and chatty on the walk back to my place, like this was just another day on the way home from school. We threw dirty snowballs at each other and placed bets on what minutia Monsieur Salinger would include on our *Promenade Parisienne* test. If anyone had seen us, they might have believed we'd only met in the last few weeks, so generic was our banter.

When we reached my apartment building, I punched in the code and then turned to face Pete. "Thanks for the tea," I said. "And for my present. See you tomorrow?"

"Hold on a sec, Sully." Pete pushed the door open behind me a little wider, his face inches from mine. "I haven't seen Marie-France in a while. Could I come upstairs to say hello?"

"Oh!" I gulped. "Um, yeah. Good thinking. She's been asking about you lately."

And just like that we were in the narrow elevator, Pete Russell's body so close to mine that I couldn't think straight. My knees locked in place but Pete just watched me blankly, like we rode tiny elevators together all day every day. When the pulley jostled and vibrated to a halt on the fifth floor, it also jostled my knees from their locked position, and I found myself pitching forward, grabbing the lapels of Pete's coat and holding on for dear life.

"Oof," I said, attempting to laugh as I pulled myself back upright. He watched me strangely for a moment, so strangely that I froze in place. But then, as if he could read my mind, he winked and then pushed the door open, gesturing for me to leave first.

I nodded as I strode past him, hoisting my messenger bag strap over my head as I went. "So, are you flying home Saturday? Because Dan said his parents are taking him on some Mediterranean cruise for the holidays, and if I have to fly home alone with Marshall…"

Pete lifted an eyebrow as he leaned sideways against the apartment door frame. "You haven't heard? Marshall's spending Christmas here. With Élodie."

"Wow." I unzipped the outside pouch of my bag and pulled out my keys. "I never thought I'd say this, but I'm a little jealous of Marshall. Christmas in France sounds like the best idea ever."

I could feel Pete's eyes on me as I fumbled with the lock. "My grandmother thinks so, too. She'll be here Saturday morning."

I lifted my eyes to his. We hadn't spoken about his grandmother's diagnosis one single time since that weekend Drew came and Pete escaped to Lucerne. I hadn't been brave enough to ask, and he had barely spoken to me until today. But as I searched his dark eyes, I could see his heart was breaking, despite the easy smile and the casual way he leaned against the doorway.

I had an overwhelming urge to hug him.

Instead, I opened the front door to Marie-France's apartment. The lights were off inside. No sign of Marie-France. No sign of Anne. When I turned back to Pete, he was standing behind me, and in the muted light from the hallway, I could see a grin widening across his face.

The apartment lights flipped on behind me, and I heard five people shout "Surprise!" at the top of their lungs. How did I not see *that* coming? It was Wednesday night, *and* my birthday.

Pete howled as he grabbed my hand then twirled me into the living room. "I can't believe we tricked you twice!"

Dan sauntered over, wearing his favorite bowtie and a toothy grin, and slapped a twenty euro note in Pete's hand. "Seriously, Meredith. Why do you always fall for his shenanigans?"

"Don't give her grief on her birthday," Harper scolded as she handed me one of Marie-France's fanciest champagne flutes. "Sorry for the secrecy, but Anne was convinced you were onto us, so we came up with the decoy breakfast. Pete bet Dan he could trick you into mistrusting your own suspicions."

I turned to face Pete and shoved him playfully. "And to think I actually believed you wanted my help studying. Hand over my half of your earnings right this second."

Pete high-fived Dan then patted me on the head. "Aw, Sully. Can I help it that you're so gullible? If I'd known all these years how easy it is to sidetrack you, imagine how rich I'd be."

He had no idea.

Anne dragged me into the living room to show me the spread. Marie-France had made my favorite meal: salmon and asparagus. For dessert, the girls had made cupcakes with the Betty Crocker mix we'd bought a while back at the American specialty store in the Marais. They'd even decorated them with twenty-one candles.

As usual, Marie-France held court at her end of the table, flipping her dark bob and flirting shamelessly with the boys. Our favorite thing about Marie-France was that she had a seemingly endless cache of funny stories about the Americans who had lived with her in the past. She never repeated a single story. My spleen hurt every week from laughing so hard, and this week was one for the books.

I scanned the faces around the table, warm in the glow of the candlelight. How lucky I was. For the rest of my life, this would be my twenty-first birthday memory: a snowy Wednesday night in Paris with some of the best people in the world.

After the cupcakes, Kelly handed me a package. "This is from all of us, but to give credit where credit is due, you should know that Anne and Pete did most of the work."

"We've been putting it together for a while now," Anne explained as I removed the wrapping paper to reveal a hardback book. "I stole the photos from your laptop every time you weren't paying attention, which is harder than it sounds since your fingers seem to be surgically attached to the keyboard."

"Har-dee-har-har," I said, flipping through the pages. "Are you sure these are my photos?"

"They're yours, but Pete cropped them. We organized them into a book a few weeks ago."

I went back to the beginning and turned each page again, more slowly this time. Some photos were of places, most were of my friends, but there was a full-page, two-headed selfie Drew had taken of us right in the center of the book. I looked up from the page to find

Pete watching me from across the table, no hint of anything in his eyes except pride in a job well done.

"And now, for one more photo." Anne ran to the kitchen and returned with my SLR camera, then handed it to Marie-France who began organizing us in front of her magical Christmas tree. She was so adamant about staging us herself that I should have known something was up. When I downloaded the images later that evening, I nearly marched back down the stairs to ask Marie-France if she knew the English word *buttinsky*, because this time, she'd gone too far.

Each of the six of us wore a Santa hat. But framed in the center of the image stood Pete Russell and Meredith Sullivan, with a sprig of renegade mistletoe dangling just above our heads.

thirty-one

Lincoln City's the sort of beach town people describe as quaint. When I was a kid, I wondered what that meant. My family had chosen Lincoln City when we moved to America because of its location midway up the Oregon coast and its cool, rainy climate, so similar to our hometown in Ireland. For me, everything about it seemed normal and, to be honest, a little boring.

But now that I'd lived in Portland and Paris, I understood why people found my hometown so magical. You know Stars Hollow on *Gilmore Girls*, with its quirky town square celebrations and caricatures masquerading as locals? Lincoln City had it all, with idiosyncrasies to spare.

Sure, the coastline was gorgeous, and you couldn't beat the weather; at least, whenever the sky wasn't spitting rain on you. But the real draw of my hometown was the traditions.

Twice a year we held a Kite Festival attended by people from all over the globe. There were also two Whale Watch Weeks, art festivals, and clam bakes, too. Not to mention a ginger contest every February called the Redhead Roundup, which I'd never won, but hope springs eternal.

One of my favorite traditions happened from October to May, when people combed the beaches from Roads End to Siletz Bay in search of hand-blown glass floats – hundreds of them, in every shape, color, and size. On Christmas break during my freshman year of high school, Ian and I had stumbled across a green, fairy-shaped float hidden behind a piece of driftwood at the beach near our house. For the rest of the school year, I'd argued with my parents. It was a sign, I told them. Our destiny lay in Ireland, not Oregon.

But that summer, after too many months of guilt, Ian admitted that *he* had bought that fairy. Then he'd waited for me to get distracted, and placed it right by the driftwood so I would see it.

I didn't speak to him for a week afterward.

But the tradition I loved best was the annual Sutton-Sullivan Christmas party: a Dungeness crab boil followed by hours of karaoke. By my count, this was our tenth anniversary. Drew's mom died the summer before fifth grade, so that year, the Suttons invited us to their house on Devil's Lake for Christmas. Ian, who's always had a secret soft spot for our friend Drew, was feeling extra sentimental that Christmas and took it upon himself to add some fun to our annual crab boil. So he set up the karaoke machine his new girlfriend had bought him two days earlier, and ten years on, the tradition still stands.

As stodgy and conservative as Drew's grandparents appeared to the rest of the world, all bets were off during karaoke. His grandmother Maureen rivaled any Broadway star, but the real treat was Grandpa Andy's annual showstopper: The Jackson Five's *I Want You Back*, performed in full falsetto with choreography executed to the exacting standards of the King of Pop himself.

Every year, I was so tempted to post the footage online. The good citizens of Lincoln City deserved to know their most beloved dentist had better moves than any boy-bander alive.

But this Christmas, the festivities ended much earlier than usual. My parents and Ian headed back to our house around ten, and Drew's grandparents were asleep half an hour later. Which left Drew and me alone on the back deck overlooking the lake.

The first time I'd come to this house, my childlike mind didn't understand this space. Why would anyone build a deck sheltered from the sun? What was the point of a room without walls, or an outdoor fireplace?

But twenty-one-year-old me understood. Every night since I'd come home, the two of us had snuggled up on the comfy outdoor sofa under a huge pile of blankets, with nothing but candles and a crackling fire to distract us. Across the lake the twinkling Christmas lights reflected on the water, and the whole world seemed bathed in happiness. And even though Drew had probably honed his late night make-out mojo here with other girls, I didn't care. This space was *ours* now.

As the clock struck the quarter hour, Drew pulled away from a very sweet, very long kiss with an expression I couldn't quite understand. "Can I ask you a question?"

"Always."

"How come we've never talked about our first kiss?"

I pushed myself a little upright and smiled. "Do we need to? I mean, I know you were jet-lagged and everything that first night, but…"

"No, Meredith. Not our first kiss in Paris. The first time we kissed *ever*."

My lungs suddenly hollowed out. For nearly two years, I'd never told a soul. Not even Ian.

In the spring of our freshman year, when Lindsay and I still lived together, Drew had invited me to a Sigma Phi Beta party at some local mansion that backed up to the Willamette River. It wasn't a formal. It wasn't even technically a date party, but there was a theme: Famous Gingers and Their Friends. So of course Drew asked me to go. And of course he wanted to dress like Anne Shirley and Gilbert Blythe.

At the time, I hadn't thought much about his choice. Drew had always been lazy about such things, and *Anne of Green Gables* was my favorite book. So I spent every free minute for two weeks combing Portland's best thrift stores to piece together our costumes.

The party itself was just what you'd expect: a hundred or more drunken college students, dressed as everyone from Lucille Ball and Desi Arnaz to Vincent Van Gogh and his missing ear. Turns out we weren't nearly as clever as we thought. Drew and I were just one of *six* Anne-and-Gilbert pairings, which had outraged Drew so much that he drank twice as much as usual.

Twice the beer, twice as fast. And that was before the whiskey.

When it became clear early on that Drew was already a mess, I stopped drinking anything harder than diet soda. By midnight he'd misplaced my favorite newsboy hat, and we spent the next half hour searching every nook and cranny of the house for it. The longer we looked, the more agitated he grew, until he stumbled out to the river dock and parked himself on the deck in defeat.

"You must be so sick of me by now," he muttered, kicking his feet in the water.

"Why? Because you always lose my stuff?" I lowered myself next to him, dangling my legs over the edge. "It's a hat, Drew. There are worse things you could lose."

"I know." He looked down the river. "I could lose *you*."

If he hadn't been so pathetic, I might have laughed. Instead, I lifted my hand to his chin and turned his face back toward me. "You'll never lose me, kid. Not even if you break my heart."

And just like that, Drew's hands were in my hair and he was kissing me. Except it was terrible – desperate, sloppy, and tasting like stale keg beer and half a bottle of whiskey.

When his teeth knocked against mine and then split my upper lip, I shoved him away. Hard. And then he threw up over the side of the boat dock.

Ah, so romantic. Exactly how I'd always dreamed it would be.

Half an hour later, we were back in his dorm room thanks to one of the sober pledges – the ever reliable Dan Thomas, as a matter of fact. I sat up half the night making sure Drew was still breathing and shoving angry tears off my cheeks, swearing to myself never to mention what happened. *Never.* Not unless *he* brought it up first.

But he never did. And by the end of that semester, he was so into Lindsay Foster that he'd gotten a summer job at a dude ranch near her hometown in Wyoming just so they could be together forever and ever. Which is why I'd never let myself wonder what that kiss had meant beyond drunken frat party hijinks.

And now Drew was looking at me like I was the one who'd betrayed *him*.

"So you *do* remember." He pushed out a phony laugh. "All this time, I just figured you were as wasted as I was that night. Maybe you should've majored in theater instead of French lit."

I breathed in steadily, then exhaled. "Why haven't you ever said anything, Drew?"

"Why haven't *you*? I kissed you, Meredith, and the next day, you didn't even blink at me funny. For a week afterward, I gave you chance after chance to say something, *anything*, but you never did. So I started hanging out with Lindsay. I figured if I was up in your face with another girl, you'd show some sign that you cared, but nope. You just carried on like nothing had changed. Cool as ever, checking off to-do list boxes, like your life was the only one that mattered. And this fall, you did it again. You just left for Paris after we spent the whole summer together, like I didn't factor into your plans at all."

I felt like I might be sick. All this time, I thought I'd been the bait for Lindsay. But she'd been the bait for *me*.

I untangled myself from the mess of blankets and blew out each and every candle, one by one, until the smoke rising between us mirrored the fog inside my brain. Drew glowered at me as I settled onto a chair by the fire, but I didn't care. I needed those extra ten feet to face him for the first time maybe ever. So I took in a deep breath, fixed my eyes on his, and answered.

"Do you really want to know why I never said anything about that kiss, Drew?"

His expression softened a bit in the firelight. "Of course I do."

"Okay, well, it sounds like you think that night changed everything between us. But what if it changed things in a way you don't realize?"

"What do you mean?"

I curled up in the chair, hugging my knees to my chest. "Have you ever considered how that night felt for *me*? You got drunk, you kissed me – so unromantically that you split my lip open, by the way – and then you passed out and left me to make sure you didn't aspirate in the middle of the night."

His face blanched. "Well, when you put it that way…"

"I'm not putting it any way, Drew. These are facts. So before you feel sorry for yourself that I never brought up that kiss, maybe use that clever brain of yours to imagine how humiliated I felt. How maybe I didn't *want* to remember that kiss, because it felt like it didn't mean anything to you. And as for Lindsay…"

Drew stood up and crossed the deck in two strides, pulling another chair plumb with mine over by the fireplace. "I know," he said, pulling my hands away from their death grip on my knees. "And I'm so sorry, okay? Using her like that to make you jealous was immature, but –"

"But what? Do you really think there is anything you can say that will make this disappear? Lindsay was *my friend*, Drew. She was the only close female friend I'd ever had until you came between us."

He stared at my hands resting in his for a long time. His fingers brushed softly over my skin as he thought, but I didn't respond. So he lifted his eyes to mine and let my hands go. "Is that the reason you moved to Paris, Fee? Because I hurt you?"

There it was. Drew had just spoken the truth that had been hanging between us since I got the Beckett Scholarship. But I'd never

166

told him – had never *wanted* to admit it – because the truth was, I loved Drew. No matter what.

Somewhere deep inside, the younger version of me rattled her cage, demanding that I stop wasting everybody's time. I didn't blame her. I finally had the one thing I'd wanted for as long as I could remember. Drew Sutton was in love with me, not Lindsay Foster.

So why couldn't I let it go? Why was any line that Drew had crossed more of a betrayal than my lingering confusion over Pete?

thirty-two

I never answered Drew's question about Paris. Well, not with words. I kissed him, and I guess that was the answer he wanted, because he kissed me back like it was all he needed to know.

The next morning we went snowboarding on Mount Bachelor with our high school friends. Drew ate my snow dust all day long and never mentioned Paris once. In fact, he never mentioned Paris or Lindsay again for the rest of break. We ran together on the beach every day and spent New Year's Eve on a boat decked out with fairy lights. He said all the right things about starting a new year together. I waited and waited, but the Paris question never reared her ugly head again.

Eight hours before we were supposed to head back to Portland – Drew for school, me for the airport – we lit the fireplace inside my little white gabled house on Neptune Avenue and watched *The*

Sandlot for the millionth time. When the credits rolled, Drew rested his forehead against mine.

"I hate this semester already," he smiled sadly. "What am I supposed to do without you?"

"You could take up needlepoint."

"Maybe I'll become a ski bum. I need to make a trip back to Mount Bachelor anyway."

"Why? Because your girlfriend snowboards better than you do?"

"You wish," he grinned. "Hey, do you have some quarters?"

"Why? Do you need them for laundry or something?"

"Not laundry," he said, rolling his eyes. "Novelty items. Did you see that sweet claw machine at the Mount Bachelor ski lodge? I know for a fact I can score you at *least* a couple of fancy-looking rings so you don't feel frumpy next time you're invited to a ball at the Tuileries."

"Aren't you thoughtful?" I snuggled into the crook of his arm. "But don't you think I'd impress Count Halitosis von Wartburg more if I blinged the whole way out? One ring per finger, please. And see what you can do about a faux emerald necklace. It would go great with my hair."

"So greedy." He opened his hand toward me. "Come on, Fee. I know for a fact there are twelve quarters in your wallet. Be a pal and hand them over, okay?"

"Wait, how do you know that? Did you dig through my purse?"

"Look, *mademoiselle*, I'm not sure whether you've heard this or not, but the French are so snobby that they refuse to take American money. And since you insist on leaving me tomorrow, the least you can do is hand over your spare change to fund my new collection of water guns."

"Oh, I see how it is. So all of that about adding pieces to my jewelry collection was just a trick to fund your prank arsenal? You are aware that you're nearly twenty-one years old, right?"

"This isn't an either-or situation, Fee! I'll win you all the jewels you could ever wear, just so long as your quarters score me a water gun or two."

"Why? Are you heading back to Wyoming this summer to work at the dude ranch?"

"You're hilarious," he scowled. "No, see, there are all these superlative pictures lining the staircase at the frat house. You know, *Best Attendance. Most Philanthropic,* blah, blah, blah. For two years in a row, Russell's gotten the highest GPA in the whole fraternity, and his picture is at the top of the stairs. Every morning when I walk downstairs for breakfast, there he is, judging me. So I figured I'd counter his psychological warfare with a little passive-aggressive water therapy."

I studied Drew's expression for a moment. "Okay, I have to know – why in the world do you hate Pete Russell so much? Don't you know how much the two of you have in common?"

"I *do* know," he said softly, crossing his arms. "But we got off on the wrong foot, mostly because when he found out I knew you freshman year, he taunted me for half of October, threatening to make a move on you at the quad Halloween party."

Drew might as well have knocked the air out of me with a canoe paddle. "But... I wasn't even in town on Halloween that year. Ian made me come see him in Seattle that weekend."

"I know. That's because I panicked and told your highly protective older brother that you were getting too friendly with a senior psych major. A really, really good-looking one."

"What? Why would you do something like that, Drew?"

"Didn't you hear what I said, Fee? Russell wanted to ask you out! I couldn't let that happen. Anyway, he must have figured out my scam because from that moment on, he's had it in for me."

I breathed in deeply, then breathed in again for good measure. "If you didn't want me to go with Pete to the party, why didn't you just ask me yourself?"

"I don't know," he shrugged. "I was an idiot every day of my life until ten weeks ago. Haven't we already established this fact?"

I slid my fingers into his hair again and tugged his face toward mine. "What am I gonna do with you? Violent thoughts, compulsive lying, and auditory hallucinations are bad signs. Like, one hundred percent of the time. Just ask my imaginary psych major boyfriend."

"Why do you always ruin my fun?" He pretended to pout. "That picture's like the Mona Lisa. Shooting water in Russell's smug eyeball every time I pass will be incredibly cathartic. Hey, maybe I can send you a water gun, too, so you could squirt him in the *actual* eyeball for me."

"Drew."

"Yeah?"

"I know I'm leaving tomorrow. But I'm not going anywhere, okay? I love you."

"I know you do." Drew's face softened, and he brushed his lips against mine. "So does this mean you'll cancel that boring old Italy trip and spend your spring break with me instead?"

"You claw out that emerald necklace at Mount Bachelor, and maybe then we'll talk."

thirty-three

Three cups of vending machine espresso swirled steam into the air next to Anne when I arrived in the *Grande Salle* Monday morning, straight from the airport. Across the room, Pete nodded in greeting, then turned back to Meg. A few minutes later, Dan and Marshall joined us up front, but the rest of Meg's minions plus Harper and Kelly were nowhere to be seen. In fact, half of the room seemed vacant.

Just like in September, Madame Beauchamp held a little mini-orientation for our first day back. After she outlined the coming weekend's school trip to the Loire Valley, she explained what I already suspected about the empty chairs. The coastal Northeast had been slammed with blizzard conditions over the weekend, so nearly half of our classmates were stuck at home. Anne and Meg would have been snowed in too if they hadn't spent their holidays in France this year.

Two hours later, as Dan dragged my suitcase along the rue Bonaparte, Pete turned to Anne and me. "Do you guys have plans this afternoon?"

"Coffee," Anne pointed accusingly. "This one needs lots of coffee."

Pete turned and looked at Dan, then me. "I heard *Le Galway* pub down the street from us is replaying yesterday's NFL playoff game. Cowboys versus Giants. What do you think, Meredith?"

"Let's do it," I yawned. "Should we meet at your place after I unpack?"

"Sure," he beamed. "I invited Meg to join us. We're both huge Cowboys fans."

Anne shot me a knowing look, then plastered on a smile. "Isn't everybody? They are America's Team, after all."

Pete picked up the pace so rapidly that Dan was practically running behind him. Which might explain why neither of them noticed that Anne and I were now walking in lock step – left, right, left, right – in sisterly solidarity. Was Pete Russell delusional? When a New Yorker suddenly claims allegiance to the Dallas Cowboys, RED ALERT. Hide your boyfriend, hide your brother, your best friend, your grandpa. Most of all, watch your own back.

That afternoon, while Anne and I seethed in a corner booth of *Le Galway*, Meg held court on top of the bar as Pete, Dan, and about sixty of their newest friends cheered the Cowboys to victory. After the game, I heard Pete say that her cute pink jersey must have brought them luck. For real, Pete? The game happened *yesterday.*

I guess the laws of physics don't apply in the Meg-ozoic Era.

thirty-four

Over the next several days, it became obvious how much time Pete and Meg had spent together over the holidays. She joined us every day for lunch in the Luxembourg Gardens. She monopolized every conversation, including our sacred time by the coffee machine each morning. Her strident voice became the soundtrack to the wintry January fog, and I wondered on more than one occasion why Paris had seemed so much better than Portland only a few days earlier.

Which is why I cast all my hopes on our weekend trip to the great castles of the Loire Valley. Now that Pete and Meg were joined at the hip and the Addison girls were still stuck in Maine, our quiver of arrows was down to three.

So Dan dubbed our little subgroup "The Riders of *Bro*han," a play on something from *Lord of the Rings*. We tried to make the best of things, dutifully exploring the hallowed halls of France's royal past. Always the first off the bus, always the last back on.

But then Dan and Anne realized they'd spent the same summer in high school on different exchange programs, each of them living on opposite sides of Place Plumereau, the medieval, half-timbered quarter of Tours. Which meant I spent both nights of the trip straggling behind my friends as they journeyed together down a cobblestoned memory lane.

"Would you mind pressing pause on the charm button until we get back to Paris?" I begged Dan Saturday night when Anne excused herself to the restroom of some quaint pub they both loved. "In case you hadn't noticed, I'm a little too skint right now in the friend department to be subjected to this third wheel nonsense."

"Aw. I'm sorry, Éponine. Are you gonna start singing at me now under the lamplight?"

"Mock me all you want. But you'll only have yourself to blame when the *gendarmes* find me walking the streets alone, muttering about flying kittens and stealth bombers."

Dan laughed so hard the locals at the next table scowled. "What a visual, Sullivan. Maybe you should sign up for creative writing next semester. You've already gotten plenty of practice with all the Dan Thomas fan fic you've been feeding Anne lately."

"Fan fic?" I frowned. "There's no *fic* when it's true."

"Is that a fact?" Dan's blue eyes twinkled behind his specs. "So when you told her I didn't post much on social media because I had a stalker at Highgate named Katrina, that wasn't fiction?"

"Well, yes. But I thought it sounded better than the truth: that you actually study in your free time."

The left side of his mouth hitched up, then he slid his fist toward mine and bumped it gently. "Thank you, my fellow Brohan rider. I owe you one."

As the waiter brought our drinks, I noticed several Lafayette types invading our off-the-beaten-track bar. Dan followed my gaze, and our eyes both locked on the Russell-Green duo as they peeled off from the group and settled in a corner booth with their backs to the world. Within two seconds, Pete's arm was around Meg, their faces so close together, talking in that way couples do – eyes soft, staring at each other's lips.

Anne, who had just rejoined the table, followed our rubbernecked stares just in time to see Meg close the tiny gap between them.

"Well, perfect," Dan groaned. "I guess this means they're taking things public. Just what I need: more Green in my life." When Anne and I didn't respond, he rolled his eyes. "Believe me, what you guys see at school is nothing. You would not believe what a shambles my world has become. Meg spends every single afternoon at our apartment, right up until her host family expects her home for dinner. If I'm there, I have to hide out in my room because those two occupy every inch of the sofa. And thanks to the genius who invented video chat, I can never quite get away from the insanity. Well, except when I'm with you guys."

"Oh, I know all about the schmoopy chat dates thanks to the hyper thin walls on the seventh floor," Anne scoffed, shooting me a dirty look. "Lucky for me, there are time constraints in Meredith's case. Not that it's stopped Drew from calling her twice a day, every day."

"Not *every* day," I mumbled. "Look, guys, we all saw this coming, right? Meg Green is beautiful. She's smart, she's funny, and I get the distinct feeling she's gone out of her way to be nice to us this trimester. So maybe we should all try harder to return the favor."

176

"If the next words out of your mouth are that we want Pete to be happy, you will wake up tomorrow with L-I-A-R Sharpied all over your face," Anne glared. "Do not let Meredith fool you, Dan. She and Kelly co-author a Twitter account called *@vertismes*. It's a virtual log of all the nonsensical stuff that comes out of Meg's mouth every time she speaks."

Dan's mouth gaped. "Is *that* why you two always take out your phones whenever she's around? You're live-tweeting what she says?"

"Not live-tweeting," I scowled. "I mean, we might be taking notes for later, but it's no big deal, Dan. Our tweets are protected, and we have exactly two followers besides ourselves. One of them" – I held my hand over Anne's head and pointed downward – "was the brainchild behind the whole idea in the first place, just so you know. But more importantly, you cannot tell Pete."

"You have my word," he grinned, lifting his hand to his heart. "But only if you let me follow, too."

Pete and Meg were still smooching away in the corner, and even though she'd embarrassed me, Anne was not wrong to call me out. Really? Out of every girl on the planet, Pete chose *Meg Green*? Didn't he see how insipid she was? Of course he didn't. He's a guy. Resistance was futile against the Queen of the Fembots: that perfect body plus an aura of mystery equaled Pete Russell reduced to his testosterone-y core.

thirty-five

I defy anyone to dispute that January and February are the two dreariest months of the year. At least in the Northern Hemisphere. At home, this time of year means constant drizzle from a cold, gray sky that bleeds horizonless into the cold, gray Pacific Ocean. Minus the large body of water, Paris was no different.

So even though the Centre Lafayette was back to full capacity now that every classmate had returned, an odd sort of darkness loomed. And after one too many days indoors, Kelly came up with a brilliant plan: a weekend in London would snap us out of our funk.

So on that last Friday in January, we boarded the Eurostar with hope in our heart and a few pounds sterling in our pockets. But gloomy London was far worse than Paris. Even the silver umbrella charm I bought for my bracelet looked like it was covered in soot.

The following Friday after *Promenade Parisienne*, Harper dragged us over to Maya's of Montparnasse, our failsafe remedy for the dreary, homesick blues. The chips, queso, and margarita combo cheered even crabby old me. And, because Anne had heard nothing but glowing reviews about some new American romantic comedy called *April in Paris*, we dropped a small fortune to see it on the Champs-Élysées, certain that it would be the answer to all our February prayers.

Bad call, Anne. Every last warm fuzzy from the Tex-Mex goodness immediately faded as the latest Hollywood It Girl and her on-screen suitor gallivanted around a brightly lit, Technicolor Paris that resembled Oz more than the capital of France.

"Where'd they film *this*?" I whispered. "It rains half the year in this town."

"Probably Burbank," Kelly grimaced, her blue eyes narrowing. "Would you look at that? They have Montmartre in the southern half of the city on this wide shot. What is wrong with these people? I know they were on a budget, but come on. Not a single one of their unpaid production assistants knew how to access the map app on their phone?"

The four of us crossed our arms simultaneously in disgust.

But Harper refused to let the evening be a bust, so she invited Anne and me back to their apartment to watch the first season of *Gilmore Girls*. Paris (Geller) for the win, I say. We stayed up all night, busting out Kelly's secret Tootsie Pop stash, begging Luke and Lorelai to get together.

By eight a.m. on Saturday, I felt ten years younger and a hundred years saner. When Anne suggested we walk the four miles back to the apartment, I was happy to oblige her. We were back in love with our city again. Right on cue, the clouds broke for the first time in weeks, and a tiny ray of sunshine bathed our path in golden glory.

Weaving our way through the Right Bank down to the Seine, we stumbled across a Chinese New Year parade between the Centre Pompidou and the Hôtel de Ville. It was one of those peculiar Paris moments that had vindicated my splurge on a high-end smartphone when I first moved here. You need a high-pixel camera with a lot of extra storage when these are the sights you find just around the bend every day.

Only this time, what I found around the next bend was a string of text messages on my phone screen. One by one, the mini-diatribes scrolled in rapid succession.

Six hours later I'm still sitting here waiting

Yep I've wasted my entire Friday night on you

Trying not to imagine you dead in a ditch right now

Okay well now I'm just pissed - or terrified - no wait, both

WHY DONT YOU ANSWER ME FEE IM FREAKING OUT

Really, Drew? If you're gonna all caps me, THE LEAST YOU CAN DO IS PUNCTUATE.

"Where have you been?" Drew boomed over his microphone half an hour later when my laptop finally connected to his.

"Hey, *bonjour* to you, too," I retorted. "You know where I was. With the girls."

"All night? Doing what, clubbing?"

"No, not clubbing. We were binge-watching *Gilmore Girls.*"

"Oh." Drew glanced over at the bedside table, where his cell phone screen was now illuminating the darkness behind him. "I'm just glad you finally called. I need to talk to you."

"Why? What's wrong?"

Drew rubbed his eyes with the palms of his hands and then crossed his arms over his chest. "I've been doing some work for my granddad's practice, organizing digital files remotely, and he's paid me just enough that I could buy you a ticket home for spring break. I know it's last minute and you've already got plans with your friends to go to Italy, but…"

My initial reaction was fury. For some reason, since I'd come back to Paris, it seemed like every conversation with Drew had devolved into a fight over my spring break plans. And even though the last month on the ground here had been wretched, I didn't have the rest of my life with these friends. In June, we would scatter to the winds, and who knew when we'd all be together again.

I guess Drew took my pause as a good sign, because he smiled. "Today is twenty-eight days out from the start of your break, and I was thinking, if you could come home a couple of days early, you'd be here just in time to celebrate my twenty-first birthday. What do you think?"

"I don't know." I straightened my torso while Drew shot another glance at his phone, which had been blinking non-stop like a strobe light since he called. "Do you need to get that?"

Drew shot me a look, then grabbed his phone and turned the screen toward the camera for me to read.

"L. J." I scrunched up my nose. "Who's that?"

"It's Jack Chisholm. The guy from Medford?"

"Oh, yeah," I nodded casually. "How'd he get that nickname?"

"Jack. Lumberjack. *L. J.*" With his phone still turned toward me, he went to his contacts, and pulled up L.J., who was, in fact, Jack

Chisholm. Then he fixed me with a smug grin. "You thought L.J. was a girl, didn't you?"

"Why would I think that?"

Drew slammed his phone down, then looked back up at me. "You know what? Forget it. I'm going to sleep now. My friends are all headed home for the night so there's no point in leaving now."

I hadn't yet done the math on the time difference. It was a quarter past two at home. "Hey, I'm sorry I made you miss out on the fun. And I love your idea, Drew. I really do. But I don't think I can back out on Italy. Other people are counting on me."

"But this is a win-win, Fee!" I hadn't seen that softness around his eyes since Christmas Break. "It's a free trip home, you won't have to spend any money on overpriced European hotels, and most importantly, you'll be with me."

"But everything's booked, even our train tickets. Kelly's even typed up an itinerary."

"Oh, well, if Kelly's typed up an itinerary," Drew scoffed. "Are you kidding me with this right now? Itinerary or not, you see your friends every day. I am your *boyfriend,* Meredith."

"It's not about that, Drew. You know I want to see you. But I can't come home. Not yet."

"No need to finish. I have this answer memorized." He cleared his throat, then shifted into a falsetto. *"The six of us only have this tiny window of time to be together, Drew, so we have to go everywhere as a group. Especially to Italy."*

"Was that supposed to be me? Because it sounded more like Mickey Mouse."

Drew's eyes narrowed. "You do realize that what I'm asking isn't outrageous, right? That you should *want* to spend more time with me than with people you didn't even know this time last year?"

I closed my window so the whole building wouldn't hear, then sat calmly back in my chair. "You promised me you would do whatever I asked to make this work. Those were your words, Drew. I can screenshot your dorky card if you don't believe me."

"I know what I said, Meredith. I just didn't expect you to take such an active role in the obstacle portion of our relationship. Do you even miss me? Because you sure don't act like it."

I dropped my head into my hands, searching for the right words as I pushed back the tears. "Why can't I make you understand? I didn't move to Paris to make your life difficult."

"No," he laughed ruefully. "You moved to Paris to punish me for breaking your heart."

When I opened my eyes, the connection was gone. I waited several minutes, just in case it was a glitch. But then I stood up, grabbed my phone and my earbuds, pulled on my running shoes and sprinted down to Luxembourg Gardens. I covered every inch of the park twice, desperate for the sun to warm me again from the inside out.

As I approached the northern entrance, a flurry of red drew my attention to the Boulevard Saint Michel. The same parade we'd seen earlier in the day was now headed east, its dragon dancing from side to side as red flags waved everywhere.

Like I needed help noticing the ones from home waving *right in my face*.

thirty-six

As many times as I've heard the explanation for leap year, I still do not understand the logic behind the math. Yeah, I get the need for accuracy, but really, who is going to know if we're twenty-four days short every century? And more importantly, does someone actually care?

On Thursday night, February 29th, I was standing in the garret of my room with my back to the window, staring at the clothes blanketing every surface. I had no idea what to pack. The forecast was chaos: rain in Florence, snow in Venice, sunny and seventy-five degrees Fahrenheit in Rome. And, oddly, the possibility of a hailstorm in the middle of the week. Who knew Italy had hailstorms?

Surely leap year was to blame.

I had just maneuvered around a pile of too-heavy-to-pack sweaters when my cell phone chirped from my pocket.

"Hey, Dad," I answered distractedly. "How are you?"

"Hello, my darlin' girl," he answered in his thick Irish brogue. "How's Paris? Still there?"

He asked this question every week. I don't know why, but Jamie Sullivan found it hilarious.

"Yes, Dad, still here. Hey, is everything okay? We weren't supposed to talk until Sunday when I get to Florence. You know it's Thursday, right?"

He cleared his throat, then cleared it again. "Yes, darlin', your mum and I are grand. But you see, I had this little problem yesterday..."

"Problem?" My voice escalated an octave. "What do you mean?"

"Well, the doctors, they claim I've had a little, you know – *incident* – with my heart."

My entire body went numb. "Hold on. Did you have a heart attack?"

"Me? Well, I suppose you could call it that, but really..."

There was a bit of static, like someone was scuffling with the phone, and then a female voice came over the line, strong and clear. "Meredith, please don't worry," my mom said. "Your dad's comfortable for now, but the doctors plan to do open-heart surgery on Saturday."

"*This* Saturday?" I crumpled against the nearest wall, a knot forming in my stomach. This couldn't be real. "Is he...? Mum, how bad is this? Tell me the truth."

My mom paused just long enough for me to know her reply was only partial. "Don't you fret, love. Just go on to Italy and check in with us once you're settled. Greg has already got your brother on the next flight out of whatever far-off land he's been visiting this week, so you go on with your friends. We'll be grand."

"I'm not going to Italy!" I choked. "You need help, Mum, and I want to be there. Can't I use Ian's miles to come home, too?"

She sighed, and her voice was suddenly one among many as she stepped into the hallway. "Of course you can, love," she said in a muffled tone, like she was covering up the phone. "Your brother said you can speak with the ticket agent at Charles de Gaulle airport. Do you know his air mile account number?"

"Of course I do. Ian made me memorize it ages ago. I assume you're in Portland?"

"Yes. We're at St. Joseph's, near your school. I'm staying down the street in a hotel."

"That's good. Are the Suttons with you?"

"No. They flew to Florida a few days ago for a Caribbean cruise, and your father doesn't want me to bother them. They'll be home early next week anyway."

"What about Drew? Have you called him yet?"

"No. I thought you might want to tell him yourself that −" Mum's voice cracked as it trailed off. "Listen, love, they're quite strict about using your mobile in here, so I should go. Can you text me once your flight is sorted? I'll do the same if I hear back from Ian."

When I hung up, I opened the metal *volet* shutters on the window so violently that the boys probably heard the clatter up on rue Guénégaud, but I did not care. I was suffocating.

Anne suddenly burst through my door, her face as white as the walls. "Are you okay?"

I folded into myself like a little kid and slid down the nearest wall. Anne lowered herself next to me as words spilled out as fast as my mouth would move. I realized as I neared the end of the story that I was holding my cell phone in one hand and the scarf I'd been about to pack in the other. Anne, who was not a touchy-feely sort of person, tugged them both free from my hands, then wrapped her arms around me as I sobbed into her shoulder.

Every neighbor across the courtyard must have thought those crazy American girls on the top floor had finally cracked from too much wine or culture shock.

When I finally composed myself, Anne went into drill sergeant mode, dictating with no hesitation which items to pack for home and which to put back in my closet. If she hadn't been there, I would have just stared into the void until my eyes bled. Instead, she handed me items, and I placed them obediently in the bag.

If I ever made it back to Paris again, I might relinquish all decision-making privileges to Anne. Never underestimate a friend who thinks clearly under duress.

thirty-seven

By five the next morning, Anne and I were both out the door – Anne to the train station to meet the rest of our Italy-bound friends, and me to Charles de Gaulle to catch a flight home. I left a note downstairs in Marie-France's apartment about what had happened, and gave her and Anne both a list of fifty numbers where they could reach me.

On the way to the airport, I tried to call Drew again for the fifteenth time since the previous night. Then I tried again. And again.

No answer. No answer. No answer.

Ever since our fight last month, things with Drew had shifted. Our Valentine's Day video chat "date" had been a bust, and when I called on the 28th to wish him a happy birthday, Drew's glib responses made me feel like a telemarketer. He was like, "Oh, hello. Thanks for the birthday wishes. Let's talk about everything *except* Italy this time. Yep, yep, the weather's rainy as usual. Okay, gotta go, goodbye."

And now that he was getting his way, now that I'd be home for spring break after all, now that I *needed* him, Drew was ghosting me.

When I arrived at the counter for Ian's preferred airline, I explained my situation to the agent. I gave her my brother's frequent flier number, but there were no reservations listed from Paris on his account. "And since you're not on the list of authorized users," she purred, "I'm afraid my hands are tied."

"Oh. Okay." I willed my lips into a smile. "Then could you help me purchase a one-way ticket to Portland?"

"Of course, Miss Sullivan. For today's flight via Dallas-Fort Worth?" The robotically polite lady replied. "That will be three thousand, five hundred dollars. Cash or charge?"

"Thirty-five..." I sucked in a breath. My credit card limit wasn't even half of that amount. "Look, don't I qualify for an emergency fare? My dad's having open heart surgery tomorrow."

"That *is* the emergency fare," she countered, oozing faux sincerity. "It's the best I can do for an open-ended, last-minute ticket into the United States. I'm sorry. You must understand security protocols these days are quite restrictive."

"Fine," I growled. "Can you just hold that seat? I need a few minutes to figure this out."

"Certainly, *mademoiselle*, but not for long," she cooed, never dropping that well-honed customer-friendly veneer.

I went into overdrive. First I called my mom. Maybe her phone was off, or she was on the other line, but it went straight to voice mail. I called my dad's phone, just in case. And the hospital room.

Nothing.

And then, because I was desperate, I tried Ian's phone. There was a chance he was in an airport lounge somewhere, tapping away on his laptop. Surely he hadn't forgotten about me? But the more I thought about it, the more terrified I became. If Ian was that distracted, things at home were worse than I knew.

As a last-ditch effort, I tried Drew one more time. I called every place I could think of, but every line just rang, rang, rang, and then rolled to voicemail. Then, because leap year hates me, my own phone buzzed back: *10 Percent Battery Remaining. Engage Low Power Mode?*

I hadn't slept more than a handful of minutes last night. The concrete pole I was leaning against was no longer enough to keep me upright in my exhaustion. So I sank to the ground, slumped against my suitcase like it was my only friend left in the world, and began to weep.

For years, people had been making these sorts of decisions on my behalf, and now that I needed to be resourceful, I had no coping skills. For the next few minutes, I just sat there curled between the pole and my bag, sobbing silently into my scarf like some sort of security blanket.

Then a hand touched my shoulder. "Sully?"

thirty-eight

I looked up to find Pete Russell crouched before me. With both palms, I shoved the tears off my face and tried to smile, but it was no use. If I tried to talk, nothing but a sob would escape.

In one single movement, Pete lifted me gently to my feet, then wrapped both arms around me. "Meredith, talk to me," he said quietly into my hair. "Did something happen?"

"My dad had a heart attack." My lips trembled against his shoulder. "He's having surgery tomorrow morning, but the ticket agent says it's going to cost thirty-five hundred dollars for a one-way ticket. How am I going to pay for that? My family won't answer their phones, and Drew…"

As soon as I said his name, my voice quavered and the rest muffled into sobs. Pete held me tight, hugging me against his chest like it was the only thing on his agenda for the day. "Don't cry, Sully. We'll get you home."

He held me until I stopped trembling, and then a little bit longer, just to be sure. Then he grabbed my suitcase and deftly maneuvered both our bags into the Priority Access lane, where an even more polite woman greeted us. Air mile account numbers were recited as a keyboard clickety-clacked. Before I knew it, I was booked into a seat next to Pete from Paris to Dallas-Fort Worth, and then on to Portland, with a return flight on St. Patrick's Day, the last day of our break.

When Pete handed me my ticket and steered me by the elbow toward passport control, my addled brain finally kicked back into gear. "Wait a minute, Pete, I can't let you do this. How will..."

"Stop that, okay? I'm not leaving you in Paris when your dad is sick. Look, it's no big deal. My grandfather flew all over the world for his job. Trust me, our air mile account is flush."

"But..."

He stopped walking and pulled me off to the side, both hands on my shoulders. "Sully, you're going to hurt my feelings if you don't let me help you out. Come on. We need to get going."

He gestured for me to follow him over to security, where we passed quickly through the gazillion steps of international departures. At the gate, Pete left me alone with the backpacks to find us coffee and something to eat. I was texting my mom with my flight information when he returned.

Pete handed me the biggest coffee in France and a chocolate croissant. "Is that Sutton?"

"It's my mom." I grabbed the two napkins he was offering me, and managed a weak smile. "After a couple dozen non-responses, I think it's safe to say Drew is busy."

Pete's eyes went wide, then he scowled. "He hasn't heard about your dad? Wait, did you try calling him at..."

"I've called everywhere."

Pete cursed under his breath – something I'd never heard him do – then took out his phone.

"Please don't," I said, so quietly that I felt like a child. "Look, I appreciate what you're doing, but I've already called the Sigma Phi house phone a few times. You don't want the guys thinking I'm a stage-five clinger, do you?"

He laughed. A very Pete, very heart-warming chuckle. "You are *not* a stage-five clinger, Sully. But shouldn't we keep trying? Won't he want to be at the airport when we get home?"

Maybe it was because I was out-of-my-mind worried about my dad. Maybe it was my lack of sleep, or the fact that my entire support network had just ghosted me. But for the first time all morning, it occurred to me there was a reason Pete wasn't on his way to Italy.

I wrapped my hand around his wrist. "Your grandmother?"

"Yeah." He attempted to smile. "Her nurse called. They brought in hospice yesterday."

thirty-nine

Before I could respond, the gate agent started calling our group to board. Then Pete's phone rang in the Jetway and, even if I hadn't heard that unmistakable voice, I would have known it was Meg. I scrolled my own phone in an attempt to give them privacy, but I still heard plenty.

Like the fact that she was meeting her parents tomorrow in Rome to set sail on a Mediterranean cruise for two weeks with at least one of her minions in tow.

Or the things Pete *wasn't* saying, like the news about Gigi. Or the fact that he was on a plane home instead of to Italy. Or that one of *his* minions had hitched along for the ride.

When we got to our seats, I wanted to laugh: we were in the bulkhead on the right hand side of the plane. The same two seats from August. I found myself smiling at the memory of that day. I didn't even recognize that Meredith anymore.

While Meg blathered on in Pete's ear, he grabbed my black tote from me and placed both of our bags in the overhead bins with his free arm. I slid gratefully into my seat by the window, and had barely strapped myself in when exhaustion overtook me. We were thirty thousand feet in the air and somewhere over Ireland before I woke up again.

Pete slumped in his seat as if every cell in his body needed rest. There were those same rosy cheeks again that I'd noticed when we'd flown to Paris in August, but today, it made me want to hug him. Having grown up traveling with both Ian and Drew, it struck me as odd that Pete was neither snoring nor sleeping with his mouth open. He was just… peaceful. And beautiful. The cropped haircut he'd had at the beginning of the year was now longer, and though it was not the lion's mane he'd had in previous years, the curls around the crown of his head were the perfect kind of messy, like he woke up that way and wondered why you didn't.

I watched Pete sleep for a lot longer than I would ever admit, wondering how someone I'd once considered the boorish bane of my existence had just appeared by my side when I needed it most. If any one of my people had answered my calls over the last few hours, I might not have even seen Pete this morning. Now, neither of us were alone.

When the flight attendants rolled the lunch trolleys down the aisle, Pete jerked awake. He rubbed his eyes hard, glancing first to his left, then back at me. "Oh, hey. You're awake," he smiled. "Sorry, did I snore?"

"Not yet," I grinned. "But you did recite bits and pieces of the Gettysburg Address."

He stretched his arms above his head and yawned. "Weird. Usually it's *The Wasteland.*"

Then he smiled wider, and I couldn't help but wonder if he missed our banter as much as I did.

The flight attendants arrived at our row, chirping 'chicken or pasta' in all directions. And although we'd both inhaled our croissants earlier, I guess exhaustion had induced starvation, because Pete and I shoveled everything on our trays into our mouths.

"That was definitely *not* Florentine pasta," Pete sighed after the flight attendants had cleared our tray tables on their return trip through the aisle. "Do you need somewhere to stay tonight? Because it's not a good idea for you to drive to the coast when you're exhausted. That last forty minutes before Highway 101 is tricky, especially in the dark."

"It's the trees." I picked at the tiny dinner roll crumbs on my sleeve, then brushed them onto the floor. "They make an extra canopy so you can't see the moon, not to mention all the curves in the road. But don't worry, my dad's in Portland. The Lincoln City hospital is sort of small, so they usually send emergencies to the big city whenever they can."

The color drained again from Pete's face. His breath became twitchy as his chest rose and fell against my elbow. Then his eyes locked with mine, and suddenly it felt like I was looking at a person I'd known all along but never really noticed before.

Pete watched me hesitantly for a moment, then turned his whole body to face me. "I've never told you this before, but I've been to Lincoln City."

"You have?"

196

He nodded. "Twice as a kid, and once just after high school. Never since."

"Really? You never told me that."

Pete's eyes went soft. "Well, it was before I knew you. And it's kind of a long story."

I pointed to the in-flight map flickering on the wall screen before us. "You've got a captive audience for a few hours. Even Greenland is listening."

"Well, if Greenland is listening…" Pete smiled, but it didn't reach his eyes. "Okay, so, once upon a time, there was a goofy high school graduate who somehow got into Stanford."

"*Stanford*? Are you serious?"

"Completely. My parents met there, and for my whole life, that was the only place I wanted to go." A wistful look crossed his face. "When we found out orientation started July 5th, my parents decided to make a family vacation out of it. You know James, the guy I worked for in Shanghai?"

"Yeah?"

"His mom and my mom were roommates in college. They're our family friends, like –"

"My family and Drew's?"

"Well, I hadn't thought of that, but yeah," Pete nodded. "I spent Fourth of July with my parents at the Logans' house in Palo Alto, but after I got settled in the dorm the next day, I never called or texted them once. I was too busy making plans, making friends. It felt like my whole life had been leading up to that moment, you know?"

I did know. That's how I'd felt at Highgate's orientation.

"There was a huge party the night before I left," Pete continued. "I came home at five a.m., totally wasted, to find my parents waiting inside the dorm lobby. They'd been calling me all night to let me know we were leaving early. So, when I didn't answer, they got worried."

"Sounds about right. Were they pissed?"

He laughed again under his breath. "If they were, they didn't show it. They just went with me up to my room and shoved all of my stuff into my bags while I hung out with my head in one of the disgusting dorm toilets."

Now I was laughing. "Wow, Russell. That's quite a mental picture you've given me."

But Pete wasn't smiling anymore. "I was such a little jerk, Sully. Before we'd even left the dorm parking lot, I'd passed out in the back seat."

"Well, you're hardly the first person who's done that, you know." His face went pale again and suddenly contorted, the pain in his eyes so bright that tears pricked my own eyes. "Hey, you're tired," I said, laying my hand over his. "We can talk about this later if…"

"No," he said flatly, his eyes meeting mine. "Let me finish. See, they'd been planning all week to surprise me with this drive back along the coast. Every time we'd gone to visit the Logans over the years, I'd begged my parents to take Highway 101, but we'd always been in too big of a hurry to get home. But that day the whole point of leaving early was to see the sunrise over the ocean together. When I finally woke up, the sun was high in the sky, and we were already two hours into Oregon. I had missed all of California."

"Pete, I'm sure they understood. They were in college once."

"I know. But they'd been looking forward to surprising me, and I ruined it for all of us. Of course I apologized, but all day I felt like

I'd sucked the joy right out of life. When we reached Lincoln City, my dad decided we'd driven far enough…"

"Because of the tree canopy?"

"Obviously," he smiled. "So, we checked into a motel somewhere on the south side of town near Siletz Bay, then headed north to find somewhere to eat."

"North?" I sat up straight. "Sullivan's is on the north side of town."

Pete paused, his eyes fixed on mine. "I know. That's where we went."

Like those sped-up flashback sequences in a movie, my mind finally registered who Pete Russell really was. He hadn't seemed familiar to me for the last three years because he resembled Chris Pratt. No, it was Pete himself I recognized.

The dark curly hair. The laugh lines around the eyes. The hopeful smile.

Four years ago, on the night of July 8th, a family of three was leaving Sullivan's when they turned south on Highway 101, and a drunk driver collided head-on with their car. And I was standing on the front steps of the restaurant, just a couple hundred yards away.

forty

You know that thing that happens when you're trying to smile your way past the tears, and you end up looking like a Halloween mask? That was Pete. And I just couldn't take it anymore.

So I yanked off my seatbelt and threw my arms around him, squeezing him so hard I thought I might cut off his air. His entire body seized up at first, but I refused to let go. After a handful of seconds, he buried his face in my shoulder, his breath hitching in his throat as he fought back tears. But that didn't stop me. I kept holding on, because all my words had escaped me.

The night of the accident, I was waiting for Drew to finish his shift so we could meet some friends at the movies. I had just walked outside when I heard the unforgettable sound of metal crashing against metal. I didn't see the accident happen, but I saw the two cars once the dust settled. In my terror, I had run back into the restaurant to find my dad, screaming at everyone I saw to call 911. I was shaking so badly that Drew grabbed me and took me back to my parents' office. Jamie Sullivan held both of us tight as he spoke to the police.

I'd heard the ambulance sirens arriving on the scene while Drew and I huddled together on the sofa in the office, safe and sound and hidden away from the outside world. Employees ran up and down the hallway, helpless to know what to do. We didn't leave the building until long after closing. By that point, nothing remained of the accident but tiny shards of plastic from the headlights.

The next morning, a policeman came to our house to get a statement from each of us. He explained that the driver – a young woman celebrating her twenty-first birthday – had survived the crash, but the front seat passengers in the other car had died en route to the local hospital. Their eighteen-year-old son had been Medevac'd to a trauma center in Portland with critical injuries.

That's all my family ever knew. For a while after the accident, we'd tried to find out what happened to the boy, but at the request of the family, none of the victims' names were ever released to the press. But that didn't stop us from praying for the son every single night for a year.

None of us had ever forgotten about that boy. We talked about him a lot, actually, even as recently as Christmas. Was he still injured? Had he gone to school? Where *was* he now?

He was here, right in front of me. Where he'd been all along.

"I'm sorry," Pete whispered as he pulled away, wiping his cheeks. "You have no idea how many times I've wanted to tell you. When I saw your Sullivan's shirt the first day of school, I knew exactly who you were. I'd seen you that night in the restaurant. You walked us to our table."

"You *remembered* me?"

"I mean, what kind of question is that? I don't meet feisty redheads every day." He gave me a watery smile. "Anyway, I panicked that first day of class, and I immediately wanted to take back what I said, but I couldn't without explaining myself. And then so much time passed that the truth felt outrageous."

I grabbed his hand and squeezed it gently. "Well, at least this explains why you hated my Sullivan's t-shirt so much."

He rubbed away a tear with his free hand, then laughed under his breath. "I did *not* hate it. You look really pretty in green."

Raw panic bloomed in Pete's eyes, like he'd stepped too far over the line. But for me, in that moment, it was as if he'd set a bonfire in a cave of shadows.

As if I'd just seen the real Pete Russell for the very first time.

Pete wiped a hand past his eye just as a tear breached his lashes, then he stood. "I think I'm going to stretch my legs a little. You need anything?"

"No. But Pete? Thank you. For finally telling me."

Pete nodded self-consciously, then headed to the back of the cabin. Sitting there alone, listening to the steady rumble of the jet, I couldn't help but think what an idiot I'd been. How many times I'd chosen to believe whatever I wanted about Pete without a shred of evidence. How foolish I'd been to let Drew stunt our friendship. How petty I'd been to punish Pete for choosing Meg.

The true reason Pete had never told me about the accident had very little to do with himself and everything to do with me. From the second we'd met at Highgate, I'd failed Pete Russell. I was a judgmental coward with selfish, shallow dreams. And all this time, Pete had deserved so much more from me.

forty-one

You can wait for arriving passengers pretty far into the terminal at Portland's PDX airport, and I could see my brother waiting almost the second we stepped out from the gate. Ian grabbed me and then Pete into his usual bear hug and held us both so tightly that Pete blushed a little. But by the smile he gave me over Ian's shoulder, I knew he didn't mind much.

"So, is your family here?" Ian asked Pete, glancing around. "I'd love to meet them."

I panicked. Such a normal question to ask, yet so very *wrong*.

"No," Pete said unblinkingly. "I always catch a shuttle home."

"What? No way. Meredith and I will drop you off. Where do you live?"

"Um, Dunthorpe? Near Bishop's Close?"

That was quite a swanky part of town. But either Ian didn't know or he didn't care. "Grand," he said, grabbing my bag. "Sit up front and show me the way."

It turned out that Ian had arrived six hours before us after a thirty-eight hour transit from Estonia via Copenhagen, Reykjavik, New York, Chicago, and finally Seattle. And he thought he *had* booked me a ticket, but he realized at some point in transit that he'd never gotten confirmation.

"I threw up twice in the transit lounge at LaGuardia," he said, his voice a little wobbly. "I had a full visual of you alone at Charles de Gaulle with your hair in a messy top knot, sobbing into your scarf."

Pete's eyes met mine. "No way," he smiled. "Not Meredith."

As I listened to my brother swap travel stories with Pete, my brain couldn't believe what it already knew. They had everything in common: the vagabond-around-the-globe past, the sharp intellect, the disarming wit. Most people seemed slightly intimidated by Ian, but not Pete. They'd only met that one time at Marie-France's apartment, but to hear Ian and Pete laughing, you would have thought they'd known each other long before either of them knew me.

Before Ian's car came to a halt in the driveway, the front door of Gigi's Tudor-style house opened, revealing two women. The one in the nurse's scrubs was obvious, so the elderly woman in a black turtleneck and jeans had to be Gigi. Pete had told me she was in her mid-seventies, but her salt-and-pepper hair and youthful face seemed at least two decades younger, despite her poor health.

Pete didn't even shut the passenger door behind him. He just ran to his grandmother, pulled her gently away from the nurse's steadying hold, and hugged her as fiercely as anyone could hug someone so fragile. She looked terribly tiny against his large frame as she peeked around his arm to smile at Ian and me. "You brought friends home with you?"

With one arm still around her, Pete turned to face us. "Gigi, these are my friends, Meredith and Ian." He motioned for us to come closer. "Meredith studies with me in Paris."

Gigi's eyes flicked between Pete and me. Then she grinned so widely that her dark eyes crinkled. Just like Pete's. "I was hoping you would bring Meredith home to meet me," she beamed, squeezing his waist.

Pete's eyes met mine for a second, and his grin went a little lopsided. "Gigi, Ian is Meredith's brother. They've both flown home to visit their dad. He's having surgery tomorrow."

"Oh?" A shadow crossed Gigi's face. "I'm so sorry to hear that. Do you two need somewhere to stay? We have plenty of room here if you'd like."

I had to bite my lip to keep my eyes from filling again with tears. Who offers shelter to two complete strangers when she's days away from her own death? I opened my mouth to speak – twice – but no words came out.

Luckily, Ian was oblivious. For all he knew, the woman in the scrubs was Pete's sister. So he stepped forward and took Gigi's hand in his, and said the very thing any normal person would. "Thank you so much, Mrs. – um..."

"Margaret. Please call me Margaret."

"Thank you, *Margaret*," he said, winking. "You're so kind, but our whole family is staying in a hotel near St. Joseph's. In fact, I promised our mum I'd get Meredith to the hospital as quickly as possible, so we should probably head out, if you don't mind."

Gigi smiled warmly at Ian, patted his hand, then turned her attention to me. "You'll come back to visit, won't you, Meredith? Maybe Sunday, if your dad has stabilized?"

"I will," I nodded. And then, for some reason even I couldn't explain, I closed the gap between us and hugged Gigi as tightly as I could without hurting her. "Your grandson is just like you," I whispered quietly so only Gigi and Pete could hear. "His mom and dad would be proud."

When I pulled away, Gigi took my face in her hands, looking so deeply into my eyes I thought she might put a spell on me. Then she turned to Pete and smiled. "Oh, I *like* this one," she chuckled. "Peter, come inside after you've said your goodbyes."

Ian grabbed Pete in one of his best, big brotherly hugs – one flat palm pressed against Pete's back, his solid fingers curved around Pete's shoulder. Watching the two of them, I felt a giant twinge of guilt. Drew idolized my brother. I hoped he never had to see this. It was one Sullivan too many in Pete Russell's court.

And just like that, Ian was back in the car, turning the engine over before my mind even registered that he was gone. Pete stepped toward me, wrapping his hand around my elbow.

"Hey." Pete's dark eyes were full to the lashes with grace. "This might sound crazy, but I don't believe it was an accident that I ran into you this morning. Truth is, Sully, I think I might be able to face these next few days now that you're here, too."

I nodded, wrapping my arms around his waist and burying my face in his chest. "Pete?"

"Yeah?"

"Does it make me a bad person to pray that the Italian trains go on strike? I mean, not for the *whole* two weeks that Dan and the girls are traveling. But maybe just long enough that they get stuck somewhere gross and industrial for a day or two?"

Pete's chest vibrated against my cheek as he chuckled under his breath. "Does it make me worse than you that my prayers were more specific? Because while you were asleep earlier, I prayed that every single track leading to Venice would burst into flames *and* fall into the Adriatic."

"Wow." I burrowed tighter under his arm. "I'm taking back what I said to your grandmother, Russell. Poor Kelly had more on the Venice itinerary than anywhere else."

"Why do you think I got so specific? It was altruistic, really. I love that girl, but her itinerary was nuts. She'll only have herself to blame if Dan shoves her into the lagoon."

forty-two

"Well, if it isn't our darlin' girl, all grown up and Parisian now."
My dad's lilting Irish brogue spilled out into the hallway before I
could even breach the hospital room doorway. He was sitting upright,
his arm draped around my mom's waist, the twinkle in his green eyes
breaking my heart into a million tiny pieces. I dropped my backpack
on the floor and ran to his bed, throwing my arms around them both,
then felt Ian encircle us, too. I had never, ever been so happy to see
three people in my life.

"Would you look, Molly?" Dad mumbled into my cheek. "Our
two babies flew across an ocean and an entire continent to see their
favorite dad. I told you my evil plan would work."

Ian pulled away, but I stayed right where I was, pinching my
dad's chin playfully. "Are you in cahoots with Drew, Jamie Sullivan?
Because if you faked a heart attack to get me home…"

"Wouldn't you like to know," he grinned. "Now, did you have much turbulence? I hate flying across the Atlantic. Too many patches without land, especially on this side of Greenland."

For the next thirty minutes, my dad beamed as he listened to Ian describe his nightmarish trajectory home. Hearing it the second time around, I thought about what Pete had said earlier and a sudden calm drifted over me. He was right. Our meeting was not an accident. All the 'what ifs' in the world couldn't convince me otherwise now.

By the time the nurse came by to tell us visiting hours were over, my mom kissed my dad on the cheek, and the look that passed between them was... well, I knew that look. After thirty years of marriage, those two knew everything there was to know without saying a single word. As we shut the door behind us, my legs nearly caved in on themselves as I realized that by this time tomorrow, my dad might not be with us anymore. And then they nearly caved in again when I saw who was standing at the nurses' station twenty feet away.

Drew reached my mom in three seconds with his long stride, hugging her so hard I think even she was surprised. He muttered some sort of apology for not being here sooner, then turned to me, his eyes so full of accusations that I burst into tears. Again.

He didn't say a word as he wrapped his arms around me. At first I kept my arms between us in silent protest. The cloying stench of whiskey flooded over me from every surface – his clothes, his skin. His breath against my cheek.

But when Drew took my hand in the elevator, I didn't fight him. The four of us walked silently to Ian's car, and once my mother was securely fastened in the front seat, Ian motioned for Drew and me to follow him out of earshot behind the car.

"Let's cut to the chase, Andrew," he hissed. "The whole world can smell that you just turned twenty-one. I get it. We've all been there. But there's no excuse for your getting behind the wheel tonight, not even to come see us."

"I'm not a moron, Ian. Someone drove me here."

"How convenient." Ian cocked his head. "Who was it?"

Drew blinked. "Why does it matter?"

"Because I'd like to shake this mystery person's hand. Must be someone powerful to convince you to join us after you've ignored my mother, my sister, and me for the last thirty hours. Someone like, oh, I don't know. Maybe like Mr. Darcy? You know who that is, right?"

Drew stared at Ian, motionless. Even intoxicated, he knew when to stay quiet.

Ian steepled his fingers together, his eyes still fixed on Drew. "So, here's the plan: when we get to the hotel, I'm going to give you a few minutes alone with Meredith while I get Mum settled, and then I'll drive you back to that rat hole of a fraternity house. But I warn you, Andrew, I am exhausted. I don't have time for any of your usual nonsense. Now get in the car."

Without another word, Drew climbed in the back seat like a little kid in a carpool line.

forty-three

Drew did not say another word on the six-minute drive to the hotel, and I couldn't help but notice how out of place he seemed. Like a visitor from another planet. Or a time traveler from another century.

The second Ian and my mom disappeared into the hotel, Drew shot me a look. "Out of all those calls and texts, you couldn't leave a single message to let me know Jamie had a heart attack?"

"What would I have said, Drew? 'Hey, guess what? You got your wish! I'm skipping out on Italy so they can crack open my dad's chest instead. Wanna hang out on Saturday?'"

My breath actually hitched in my throat as Drew's face scrambled into a million pieces, but I refused to cry. The more he sat there blinking at me, the more cartoonish he appeared.

He didn't hug me. He didn't touch my cheek or my hand. He just glared at me for half a minute before he started back in again. "Why haven't you asked who brought me to the hospital tonight?"

"Because I don't care, Drew. Not unless it was the tooth fairy."

His rueful laugh sent a chill through my heart. "Don't play cute, Meredith. It was your little boyfriend, Pete Russell. He called every person we both know until he tracked me down tonight. Then he came to the bar and dragged me to the hospital right that second."

My mouth went dry. "But… I didn't…"

"Oh, don't worry. He made it very clear whose idea it was. But you know what question he refused to answer? Why he's here in Portland with you when he's supposed to be in Italy. Maybe you can enlighten me?"

If he had slapped me across the face, it would have hurt less. I was suddenly so tired I couldn't see straight. "That's a long story," I sighed. "You think we could press pause for tonight?"

"You know what? Don't bother," Drew scoffed, sounding more lucid than he had all night. "You think I don't see what's going on? That guy doesn't care if you're in Paris, or Italy, or the dark side of the moon, just as long as you two are together. Ian had no idea how right he was. Pete Russell really is Mister Freakin' Darcy, saving the day so he can cuddle up to the girl of his dreams."

"Get over yourself, Drew." I felt my eyes narrow. "Pete didn't come home to *cuddle up* with me. His grandmother is dying."

He sucked in a breath. "What?"

"You heard me. It's only a matter of days now and he just wasted precious time tracking you down. What a crazy idea, right, thinking you'd want to be with my family and me? How dare he be so foolish?"

Drew blinked at me several times, then frowned. "Why didn't he say something?"

"You're missing the point. Pete's grandmother is the only person he has left *period*. You get that, right? How it feels to lose the person you love most in the world?"

The air seemed to leave Drew's lungs as his eyes widened. Then, just like that, his expression shifted again, and there was Andrew Sutton, the boy I'd known since kindergarten. The one I'd loved for as long as I could remember. Only now I could see that he would have been less wounded if I'd slapped *him* across the face.

In all the years I'd known Drew, I'd never taken someone else's side. Not even Ian's.

Until tonight he'd never given me a reason.

forty-four

Just before noon the next day, the surgeon came in and told us they'd had to do five bypasses on my dad's heart, but he was doing well. Just like that, a peace came over me that I hadn't experienced in… well, ever. Half an hour later, the nurse came in to tell us Mr. Sullivan was awake and we could see him two at a time.

I volunteered to stay in the waiting room while my mom and Ian went first. I could tell by the look on my brother's face that he knew what my ulterior motive was, but, wise man that he is, he did not say one word. The instant the door shut behind them, I called Drew.

"Hey," he said lazily, like this was any old Saturday. "How's Jamie?"

How's Jamie? Was he serious right now? He could have said anything right this second and it would have been more acceptable. *I'm so sorry, I was kidnapped by aliens last night who wanted a sample of my perfect DNA.* Or, *I would be there right this second, but*

I somehow got trapped under some driftwood. He could have given me *any* explanation why he was skipping out on what was arguably the worst day of my family's life. Instead, he asked about *Jamie*, like he was talking about some character in a show I was binge-watching instead of my one and only dad, whose life hung in the balance.

"He's... out of surgery." I clipped my response before I added *you gigantic flake*. "My mom and Ian are already visiting him as we speak. You want to come up and tell him hello?"

Drew sucked in air slowly, then clicked his teeth. "Here's the problem: this weekend is initiation, you know, for the new pledges? I was on my way over to see you guys this morning when our usual venue called to say they've got a mice infestation, so now I have to find another place, like, yesterday."

"Oh." My mind suddenly felt dull, like someone had thrown a blanket over me in the dark. "Can't you get someone to help you?"

"No, Meredith. This is my responsibility. Look, I know this is the worst timing ever, but do you really *need* me there? Your dad's in good shape. Plus, you must be jet-lagged. If I came over, I'd probably just sit around watching you and Ian sleep all day."

Maybe he was right about the jet lag, because I could hardly wrap my mind around what he was saying. Less than a month ago, Drew was begging me to come home, and now that I was here, he was too busy to see me? And what about Jamie? Even if I wasn't here, Drew should have been here checking in on my dad. The last thing I wanted to be was *that* girl, but I couldn't help wishing Drew would tell his so-called brothers to fix their own problems.

"Meredith, I'm sorry," he pleaded. "But just think about this rationally. If I leave right now to come sit with you, we'll be ruining an entire pledge class's one and only initiation night. Plus, you know I'm running for president soon. Do you want to hurt my chances?"

"I wouldn't dream of it." Nor was I trying to hide my sarcasm at this point. "So I guess I'll see you tomorrow sometime?"

"I don't know, sweetie. I'll text you, okay?" And just like that, the line went dead.

Sweetie? I hated that word, and Drew knew it. Hoping to drown my sorrows, I escaped to the vending machine room at the far end of the ICU waiting area. But as our conversation replayed inside my mind, my blood pressure skyrocketed. When my coffee cup got stuck in the machine, I began to smack every button on the panel with the palm of my hand, imagining Drew's face floating behind the plastic cover.

"Don't hurt me," someone whispered in a creepy falsetto behind me. "Skynet is watching."

I turned to find Pete Russell leaning against the doorway, watching me. "Hi," I said, scowling. "Welcome to the dark side of decaffeinated Meredith."

"Are you sure they put the right Sullivan in the hospital? That vein in your temple's about to burst." Pete stepped forward, reached over me, and gently excised the cup from the machine. "Here you go."

"Amazing. I've been wrestling with that thing for two minutes. But you waltz up and suddenly all is right with the world."

Pete smiled, then shrugged. "Well, you know. I have my moments."

Oh, hey there, butterflies. Thanks for showing up right on time. I took a sip of my coffee to steady my nerves. "Shouldn't you be at home with your grandmother?"

"Who do you think sent me here?" Pete leaned against the coffee machine, crossing his arms over his chest. "Gigi said I was fussing over her too much and that I needed to take all my stuck-in-a-plane-for-too-long energy elsewhere. So here I am. Is Sutton in your dad's room or something? I didn't see him in the waiting room when I came in."

I drained my cup, then turned to the machine for round two. "Drew's at the Sigma Phi house doing more important things, like making sure all your new pledges love him. Could you help me remember to plan better next time so my family drama doesn't interfere with his presidential campaign?"

When I turned back to Pete, I expected him to list all the reasons Drew's excuses were suspect. But to his credit, Pete just smiled and followed me back into the waiting room, where Ian and my mom sat huddled in quiet conversation.

"How's Dad?" I asked when we reached them. "Everything okay?"

"Of course, love," Molly beamed as she rose to her feet. "Who's your friend?"

"Oh, sorry." I took my mother's hand then pressed her forward by the elbow. "Mum, this is…"

"Hi, Mrs. Sullivan. I'm Pete." He extended his hand in my mom's direction. "Meredith and I go to Highgate together. I'm glad to finally meet you."

My mother's eyes traveled over Pete's face like she had a sense that she knew him from somewhere. And as I watched him shake her hand, I felt suddenly protective about what Pete had told me on the plane. There was such a formal quality in the way he'd spoken to my mom. He wore that polite smile like a mask, like he was meeting a random person instead of the owner of the last place he'd seen his parents alive.

Last year I wouldn't have noticed the difference. But now I saw pain brewing in his eyes.

Ian stepped forward and put his hand on Pete's shoulder. "This is the guy I was telling you about, Mum. We have him to thank for getting our girl home yesterday after the disaster with my airline miles."

"Oh!" My mom's face brightened again, and she lifted her hand to Pete's face, touching his cheek. "Call me Molly, love. After all, you saved our girl. You're part of the family now."

Maybe it was because it had been so long since Pete had felt a maternal touch, but he instantly relaxed into her grasp. My mother, who is even taller than I am, suddenly straightened to her full height, and put her arms lovingly around my friend. Pete curved his chin over her shoulder as she squeezed him tight. And when he lifted his eyes to mine, they were brimming with tears.

forty-five

You know how sometimes you want to disappear into the nearest sewer grate when you have an abnormal reaction to something? When Pete finally let go of my mom, he seemed completely mortified as he brushed away the two or three tears that had just spilled onto his cheeks. "Whoa, what are these?" He laughed, pointing at his face. "Jet lag is a beast, am I right?"

I'd never seen Pete splutter and stammer around the way he did for the next five minutes as we walked down to the hospital cafeteria for a late lunch. But it didn't take long before he relaxed into his normal self again, mostly thanks to Ian's wicked sense of humor and my mother's warmth. If you had seen the four of us laughing and entertaining one another around the table, you might have believed Pete had known us forever.

I spent most of lunch imagining how my mom and Ian would feel knowing that Pete was the boy we'd prayed for all those years ago.

Pete's phone vibrated about thirty minutes into lunch. When he looked up from reading the text, his expression was grave. "I'm really sorry about this," he said. "But I have to go home. Gigi's usually alert in the morning and sleeps in the afternoon. I told the nurse to text me if she woke up, so…"

"You want Meredith to go with you?" Ian said, looking back and forth between Pete and me. "Dad's sedated so there's really no need for all three of us to be here. I can pick her up later."

Pete lit all the way up. "Really? Gigi would love that. Are you sure it's okay?"

"Believe me, you'll be doing us a massive favor," Ian huffed. "When Meredith gets this crabby, we usually make her organize the kitchen cabinets or something. Good luck, bro."

Moments later, I was sitting in Pete's car. Why did I suddenly feel like we were on a date? I convinced myself it was because I'd never driven anywhere with him before. But as Pete shuttled me around his neighborhood, I might as well have been sixteen again, alone in a car for the first time with some boy I'd had a crush on for much longer than I'd even admitted to myself.

"Here's my old school on the right – St. Francis Prep." Pete shot me a sidelong glance as we turned in to the campus. "Hey, what's that smile for?"

"Oh, you know. I'm just thinking about little Petey Russell, team captain of the Ducky Firecrackers, trying and failing to make Old Lady Brooks fall under his spell."

"Do I need to keep driving?" Pete smirked as he made a dramatic U-turn out of the parking lot. "Because there's a pub around the corner from my house, and every Saturday night, they have Irish step dancing lessons. Don't make me force you on stage, kid. You know I'll do it."

Pete's teasing me was not a new thing, but alone in his car... well, it certainly *felt* new.

"So, what's the deal with this initiation tonight?" I blurted as we turned onto a tree-lined street so perfectly paved I had to wonder if they resurfaced it nightly. "Do you dress up in cloaks and chant around a bonfire in the woods? Or do you just sit around drinking beer in your underwear until the last little pledge passes out?"

Pete laughed so hard he actually snorted. "You'd be so disappointed by the truth. But you know I can't tell you."

"I know, I know. Secrets of the brotherhood and all that. But it wouldn't be too scandalous to tell me what time it starts, would it?"

Pete paused for a moment, then gave me a knowing look. "Midnight."

I felt the vein in my temple begin to throb again. "Ah," I pushed out a puny laugh. "Well, let's hope my very important boyfriend gave himself enough time to get done *all the things*."

Pete pulled into a circular driveway – his driveway, it turned out – and shut off the engine. "Seriously, Sully. *Why* are you with him? Because the way I see it, when your dad is in the hospital, your boyfriend should be there by your side, no matter what else he has going on in his life."

"Believe me, I don't understand what's going on any more than you do." I breathed in deeply to thwart the sob rising in my throat.

"Drew loves my dad, Pete. Maybe he can't face what's happening. Heart problems – that's how his mom died."

"Don't make excuses for him. You deserve better, Meredith. If I were Sutton, I would be spending every single second I could with you while you're home. That's what you do when you love someone. You're there for them when they need you."

Tears filled my eyes before I could blink, so I looked out the window, away from Pete. I felt his hand close around my shoulder, which only made the tears fall faster.

"Hey." He squeezed again gently. "I'm sorry. This is none of my business. I just don't like to see you get hurt, that's all."

I looked over at Pete and smiled grimly. "You know those rickety old suspension bridges in the middle of nowhere? The ones that have ropes on either side, but half the slats are either broken or disappeared altogether?"

"Yeah?"

"Well, that's how my life feels right now. It might appear dilapidated to everyone else, but it's mine, so I know how to navigate the rotten parts. But if one more thing changes, even the tiniest little bit, I'm scared the whole thing might disintegrate into the gorge and take me with it. So I'm clinging to what I know. Even the messy bits."

Pete watched me silently for a minute, then nodded. "Okay, Sully," he said. "I hear you. And just for the record, I was captain of the Ducky *Shin*crackers. Heaven forbid you disappear down that gorge with the wrong name in your head. I know how much you hate being wrong."

forty-six

Gigi was asleep in her wheelchair by the floor-to-ceiling window that looked out onto the driveway. Her face, which had seemed so youthful the night before, was now sunken and gray. It had only been eighteen hours, and already, she seemed twice as old.

Pete clenched his jaw so tightly that the veins in his neck bulged. "I thought you said she was awake?" He whispered to the nurse, Patty, who'd just walked into the room.

"She was. Poor thing." She shook her head. "When the fatigue sets in, she just can't fight it. And she'll be so disappointed, too. Margaret was really hoping you would bring Meredith back with you, Peter."

As Patty rolled Gigi out of the room and back to her bedroom, Pete motioned for me to follow him into the kitchen. The breakfast nook at the far end had an enormous bay window with a breathtaking view of the Willamette River and, in the distance, Mount Hood. This was the same view I'd had from my dorm room last year at Highgate, which was only a couple of miles south down the river. But here no trees blocked the view. There was nothing but a gazebo off to the left.

I could hear Pete tinkering behind me, but I never turned around, mesmerized by the golden light lingering above the horizon of the river. I stood at the bay window for several minutes, staring at the changing colors of the late winter afternoon sky.

"What do you think?" Pete handed me a cup of coffee and motioned for me to sit on the window seat. "Gigi and Pops bought this place when my mom was a little kid. I guess it's been in our family nearly fifty years."

"Fifty? How old were your parents when...?"

"Forty-six," Pete smiled weakly. "Both of them. Hey, why do you think no one ever asks me about my parents? Do you think everyone assumes I don't want to talk about them?"

"Maybe. That's why I've never asked. What were their names?"

"Elizabeth and James," he said, the crinkles tightening around his eyes. "But nobody called them that. It was always Liz and Jim."

"What were they like?"

"I think you would've liked them, Sully. Both my parents were hilarious. You know those people who always say the one thing you'd never expect, and you end up laughing so hard your gut hurts for the rest of the day?"

"You mean people like you?"

Pete frowned. "I'm not funny. I'm just a dork."

"Did I say you weren't? But being dorky doesn't mean you're not hilarious. Now tell me, was it weird to have your mom as a teacher? Did the other kids give you a hard time?"

224

"No," he said quietly, his eyes drifting outside. "Everybody loved my mom. I was so proud of her. She sang songs to get us to remember stupid grammar concepts or vocabulary, and she always told these really funny stories about living in France to teach us the culture."

"And your dad? You told me last fall he was a photojournalist. Was he gone a lot?"

"Not as much as you might think," Pete said, turning back to me. A smile began to spread slowly across his face. "You want to see some of his pictures?"

I nodded and followed Pete to a gigantic bookcase in the living room. He pulled down a couple of large format photo albums from the top shelf, and for the next couple of hours, we sat on the sofa while Pete showed me hundreds of his dad's photographs taken on every continent, including Antarctica. Next, he showed me a few family albums, some from his childhood, some from his teenage years, so I could see his family, just as they were.

And, because I asked nicely, Pete caved and showed me the Ducky Shincrackers' highlight DVD from his senior year. Tears streamed down both of our faces as we relived all his greatest hits: behind-the-scenes practice footage, pep rallies and games, even a regional competition in costumes so authentic I felt like we'd been transported back in time seventy years.

For hours, I watched Pete Russell, my mind tumbling and spinning, trying desperately to remember the reasons I'd loathed him back in the day. Maybe then I could stop my traitorous heart from crossing that line I'd been toeing for far too long.

forty-seven

Drew never texted me that night. I kept dreaming that he had, and every time I woke up and checked my phone, the blank home screen mocked me. Then I would lie awake for an hour or so until exhaustion took over, and the whole cycle would start over again.

At the hospital my dad was alert, but he was fighting the breathing machine. The nurses claimed this was a good sign because it meant that his body wanted to breathe on its own. But every time I went in to see him, he scrolled his fingers around on my palm, trying to write secret messages. The first time, he shifted his eyes in the direction of the nurse, then spelled out several words still banned from television by the FCC. I have never heard my dad use that kind of language in normal life, so the shock on my face and the uncontrollable laughter probably set back his progress for days.

Life hack: never make a heart attack victim laugh while they're still on a ventilator.

Something about my dad's newfound sass made me think of Pete's grandmother. So when Ian headed back to Lincoln City that afternoon to pick up some things for my mom, I asked him to drive me over to Gigi's house.

I'm not sure why, but the half-timbered, Tudor-style house appeared way more intimidating than it had the other two times I'd been there. Maybe it was because I was alone. Maybe it was because I didn't make a habit of walking up to houses listed on the National Register of Historic Places (according to my brother, who spotted the telltale plaque hiding just above the bushes). Or maybe it was because I was feeling extra self-conscious from everything rattling around inside my heart. But before I went too far down *that* rabbit trail, Nurse Patty opened the door.

"Meredith!" She beamed, brushing her dark hair behind her ear. "Did Peter know you were stopping by? He's just gone to run some errands for Margaret."

"Um, no, actually… I came to see if… I mean, is she feeling well enough for visitors?"

Patty's whole face smiled back at me. "You're in luck. She's been quite alert today. A second wind, if you will." She looked over her shoulder inside the house, then shut the door behind her, joining me on the front step. "I don't want you to misunderstand me, Meredith. This happens a lot with terminal patients. They have a surge of energy a few days before the end. I'm afraid it's just part of the process."

Something made me close the gap between us and wrap my arms around Patty, who didn't fight me when I squeezed her tight. "I don't know how you do this job every day, Patty. You must be a very strong person."

"Not this time. I don't usually let myself get attached, but this time is… well, I've cried twice already today." Patty pulled away and motioned for me to follow her. "Margaret is out back in the gazebo. We had just gone outside when I heard the doorbell ring."

"But it's freezing today!"

"Don't worry. She's all bundled up. Besides, the sun is shining. Who knows how long it will be before we have another sunny day like this one?"

For Gigi? Maybe never.

As we approached her, I noticed that Gigi's color was much better than yesterday. The cool air had left a flush on her cheeks, and she looked calm and serene. "Oh, Meredith!" Margaret smiled broadly as Patty and I stepped up the ramp into the gazebo. "Peter said you came by yesterday when I was asleep. I'm so glad you came back today."

I took in the same view I'd admired yesterday from the bay window; it was even more spectacular from the gazebo. "Wow," I said. "No photograph could ever do this place justice."

"It's a little cold to be outside, I know," she said brightly. "But this is my favorite place in the world. Well, in America at least. It's probably a tie with the view from the Pont des Arts in Paris. Have you been there?"

"Of course," I laughed, sitting across from her on the gazebo's built-in bench. "There's no better view in Paris than the one from that bridge."

"Has Peter told you that my husband and I got engaged there? It was very romantic."

"No! Did your husband study in Paris, too?"

"Yes," she replied with a faraway look. "He was a Naval Academy graduate. They have a special scholarship for their top students to complete a master's degree at Addison College. Their campus used to be at the Centre Lafayette. That's where I met Pete Beckett."

I remembered Pete telling me at Normandy that he was named after his grandfather and great-grandfather. Three generations of Petes. And three generations of smarties, too. Addison College had the best modern languages department in the country. Their graduate program had moved to the Right Bank, but we had a few Addison undergrads at the Centre Lafayette, of course – Anne, Harper, and Kelly. Those three walked around speaking French like it was their mother tongue every day of the week. And Pete fit right in.

"I'd been planning to find myself a dashing Frenchman, of course," Gigi continued. "But Pete Beckett was so handsome and smart and hilarious that by Thanksgiving I was totally over the moon in love with him. He was still corresponding with a girlfriend back home at the time, but I didn't let it bother me."

I had to laugh. Gigi was my kind of sassy. "Did you get engaged later in the school year?"

"Yes, it didn't take long." Her deep-set, dark brown eyes appeared so youthful as she spoke. "And then we married as soon as we returned home. We knew Pete would be sent to Vietnam soon thereafter. He trained first in California, but then he got deployed when I was just a few months pregnant with Elizabeth."

"She was born while he was in Vietnam?"

"He didn't even see her until she was six months old." Gigi's face grew grim. "But he was safe, and for that, I am forever grateful. He continued to fly for the Navy until his commission was up, so the three of us jumped around the globe for a while. Then we moved back to Portland, and Pete began to fly for the airlines."

Well, that explained how her grandson had convinced the ticket agent so easily to let me on his flight. His grandfather flew for business, huh? Ever the question mark, that Pete Russell.

"Why did you move to Portland, um… Mrs. –?"

"Meredith, please. Call me Margaret," she smiled. "We moved to Portland because I grew up here – in this neighborhood, actually. My father earned his living in the timber industry, and I was an only child. Then I only had one child, and she only had one child. Unfortunately, we have a bad habit of leaving our children alone in this family."

Regret was thick in her voice. I had no idea how to ease Gigi's mind. "I guess that explains why Pete is so strong," I managed to say. "We all think he's pretty unflappable."

"Do you?" She laughed a little. "Yes, poor Peter has had to carry a lot in his young life. My husband died eighteen months ago. His heart just gave out one morning. I'm afraid losing Liz and Jim has taken a toll on us all."

I reached between us and squeezed her hand. "I can't even imagine."

Gigi sat up a little straighter in her wheelchair and fixed her dark brown eyes on mine. "Meredith, I'm so glad you came to see me today. Normally, I would find it extremely distasteful to share this sort of information with you, but in this case, I think it's best you know the truth. I assume you are aware that Highgate's Centre Lafayette scholarships are funded by something called the Beckett Endowment. There's a reason it bears my last name. Maybe this coincidence has already occurred to you?"

No, it had not. Never in my life had I been so dumbfounded. I tried to put a sentence together, but my mouth felt like it was full of sawdust. "Mrs. Beckett…"

"Meredith, I insist that you call me Margaret. You are a lovely young lady, and I'm as proud of you as if you were my own granddaughter, even though we've just met. Madame Beauchamp has been sending me regular e-mails on everyone's progress, and you have more than lived up to your end of the bargain."

I squeezed her hand as tears splashed down my cheeks. "Margaret, if I'd had any idea, I would have thanked you Friday night. You could never know how much living in Paris has meant to me. Thank you seems too feeble a phrase for what you've done."

"You are quite welcome," she said, smiling kindly as she placed her free hand over mine. "But, as I said, you don't need to thank me. And this is where the story gets a little… uncomfortable."

I felt like I was in an elevator that had just skipped five floors. "What do you mean?"

"Well, as you know, the endowment covers all tuition and fees for three Highgate students each year. It has been that way since my husband and I set up the fund in the mid-1980s, and it will go on that way after… well, you understand. But this particular year was different."

"Right. This year, there were four scholarships."

"No, Meredith," she said slowly. "Three students went to Paris on the Beckett Endowment scholarship. When you took your exam last spring, the student with the highest score was Peter's friend, Dan Thomas. Second place was a Marshall… oh, forgive me…"

"Freeman?"

"Yes, thank you," she smiled. "But the student who placed third on the examination was my grandson."

Before Gigi even finished her sentence, I understood. Despite my year-long sequester, I had only placed fourth on that exam. Everything I'd felt last summer – the entitlement, the disgust at Pete's inclusion as "fourth" – it all tumbled down into a pit of shame where my pride had been.

"But if Pete was third, how did…"

"Your department chair, Dr. Sweeney, called Peter the Friday before they announced the scholarship because… well, it was an unusual situation," Gigi smiled. "For the rest of the weekend, it was as though a thunderstorm had moved in where my grandson's soul ought to be. I have never seen him so pensive in all his life. At least not like that."

I thought back to those moments after the exam when I'd fallen apart in the hallway. Pete had walked past me that day, and then he'd turned around and hovered nearby for a very long, very uncomfortable moment. I hadn't dared look up. But I wished now that I had.

"On Monday morning," Gigi continued, "Peter sat down for breakfast dressed in a button-down shirt and his best slacks, like he had a presentation to make. He looked me in the eye and said he'd made up his mind. He was giving up his spot so the fourth-place student could go instead."

My breath hitched in my throat. "But that's crazy. Why would he do that for someone he barely knew?"

"You may rest assured, young lady, that Peter and I have never had harsher words between us than we did that day. But he was not to be dissuaded. 'Listen, Gigi,' he finally said. 'I am your grandson. This is the very definition of nepotism. But the bigger problem is that Meredith Sullivan wants to live in Paris more than anything else in the world. She poured her whole heart into that test, and she deserves to go. So I'm meeting with Dr. Sweeney this morning to remove my name from the list. If you try to stop me, I'll run back to Shanghai. You know I will.'"

"I take it you believed him?"

Gigi's eyes softened. "I'm sure you know Peter well enough to know that when he believes in something, he can be rather persuasive. Dr. Sweeney accepted his decision, and that, my dear, is how you came to receive your scholarship."

I wanted to speak, but I could not. My mind was too busy putting the puzzle pieces together.

"I wish you could have known Peter when he was younger," she said, leaning toward me. "What an open, loving child he was. Outrageous and charming and so carefree that I worried he'd end up spoiled. But Peter was very close to his parents. Ever since the accident, he's kept his guard up so well that most people think he's a clown."

I nodded. "He uses humor as a shield."

"Exactly. It's good that you know this about Peter, since you are the person with the most potential to harm him." Gigi's dark eyes flickered for a moment. "He may not want to admit this to himself yet, but my grandson harbors deep feelings for you. I think he has for a very long time."

"No, no," I laughed nervously. "Listen, Margaret, you've misunderstood. Pete's girlfriend is the most beautiful girl at the Centre Lafayette. They're crazy about each other."

Gigi laughed, a full and throaty laugh, just like her grandson's. "Meredith, I've met Meg, and you're wrong. Peter does not speak about *anyone* the way he speaks about you. Even if that wasn't enough to persuade me, you are the *only* young lady he has ever invited to our house. Well, apart from our neighbor Brooks."

I started to protest again, but Gigi raised her hand to stop me. "We don't have much time. Peter will be home soon, and this is likely the only chance that you and I will have to speak. I understand that you now know of your link to his parents' death."

I nodded as tears pricked at my eyes. "He told me."

"I do not believe in coincidence, Meredith." Gigi reached for my hands again, then folded them between hers. "You and my grandson had a connection long before you met at school. And even though you were not directly involved in their accident, Peter will always associate your family with the death of his parents. Can't you see why Peter might be frightened by his feelings for you? It's a bit cruel, really. The one person who could bring his greatest happiness would also be a constant reminder of his greatest tragedy."

She paused for a moment, her eyes searching mine. "If you care about my grandson, let him know someday. Peter is the most loyal person you will ever meet. He's kind and protective – he gets that from his grandfather. I know I'm biased, but I always hope other people see in him what I have always known to be true. If you let him, Peter Beckett Russell will be your greatest champion."

I shifted my hands to squeeze hers. "I know that, Margaret. He already is."

forty-eight

The sound of a door opening drew our attention across the yard, where Pete was striding out of the house. "Good thing we've finished our little chat," Gigi winked. "Thank you for coming to see me, Meredith. You really are a beautiful person. I'm just sorry I won't get to see how this story ends."

"Sully?" Pete bounded up the gazebo ramp in one and a half strides. "When did you get here?"

"A while ago," I said, smiling widely at Gigi. "I came to visit Margaret, just like I promised I would."

"Yes, Peter, we've been having a nice little chat about Paris and how I met your grandfather," she grinned. "Now make yourself useful and roll me back inside, please."

Pete helped Gigi down the temporary wheelchair ramp, and the three of us returned to the living room where we regaled Gigi with tales of our Parisian adventures. Pete did an excellent impression of

Monsieur Ludovic that had Gigi in hysterics, and then I told her about my birthday celebration and how our friends surprised me twice in one day. She beamed at my story, shooting me a triumphant look every now and again as if to say, *See? I told you so.*

But around six Gigi grew tired. Pete called Patty into the living room and she was about to roll Gigi back into her bedroom when she suddenly sat bolt upright, her eyes a little bit wild. "Meredith," she whispered, her voice husky from too much effort.

I crossed the room and knelt before her chair. "Yes, Margaret?"

"You'll remember what I said about coincidence?"

"There's no such thing," I nodded. And with that confirmation, she relaxed into her chair, blew Pete a kiss, and motioned for Patty to take her away.

Neither Pete nor I said a word on the way back to the hospital, but instead of feeling awkward, it just felt… normal. After three days in Bizarro-land, I let the feeling wash over me without a thought beyond that moment.

"Gigi likes you," Pete finally said as we rounded the curve to the hospital. "You want to tell me what you were really talking about?"

"Well, let's see." I pretended to count down an imaginary list on my fingers. "We talked for a long time about your grandfather. We talked about Paris. Something about the third place winner of the Beckett scholarship losing his mind and giving up his well-deserved spot last spring. Oh, and cheese fries. That woman is nutso for greasy, cheddar-y goodness. Who knew someone so refined would love something so bad for you?"

Pete's face drained of all color as he pulled into a parking space just beyond the front door of the hospital, then shut off the car. "I can't believe she told you about that."

"Why not? Cheese fries make the world go 'round, my friend. Especially the loaded kind."

"I'm serious, Meredith."

"So am I. Why in the world did you give up your spot for me?"

Pete's dark eyes searched mine for a moment. "I beat you by one point on that exam. That's all it was, just one stupid point. That's like, what? A helper verb's difference. Or two accents."

"I did *not* miss any accents."

"Whatever. It felt wrong, and I wanted to set things back on track. So go ahead and rant at me, but I stand by my decision."

"No rants tonight, I promise. But would you mind explaining how you ended up in Paris? Was Dr. Sweeney so moved by your generosity that he embezzled funds on your behalf?"

"Uh, no." A muscle twitched along Pete's jawline. "My sweet little grandmother walked into Dr. Sweeney's office on the Thursday before we left last August and accused the department of academic impropriety by giving away my spot without her permission."

"But wait, I thought…"

"Oh, don't worry. That accusation was just phase one of her master plan." He tapped out a little beat on the top of the steering wheel. "See, Gigi agreed one hundred percent that you should take my spot. But then she got that cancer diagnosis and didn't want me knowing the full picture."

I swallowed. Hard. "She sent you away so you wouldn't see her deteriorate?"

Pete rubbed his hands through his hair, then nodded. "Her act was so compelling that Dr. Sweeney thought it was *his* idea to let her pay for a fourth scholarship. On Friday I was at the Sigma Phi house helping with recruitment, and by Sunday I was on a plane with you."

I watched him fiddling with the steering wheel gash for another few seconds, then I unbuckled my seatbelt. "Well, then," I said, opening the door. "Looks like I was right after all."

"About what?"

"When I told Gigi the other night that you were just like her. Oh, and also when I told her your mom and dad would be proud… of you both. Even if you *are* both terrifyingly good liars."

He laughed, then his forehead scrunched up. "Oh, man. I just realized something I've never thought of before. Marshall Freeman scored higher than *both* of us on that qualifying exam, Sully. How is that even possible?"

"Chocolate, my friend. And kale chips. The kid knows his brain food."

"You may be right," he smiled. "No wonder he impressed Élodie. Watch out, world."

forty-nine

Monday and Tuesday passed by like they'd never happened at all. I read ahead for school then jogged for miles around the hospital's rooftop track to clear my head. Ian tapped away on his laptop while my mom sat quietly in the corner of the waiting room, staring into the empty space like the walls held answers that the rest of us couldn't see.

But at noon on Wednesday, Drew burst through the waiting room door carrying Ian's favorite pizza and a stack of mystery novels by some Irish author Molly Sullivan loved. "Hey, guys!" He grinned from ear to ear. "How's Jamie today?"

For the next few minutes, Ian refused to look at Drew, much less *speak* to him. Even my mother, who earned a living by making people feel welcomed, seemed at a loss for words. And Drew, who finally saw how deeply he'd burrowed, slumped in his seat without another word.

When visiting hours came and my dad was still sleeping, Ian fixed the same elder brother glare on Drew as he had the other night, then suggested he should take me somewhere nice until the next visiting hours rolled around. So Drew took my hand and led me away from the waiting room as quickly as our feet would allow.

When we got to his Jeep, Drew didn't unlock the door right away. He took me by the waist and held me against the door as he traced a line along my bottom lip with his thumb. "Hi," he said softly.

"Hi, yourself," I said back. There was something almost predatory in the way he was looking at me, and my heart was pounding so hard in my chest that it actually hurt.

I let him kiss me, slowly at first, and then with such fever that I could hardly breathe. Before I knew it, his lips had found their place along the curve of my neck. But instead of leaning into his touch like I normally did, I flinched. Drew pulled away, ran his fingers through his hair, then lifted his eyes to mine. And there it was again, the same accusatory look he'd worn Friday night when he walked through the doors. Only this time, I wasn't jet-lagged. This time, I'd had enough.

I grabbed Drew's key fob from his hand. With two clicks of a button, the doors were unlocked and I was inside, willing myself to breathe in, then out, then in again until I could access the rational part of my brain. After much longer than necessary, Drew stepped into the driver's side and sat unblinking as I handed him the keys. But he didn't start the car. He just stared blankly ahead, like he was waiting for me to start whatever came next.

I watched Drew for the longest time, my heart shattering into a thousand pieces. I should have told him the truth about Pete when he came to Paris, but I'd wanted to believe his showing up like that was the only thing that mattered. I'd always imagined I'd be in love with

Drew my whole life. That all those years of taking care of each other and standing by each other's side meant we were soul mates.

Always, that is, until I fell in love with Pete Russell.

Drew sighed hard, then turned to face me. "I'm so tired of fighting. Aren't you tired?"

I nodded, and Drew leaned his head back against the headrest. Without opening his eyes, he said, "You want to tell me now what I interrupted between you and Russell the day I got to Paris?"

"Does it matter?"

"It matters to me."

"I know that's what you think." My lips began to tremble. "But what you really wonder is if *you* matter to me. You do, Drew. You always will. I wasn't lying when I said I loved you. And I chose you in October because in my mind, you were always the one for me. Always. I'm as surprised as you are that Pete came between us. Until Paris, I'd never given him a single thought. Not like that anyway."

Drew's lips pursed together and he nodded, eyes still closed. Then he reached across the car for my hand and lifted it to his chest, holding it against his heart just like he had in the boat that night last summer. "I'm sorry I haven't been here with you this week. I might have been able to handle Jamie being sick if everything was okay between you and me. But when I saw you Friday night, I knew we were over. And I just couldn't face it." He paused and breathed in deeply. "Think you'll ever forgive me?"

I squeezed his hand and let the tears pricking my eyes spill onto my cheeks. "Don't you remember what I told you? You'll *never* lose me, kid. Not even after we've broken each other's hearts."

He turned and looked at me. "And what if I'd been brave on the boat that night last August? Where would we be now if I'd told you how I really felt?"

In the dark blue of Drew's eyes, I could see myself looking back at him, and I smiled. "If you'd told me how you felt, Drew, I never would have left."

There is a kind of splintering that happens when the plan you'd always imagined for your life is no longer possible. For years, I'd clung to the belief that once Drew realized he loved me, we'd be together from that point until forever. But when Drew kissed me again for the last time and then drove me over to the hospital entrance, those imaginary ropes I'd been gripping pinged and snarled against my hands. Thread by thread and plank by plank, everything I thought I knew crumbled right out from under me.

I stood outside the hospital for a long while after Drew drove away in his Jeep. I'm not sure how long I lingered, but soon, a passerby with shaggy gray hair and a Santa Claus beard was standing before me, waiting for a response to a question I hadn't heard.

"I'm sorry," I stammered. "Were you talking to me?"

"Your phone, miss," he smiled. "I think it's beeping at you."

I looked down at the phone in my hand. The home screen showed two missed calls and a message notification that stopped my heart:

call me the second you see this

fifty

I started dialing Dan's French cell number, regardless of international roaming fees. If it was four p.m. here, it was one a.m. in Italy. That could only mean one thing: someone was hurt. Or worse.

"Meredith?" Dan answered. "Oh, man, I'm glad to hear your voice. How's your dad?"

"He's doing okay. But your text – tell me what happened, Dan."

He paused for a second, then exhaled. "Pete just called."

"Oh, no," I whispered. "Gigi died?"

"Yes, just a little while ago. She was fine until yesterday evening, and then she took a sharp turn for the worse. Pete had run out to get dinner for himself and the hospice nurse, and he said when he came home, it was chaos. The nurse told him Gigi's blood pressure started dropping just a couple of minutes after he left."

"Why? What happened?"

"They don't know for sure. I guess it's pretty common. Someone can seem fine one day, and the next, their vitals just crater."

Just like Patty had warned me. "Did they take her to the hospital?"

"No." I could practically hear him brushing his hair out of his eyes. "She had an advance directive not to do anything heroic, so the nurse couldn't really do much except keep her comfortable. Pete said he stayed up all night with Gigi, and then a couple of hours ago, she just stopped breathing."

I began pacing in front of the hospital doors. "How did he sound?"

"Exhausted. I've never heard his voice so hollow before, like a robot. He was so matter-of-fact, you know? I'm worried."

So was I. "Did he say anything about the funeral?"

"It's still too early to say, but he was hoping for Saturday. I told him I'd let you know. Listen, Meredith, we all feel a little helpless over here. There's no way we could get to Portland by Saturday even if we tried."

"Don't worry, Dan. I'm here." I chewed briefly at the inside of my lip. "Do you think it would be okay for me to go over to the house? Or would he rather be alone right now?"

Dan was quiet for a moment. "You should go to the house. If there were anyone he'd want to see right now, it would be you. The two of you are in this thing together, you know?"

"Okay. I'll go right now. His house is just a couple of minutes away." Tears filled my eyes again. "How is any of this fair, Danny? Pete Russell is twenty-two years old, and he's already lost *everybody*."

"Not everybody, Meredith. He still has us."

That's all it took to rally me. After I said goodbye to Dan, I called Ian to tell him I was borrowing his car. He'd given me a set of keys earlier in the week just in case. With lightning speed I reached the Tudor house, glanced in the rearview mirror in a feeble attempt to salvage my face, and walked to the front door.

A handful of people exited the Beckett house just as I lifted my hand to knock. When I stepped inside, I found Patty inside the kitchen, greeting neighbors and apologizing that Pete was unavailable. People nodded, mumbled their condolences, then left whatever baked goods or casserole they'd brought in solidarity.

Cupcakes and casseroles. Why did people do that? I had no idea.

But the blinds on the bay window were drawn, a detail no one but me seemed to notice, even though it made the airy kitchen seem dank and somber. I knew immediately where Pete was.

"Patty, this is not in your job description," I said, approaching her once the room cleared.

"I know. But Margaret was special to me. I'd like to think we became friends over the last few weeks, so I'm helping out in her honor." She lifted her red eyes to mine, then reached out to squeeze my shoulder. "You know where to find him?"

I nodded, then froze. "But what do I say? I've never done this before."

"Tell him how sorry you are. Or don't say anything at all. You will know what to do when you see him, Meredith. But try not to say that Margaret is in a better place. That's difficult to hear this soon, even when you believe that it's true."

I opened the door quietly and walked toward the gazebo with even more trepidation than I'd felt the last time I was here. Pete stood alone, leaning on the railing, his right hand on his hip as he looked out over the Willamette River, eastward toward Mount Hood. When my boot met the wood of the wheelchair ramp, he jerked his chin to the right, glancing to see who was interrupting his privacy, then turned away again. It was only for a moment, but I could see that he was crying.

I decided as I approached Pete that nothing I could say would ever be worthy of what Gigi meant to him, or even to me. Instead, I took my place at Pete's right side and slid my hand into his without saying a word. I could feel him trembling, but he didn't pull away. After a little while, Pete pulled his hand away and moved it around my shoulders, turning me toward him. I wrapped both of my arms around his waist, my left shoulder under the crook of his arm, my head resting against his chest.

We stood like that until the sun set, neither of us saying a word.

fifty-one

There were visitors all over the property when I returned to Gigi's house on Saturday after the funeral. When I walked through the front door, I could see Pete in the corner of the dining room, talking to a dark-haired young woman and what appeared to be her parents. I lingered in the foyer for a few moments, marveling at Pete's measured responses. He laughed as the mystery guest put her thumbs on his cheeks, tugging his mouth into a grin, then let himself sink into her mother's hug and then her father's. Was this the famous Brooks Darby? So much of Pete's life was still a mystery to me. I wondered if I would ever know him as well as it felt like he knew me.

I skulked up the staircase to a long second-story corridor, and when I followed it, I came to a room that was so obviously Pete's. One entire wall was covered in rows of black frames that featured photographs from all over the globe. I stood there in the middle of the room, with its massive ceiling, staring at each and every image, all printed in sepia for a unifying effect.

I wondered as I gazed if they were Pete's father's work. But then my wits came back, and I realized I was dawdling in Pete's bedroom during a wake, like some creepy stalker taking advantage of the prey's distraction.

I slid a tiny envelope out of my coat and looked around the room for an obvious place to leave it. The lamp next to his bed seemed best, so I propped it there, right next to a small photo of a very young Pete and his parents at Disneyland Paris. He was crazy cute, holding both of their hands wearing silly Mickey Mouse ears on his head, while perfect brown curls threatened to escape from underneath. And those eyes. Even as a child, Pete's dark eyes bared his old soul.

But before I could study his parents more closely, I heard someone clearing his throat behind me. "Trespassing is a federal offense, Miss Sullivan."

I turned to face Pete, who was leaning against the doorframe, rolling up his sleeves. His tie was already loosened as he hung his suit jacket on a hook by the door. I couldn't decide if my face was on fire at being caught, at what he'd just said, or simply because he looked so beautiful I felt like I might faint. I wanted to speak, but I couldn't. Not with the way he was looking at me.

Pete stepped further into the room, still keeping his distance. "What's in the envelope?"

"Cash," I said flatly. I pointed at a photo on the far end of the wall with a man smoking a cigarette while playing mahjong at a table. "I'd like a print of that shot right there. One of your dad's, I assume?"

He glanced at the image, then back at me. "No. These are all mine."

Pete nodded his head toward the photos, motioning for me to follow him, and for the next few minutes, the images took on new meaning as he once again walked me through his past. On the far left side was a very serious, very beautiful Kenyan child, scowling as she blew bubbles through a wand. Next was a landscape shot of a dozen humpback whales, all at different heights as they crashed out of the ocean together during a bubble feed.

"South Island, New Zealand," Pete explained. "Kaikoura. I took the train from Christchurch. Maybe the coolest thing I've ever done."

I pointed back to the photo of the man smoking the cigarette. "Who's your friend?"

He was someone Pete had met when he lived in Shanghai. Someone he'd played mahjong with every day during those lost months of his life. As he described this man he called Lucky, I began to realize how much Pete had allowed me behind the curtain of his well-guarded life over the past week. The Pete Russell I'd always known was confident, smart, sometimes annoying, always the life of the party. But that wasn't the real Pete. And now, here in his inner sanctum, I felt like an interloper on some private mind landscape, a place where I had not exactly been invited yet never wanted to leave.

The last image, the one directly opposite from where Pete and I stood, featured a tall, slender couple standing on the Pont des Arts. They faced away from the photographer, holding hands as they looked toward the Eiffel Tower far in the distance. "These are your parents?"

Pete nodded, smiling up at the image. But it was more like a grimace, like he was holding back what he really felt when he saw this picture. It must have been torture to wake up every morning and see what you had lost. My mind raced, trying to find some way to divert Pete's attention without being obvious. But, as always, he did the diverting himself.

"I was fourteen when I took that picture," he smiled again, this time wistfully. "It was the first time I'd used my dad's camera. I think he gave it to me so he and my mom could have some privacy for a minute. That's also the spot where my grandparents got engaged."

I pretended to inspect the image carefully, but despite everything – despite Pete's unthinkable heartache and my less significant one – all my brain seemed to register was the almost deafening whoosh of my blood through my veins as Pete stepped closer. So close I could feel his sleeve brushing against my coat.

"What's in the envelope, Sully?" His eyes stayed on the photograph for a moment, then shifted slowly back to me. "Rule-followers like you don't normally thumb their noses at propriety. Must be something important to make you enter a grown man's bedroom without an invitation."

"I didn't…"

"Is it a pirate map?" He grinned, sliding his hands into his pockets. "Because I could use a little adventure right about now. Or… wait, is it that petition you've been threatening to write? The one banning Marshall Freeman from eating chocolate bars during class? Because you know, this highly intelligent person just told me the other day that chocolate is brain food, so…"

Three weeks ago I might have had a snappy retort, but standing here in Pete's bedroom as he teased me, I was mute. He watched me quietly for a moment, as though he could see all of my words escaping into the ether. But then he offered me his elbow and guided me over to the window seat at the far end of his room.

"Have you talked to any of our friends this week?" Pete said as he fiddled with the window before pushing it open. It was unusually warm in here, I realized.

"No one but Dan," I answered. "You?"

"Same." Pete sat down across from me, elbows on his knees. "I hate to tell you this, Sully, but they are having a way better time than we are."

For the first time in several minutes, I felt like I could breathe normally. "Are they? Well, that's not a huge accomplishment. They're in *Italy*."

"Would you believe our prayers for that railway strike were heard? They've been stuck in Venice for most of the week."

"Are you trying to make me cry? Venice was the one place I was looking forward to more than anywhere else."

"I know you were. Me too." Pete smiled again, and I was suddenly aware that his eyes had gone soft. "Did Dan tell you Carnavale's still going on?"

"No! Ugh. Rude."

"That's what I said. Dan told me this creepy fog rolls in every evening. All of those masked strangers, strolling around in the haze… it's sort of enchanting, right?"

"You shut up, Pete Russell. I hate all four of them."

"I sort of hate them, too." The warmth of his gaze and the softness in his voice filled the space between us. "But maybe you'd feel better if you knew Kelly and Harper ditched the entire Venice itinerary to hang out with some guys they met who study in Seville."

"What? Why would they do that?"

"Oh, I don't know," he grinned. "Maybe because my boy finally made his move, and now Dan and Anne are so in love that Harper and Kelly threatened to hitchhike back to Paris without them."

I actually gasped. "You'd better not be joking right now."

"Oh, I would never joke about the culmination of your life's work, Emma Woodhouse." Pete laughed quietly to himself for a moment. "I guess you understand Anne better than I do because I really thought Dan was in the friend zone."

"You did?" I crossed my arms. "Why? Dan's fantastic."

"I know." Pete glanced out at the people gathered in the backyard. "But Anne's so reserved that I can never figure out what she's thinking. Even about stupid things, like the weather. Maybe it's just me. Or maybe she just trusts you more."

I shook my head. "She never told me how she felt either way. But the signs have been there all along."

"Like what?"

"Well, for one thing, Dan Thomas is the only person who really makes Anne laugh."

"Maybe the rest of us aren't funny."

"That's not true. You're hilarious."

Pete smiled to himself as he looked out the window again. "I guess I've noticed *one* thing. Every day at lunch, when he thinks no one is looking, Dan stands up first, then gives Anne his hand to help her to her feet. Every time it happens, I wait for Anne to say, 'Check your calendar, buddy. This is not 1793.' But every single time, she takes his hand. It never fails to shock me."

"That's because you know she'd give you a black eye if you even *attempted* that move."

"Makes you wonder," he said. But before either of us could say another word, there was a knock at the door, and both of our heads turned to find my brother standing in the doorway.

"Hey," Ian said, his expression shifting from stoic to confused to embarrassed all within two seconds. "Sorry to interrupt but Nurse Patty told me I might find you guys up here. They decided to release Dad this afternoon, Fee. We're going home."

"What?" I glanced over at Pete, then back at Ian. "Hold on, like right now?"

"Right now." Ian crossed the threshold into Pete's room. "Mum wants us to pack and check out of the hotel before... wait, who took these photos?"

Pete's eyes met mine one more time, and when he stood, he held out his left hand to help me to my feet. It was the tiniest gesture, one that I might never have noticed before today, but when he held on to my hand as we crossed over to Ian, I knew it hadn't been coincidence. Once we were back in the middle of the room, Pete squeezed my hand tenderly, then released it, starting over from the beginning with the same descriptions he'd given me moments earlier.

As Ian and Pete compared life notes through the photographs on the wall, the fingers on my right hand ached to slide back into Pete's. Gigi's voice suddenly filled my head. *There are no accidents. No coincidences.* Whether it was just for this moment or for all time, Pete and I were meant to be in each other's lives. No one could convince me otherwise.

fifty-two

Eight days later, on St. Patrick's Day, I parked myself on the floor in the far corner of Gate 23, pretending to sleep with my knees pulled to my chest and my face against my arms. But instead of sleeping, I mulled over every moment of the previous two-and-a-half weeks, wondering if it was possible to die of saltwater dehydration because your tear ducts had run dry. Mine certainly had.

Pete never came to the gate. I boarded the plane with my assigned group, but still, no Pete.

So when the flight attendant announced that they were about to shut the cabin doors for takeoff, I pushed the call button. Something was wrong. I knew it. So I slid open the home screen of my phone, hit redial on Pete's American number, then stared out the window at the luggage carts loading bags onto the plane at the next gate.

Someone's phone rang behind me, but since the flight attendant had not yet asked everyone to turn off their electronic devices, I didn't pay much attention. Not until the person I was calling was suddenly speaking to me in stereo.

"Sully." I turned to my left, and there Pete was, standing in the aisle, his phone to his ear.

A million questions buzzed through my mind. But one look at Pete's face, and they all disappeared. I had never seen him like this. Not when he told me about his parents. Not when Gigi died. Certainly not at her funeral or at the wake, when he'd walked around like such a boss that I'd started to believe he was superhuman.

But he was not superhuman today. Broken blood vessels dotted his eyelids and under his eyes from crying or puking or both. I hit 'end call' and watched as Pete took a seat and settled in beside me.

He didn't say another word. He just leaned forward on his elbows, the butt of his hands against his eye sockets. Soon the flight attendant arrived with her perkiest smile, which dissolved when she saw Pete hunched over next to me. Her eyes met mine, questioning at first. But I lifted my hand to her, my eyes pleading with her not to speak, and then placed my palm on Pete's back. She nodded, reaching above me to click off the call light, and when she left, I thought Pete might shift away from me. He did not. While we taxied through the safety demonstration, I could only hope that my hand resting on his back would reach the Pete I knew, wherever he was inside.

When the plane stopped to take its place in line for takeoff, Pete sat up straight and looked at me, his bloodshot eyes holding mine, like he had something to say. But then the engines began to accelerate, and Pete leaned his head against the seatback, clinging to the armrests like he might fly away without them. As the plane propelled forward, tears began sliding down his cheeks.

He didn't open his eyes again until we arrived at DFW, and on the flight to Paris, we barely spoke. After customs at Charles de Gaulle, we grabbed a cab, which seemed the best way back to school before our ten o'clock class. As the driver pulled away from the terminal, I settled into my seat, watching the Paris morning bustle outside my window, feeling more normal than I had in seventeen days.

"Glad to be back?" Pete finally said as we crossed over the Seine into the Latin Quarter.

I turned my head toward him. "I'm getting there. You?"

He just nodded. "Hey, I'm sorry I didn't call you after you went back home to Lincoln City. Things got… anyway, how's your dad?"

"Well, he's not playing his clarinet yet, but he's healing."

"I'm glad," Pete smiled. "So, that envelope you left me. In your letter, you mentioned hopping a ferry from Alaska to Vladivostok. Were you serious? Because I almost texted you a few times to take you up that offer. Though I'm not sure I've got the sea legs for it. I hear the Bering Sea is rough."

"Yeah," I sighed. "Which is probably why there's not a ferry. It was just wishful thinking on my part because I wouldn't mind disappearing somewhere. I'm sort of done with this year, aren't you?"

"Funny you should say that." Pete fixed his eyes on mine. "Maybe you've already guessed this about me, but when things get ugly, my first response is to run away. Most of the time, I figure out a way to push through it. But sometimes, it seems easier to start over."

"Sounds fairly normal to me."

"I guess so." He paused, fiddling with a tiny rip in the cab's leather seat. "But yesterday as I was walking down that long corridor to security, I just… couldn't. So I turned and walked as far as the food court, then plopped down in an empty seat, staring into the void. Some woman must have thought I was homeless because she bought me a cup of coffee then sped away."

Pete turned to look out the window at something far in the distance, and every cell in my body wanted to reach across the space between us and hold him tight. But there was a raven-haired, violet-eyed girl waiting to hold him back at school, so I stayed silent and let him continue.

"When my parents died, I was ready to run before the hospital even released me. While I was lying there immobile on the bed, I convinced myself that the pain would disappear faster if my surroundings were foreign. Gigi spent weeks trying to talk me out of it. She didn't succeed."

"Well, that explains why she helped you plan your trip. If she couldn't stop you, at least she could know where you'd be."

Pete laughed wistfully. "Man, we went around and around over every single thing. I asked her how helping James run the homeless shelter could ever be a bad thing. I accused her of wanting to keep me childlike and imprisoned in that gigantic house. I even told her she was not my mother. But Gigi took it all in stride. She kept reminding me that even if I did manage to distract myself, I was just putting off the process. The road must be walked, blah, blah, blah."

"Wow. Has Gigi always been such a life guru?"

"I'm pretty sure she's just a country music fan who ripped off a bunch of lyrics." He paused, and the smile quickly evaporated from his face. "But Gigi's not here to stop me now, Sully. Yesterday morning all of the old arguments flooded back into my mind. It doesn't take much to make a difference in someone's life. James does it every day, all day long, and he has no time to think about his own drama. So I called the Logans from the café and asked them if they knew how long it takes to expedite a Chinese visa at the San Francisco consulate."

My mouth suddenly went dry. "You'd do that? Just walk away?"

"Until twenty minutes before our flight left, I was still making my pro-con list." He looked up at the buildings outside, then back at me. "We'll be back at school in maybe five minutes, Sully. And when we walk through those doors, everyone will sweep us back into our normal lives. Except it won't seem normal to us, because you and I aren't the same two people who left."

Pete reached across the space between us and wrapped his fingers around mine. "What I needed to tell you, Sully, is that *you* are the reason I got on the plane yesterday. You were there the night my parents died. You were there when Gigi died. I think you're the only person left who knows who I really am. The only person who can bridge both worlds with me. So keep an eye on me, okay? Make sure I stay anchored to my past, that I'm still the person my family loved. It's way too easy to lose what matters when you're distracted."

fifty-three

We share a well-known expression with the French: *Plus ça change, plus c'est la même chose*. The more things change, the more they stay the same. I'd really never understood that saying until Pete and I walked back into the Centre Lafayette that morning.

The courtyard and the *Grande Salle* still buzzed with life.

The coffee machine still delivered its magical elixir.

Monsieur Ludovic still breezed into history class in his uniform. And he still seemed like he should be wearing a cape.

Marshall still chomped on his chocolate.

Dan continued to hold his hand out for Anne every day at lunch. And every day, Anne accepted.

Harper and Kelly still made everyone laugh eighty times a day.

And, just like before, Pete Russell zoomed in and out of every class with nothing more than a brief nod my way or maybe, if I was lucky, a tiny smile.

Yeah. So much for being that so-called bridge between his two worlds. I was ninety-nine percent sure I'd imagined that whole conversation. After all, it would hardly be the first time my mind had played games with my heart.

Two weeks later, April arrived in Paris, and you know what? Turns out that cliché is actually true. The gray skies disappear, the sun comes out, and *l'amour* takes over. On the Métro, in the parks, at the sandwich shop – everywhere you go, someone's smooching somebody else. Every once in a while, people smooch somebody they don't know. Why? Oh, wait, sorry. The question is: why *not*?

Thanks so much, Paris. No really. *Merci beaucoup.*

Because France was on trimesters, our friends back home would end their school year about a month before we were to end ours. So despite the blue skies, the Centre Lafayette was quite the dismal place until Madame Beauchamp called a meeting one day in late April.

"*Mesdames et Messieurs,*" she said sternly, "need I remind you that with the privilege of extra-long school breaks and an abundance of public holidays comes the terrible burden of spending extra time in Paris while your friends at home are bored out of their minds in the suburbs? Poor you. Yes. Poor, pitiful you."

The entire group laughed, but we understood. Time to get over ourselves.

"As you know, on Thursday, May 8th, the French will celebrate Victory in Europe Day," she continued. "Therefore, it seems fitting that immediately following the dismissal of Monsieur Ludovic's history course next Wednesday, we will all board the high-speed train to Provence for the final Centre Lafayette cultural trip. Be prepared. We have a lot of ground to cover while we're there."

She wasn't kidding around. The first full day of our trip, we were all over Provence visiting Avignon, Nîmes, and Arles. Even though our brains had to jump from antiquity to the papacy to post-Impressionism all day long, no one seemed to care. Best of all, Meg Green had strep throat and had to stay in Paris, all alone.

I should have felt badly for Meg. I should have offered to take notes for her or at the very least, bring her a souvenir, because four whole days *sans* Mademoiselle Verte was the best news I'd had all year. My buddies and I were back in business, and everything felt quasi-normal again. By the time I fell into bed that first night, my cheek muscles actually ached from so many hours of grinning.

On Friday morning the tour bus headed to the Côte d'Azur, stopping first at a perfume factory in Grasse. After an hour learning about essential oils and fragrance notes, Madame Beauchamp paired us in teams and tasked us with making a scent for the other person. My partner was Pete. We'd been given a worksheet to help us pinpoint the correct scent combination for our teammate, but instead of following directions, Pete had created his own questionnaire for me.

"Okay, Sully. Which animal do you prefer: giraffe or cheetah?"

"What kind of a question is that?" I scowled as I began searching through our kit for the base oil. "Come on, Pete. Just stick to the real questions."

"But these *are* real questions. Madame Beauchamp's questionnaire didn't ask what I wanted to know. Don't you trust me to make you something nice?"

"Why would I trust you? I saw you grab the gardenia-scented oil when you heard me telling Anne it makes me gag."

"Fine." Pete slid the gardenia essence off to the side. "I'm still waiting, Red. What's your choice: giraffe or cheetah?"

"Giraffe," I scowled, pouring the base oil for Pete's scent into the tiny beaker.

"Interesting." Pete propped up his notebook so I couldn't see what was going on behind it, and squeezed a dropper into his beaker, contorting his face like a mad scientist. "Okay, next question: Portland, Oregon, or Portland, Maine?"

"How do you make such high grades when you never bother to follow the assignment? Dr. Sweeney would be so disappointed in Highgate's third most talented French major."

"The assignment is to make a scent that represents your partner," Pete corrected. "Madame Beauchamp won't care that I've ditched her questions when she finds out I've made the perfect *Eau de Sully*. Now, tell me. Which Portland?"

I pretended to think for a minute. "Portland, *Ireland*."

"There's no Portland in Ireland. Even I know that."

"There is. In County Tipperary, right in the middle of the island. I have pictures of my brother and me standing next to the sign on Facebook. I'll be happy to show you."

"Which leads me to my next question." Pete resumed the mad scientist face as he dropped another mysterious oil into the base. "Which social media platform do you visit least often?"

I dropped some sandalwood oil into the beaker, then shrugged. "That's easy enough. I couldn't tell you the last time I tweeted anything."

"I can. 7:43 this morning," Pete said without looking up. "At least I assume today was your turn to post a *vertisme*. But maybe it was Kelly. She's starting to pick up your phraseology."

I whipped my head around to find Dan, but he was too busy mooning over Anne to notice my glare. When I turned back to Pete, he was watching me, arms crossed, eyes dancing triumphantly.

"Oh, look who's nervous now?" He shook his head, chuckling to himself as he dropped some unknown fragrance into the base. "Don't be angry at our Danny Boy, Sully. He never would've told me about your secret project if I hadn't forced it out of him one night last month. He was laughing so hard that it woke me out of a dead sleep. I guess my storming into his room scared him, because Dan surrendered you and Kelly like his life depended on it."

"You've known for a month?" I felt my eyes widen. "Ugh. I'm really sorry, Pete. You know we were just messing around. Please don't tell Meg. It would hurt her feelings."

He removed the notebook from between us and proceeded to clean up his station. "No problem," he said without lifting his eyes. "We broke up."

"What? Hold on a minute. Are you serious?"

"Yeah. Actually, we broke up around Easter."

"But I see you guys together, like, *all the time*."

"Oh, come on, Sully. You know how it goes. Just because you're not together doesn't mean you stop talking." The lines around his eyes reappeared. "You do know how that goes, right?"

I did know.

The day after Drew and I broke up, he'd called to see if we could set our change-in-relationship status as invisible. When I asked him why, he said we had too long a history to owe the randoms of the world an explanation.

The next week during his spring break, Drew came over to our house in Lincoln City every day to visit my dad. Afterward, the two of us would walk along the beach until the sun went down, hashing through everything we'd never admitted to one another but still needed to say.

A couple of weeks after my return to Paris, Drew had called me to say the guys had unanimously elected him president of Sigma Phi Beta. Every single brother, including Pete Russell.

And to my complete shock, my heart swelled with pride.

The next week, he'd messaged to let me know he'd driven home for Easter, that my dad was well, and that not one single person in either of our families liked Ian's new girlfriend, Kate.

I didn't even know Ian had a Kate.

So he caught me up on what I'd missed, and just like that, Drew and I were friends again. The kind of friends who care about each other, no matter what.

Now we texted once a week, Thursday night his time, Friday morning in Paris. It was like Friday Morning Breakfast, Version 2.0. That had been our tradition for a lot of years, after all.

The fact that Drew wanted to honor it now meant more to me than he'd ever know.

So I smiled down at my beaker and shrugged at Pete's question. "I might know a little something about that. But Pete?" I looked up. "I'm really sorry I tweeted those things about Meg."

Pete watched me for a moment. "It's okay, Sully."

"No, it's not. Sometimes my mind fills up with too much energy and I don't always let it out the right way. I didn't think it would matter since only the Addison girls had access."

"And Dan." Pete raised an eyebrow. "Here's a little-known fact about Dan Thomas: he may be Highgate College's brightest French mind, but he is terrible at closing his browser windows. Also, his password is *AnneWilder*. Capital A, capital W, one word."

"Guess I'd better retract that CIA recommendation. So, um… you've read everything?"

"Everything." Pete leaned back in his chair, a smile tugging at the corners of his mouth. "You got pretty prolific there in the last month, Sully. If I didn't know better, I might think some of those Green-isms only existed in that wild imagination of yours."

My mind raced back through everything we'd written the past few weeks. Not much was libel-worthy, but every single tweet was vindictive.

Except Meg's ex(!!)-boyfriend seemed as relaxed and happy as I'd seen him in months. Even the dark shadows under his eyes were gone. Pete Russell seemed like himself again, and for that alone, I was deliriously grateful.

"Here you go." He slid the small perfume bottle my way. "I hope you like it. I think the name is especially fitting."

In Pete's distinctive architect-esque script, the label read: *Jalousie Verte*.

"Green Jealousy. Aren't you clever?" As I opened the bottle, the mismatched fumes of evergreens, gardenia, and tobacco made me cough violently. "Whoa. Is this going to explode?"

"You don't like it?" Laughter danced around Pete's eyes. "They say ladies prefer a light scent in this part of the world. Go ahead, Sully. Put some on."

"Aren't you sweet? But no. This is the sort of thing you save until the day after never."

"Pretend all you want, but we both know you'll be sporting it around by the end of the day. I bet the rest of your friends will be – wait for it – green with jealousy."

"The expression is green with *envy*. And this smells like feet."

"But really well-groomed, nicely pedicured feet, right? And now for *my* signature scent, please."

I finished writing on the label, then slid the bottle across the table. "Don't break it."

Pete opened the bottle, and after he lifted it tentatively to his nose, a surprised smile crept across his face. "Wow, Sully. This actually smells nice. What's in it?"

"Patchouli, pine, sandalwood, and leather. See what happens when you follow directions? Things work out the way they are supposed to. You should try it sometime."

"Maybe I will." He took another whiff from the bottle. "So, what did you name it? *Les Orteils Qui Scintillent*. Oh, I get it. You're fluent in *franglais* now, are you? Is that supposed to mean *Twinkle Toes*?"

"Look, not all of us have a clever nickname generator built into our brains. It was either that or Soul Patch, but who knows how to say 'patch' in French?"

"*Pièce, tache…* depends on what kind of 'patch' you mean, really. But I think in this case, they've got a word for 'soul patch.' *Une mouche.*"

I stuck my hand across the table. "Hand the bottle back. Come on, hand it over."

"Why?"

"We're renaming your scent *Dictionnaire*."

"Aw. Who says you don't have the nicknaming gift, Sully? A less creative person might have settled on a more boring choice, like *Celui Qui Sait Tout.*"

The One Who Knows It All. That wasn't a nickname – that was a fact. Well, except for knowing how to mix scents, because ewwwww, that perfume he'd created smelled like a poodle smoking unfiltered cigarettes in the garden wearing three-day-old socks.

fifty-four

I don't know if she sensed our need to be together, but that afternoon, when we pulled up to our hotel on the Côte d'Azur, Madame Beauchamp put Harper, Kelly, Anne and me together in the largest room. The windows stretched from floor to ceiling and opened onto a long balcony that overlooked the Mediterranean and Nice's famous *Promenade des Anglais*. It was a gorgeous afternoon when we arrived, and while the other girls made plans to find the Old Town market, the sea was calling to my Irish-Oregonian roots.

"Do you guys mind if I skip out on the market?" I asked after we had unpacked. "I think I need to go for a run."

"Who could blame you?" Harper opened the balcony doors to let in fresh air. "We should be back by seven. The guys said they'd meet us back here about that time."

"Oh. They're not going with you?"

Kelly pushed her sunglasses on top of her head, scowling. "They're going to an arcade up the street. We are in Nice, the jewel of the Azure Coast, and those nerds want to play video games. Not explore the town. Not check out the boardwalk. Video games, you guys. Remind me again why we keep them around?"

"Because they're adorkable. Well, one of them is," Anne grinned, then sighed dreamily. And with that, I left the hotel, crossed the street, and jogged left onto the *Promenade des Anglais*.

I always felt my sanest when I was breathing steadily in and out, and the saline coastal air somehow made me feel whole again. After weeks of being land-locked, I found comfort in the sound of the waves rising and falling nearby. I couldn't help it – I come from a long line of coastal-dwelling Irishmen. Even my name meant 'guardian of the sea.' I guess it was in my blood.

On my return, the sun was inching its way slowly down to the Med, the sky turning warm shades of orange and pink above the blue horizon. That's when I noticed Pete standing on the boardwalk, pacing back and forth. I slowed to a walk, wiping sweat from my face with my sleeve. I couldn't believe how beautiful he looked standing in the fading light. Or how un-beautiful my reflection looked in his aviator sunglasses.

"I thought you guys went to the arcade?" I said in between heaving breaths.

"Dan did. I came to find you."

I steadied myself against the low wall of the boardwalk. "But won't I see you in, like, half an hour or something?"

Pete brushed a rogue strand of hair out of my eyes and tucked it behind my ear. Then he cupped my sweaty face in his hand. "Yeah," he said, stepping closer. "But this morning, when I told you about

Meg, you looked so happy. So I figured you wouldn't mind if I finally did this."

Can you make up for nine months of lost time in one moment? It's hard to say, but when Pete kissed me, I wanted that moment to last forever, even if that meant spending eternity in a sweaty t-shirt. Each time Pete's lips brushed against mine, it felt like he was showing me his side of our story, with all the parts that I'd missed, like a love letter with no words.

"You mad?" Pete said, pulling me tight against him.

"No," I smiled. "But can you tell me what possessed you to pick right *now* to kiss me?"

Pete's chest bobbed up and down as he laughed against me, at first because of my irreverence, and then, it seemed, with relief. "Well, I'm sorry. Did you have a better time in mind?"

"Let's see." I pushed him playfully away, then took the sunglasses off his face and put them on so I didn't have to stare at my disgusting self one second longer. "Any day of the week at school. Later tonight after I don't smell like *Jalousie Verte*…"

"You make a valid point." Pete pushed his sunglasses up my nose with his index finger. "Thanks for the tip, Sully. Next time *Anne of Green Gables* makes me fall in love with her, I'll pick the swooniest moment I can to let her know."

"Very funny."

He slid his hand to my hip. "So, did you *really* not know until just now? Because I'm pretty sure I've been using my best material on you since the first time we met, and… whoa, why are you scowling at me like that?"

"Because you already kissed me. There's no reason to waste your time wooing me now."

"Did you just say *woo*?" Pete's eyes slid down to my lips. "That is disturbingly hot, Sully."

"Yes, well, you're the one who likes to make out with sweaty girls in disgusting t-shirts."

He looked at my shirt, then smiled. "This is going to be our thing from now on, isn't it? You're going to make fun of me for kissing your sweaty face, and I'm going to have to explain how it was actually romantic, because I. Just. Could. Not. Wait."

"Okay, this conversation has taken a turn for the weird." I tugged at his free hand. "Come on. Let's see how far this boardwalk goes."

As we walked along, fingers entwined, my little friends the stomach butterflies arrived back in droves. Pete confessed that he'd nearly kissed me three separate times: once at the Tuileries the night of *La Nuit Blanche*, which did not surprise me. Once on my birthday, which did. And finally, in his room after Gigi's wake, when the two of us had been sitting so close that I could actually still smell his scent on me hours later up in my own bedroom in Lincoln City.

When we'd strolled half a mile, Pete pulled me in front of him at the railing, both of us facing out to sea. He slid his hands around my waist and bent his face forward so that our cheeks touched as we watched the waves rolling in and out along the shore.

"So, I have to ask," he finally said, pulling me closer. "Are you sure you're over Sutton? Because I heard a rumor that you guys still talk a couple of times a week."

"That's not a rumor," I said quietly. "But it doesn't mean what you're thinking. Besides, don't you talk to Meg?"

"That's different. There was nothing serious going on with us."

"Um, really? Because I saw you making out in Tours, and... "

"Once," he corrected. "You saw us kissing once."

I shifted around to face him. "But Dan said she was always at your house. That he couldn't get away from her."

Pete tilted his head back and laughed so hard his cheeks turned pink. "That was Dan giving you a taste of your own medicine, Little Miss Busybody. After he realized how well your slight embellishments on the truth worked with Anne, he decided to run his own experiment on you. Without my permission, I'd like to add for the record."

"So you and Meg weren't…"

"We hung out, yes." He rubbed his hand along the back of his neck. "Meg's a flirt, I'm a flirt. I ran into her and her friends on the train to Lucerne that weekend after *La Nuit Blanche*, and to my surprise, we got along well. But we both knew it wasn't going anywhere. Meg's still on-and-off with her high school boyfriend, and I'm pretty sure she knew how I felt about you. Which is why I keep asking about Sutton. Come on, be honest with me, Sully. You don't just get over someone you've loved that long in a couple of weeks."

I couldn't help but smile. "You're pretty cute with your heart on your sleeve, did you know that?"

"Am I?" He grinned. "What took you so long to notice?"

"Look, in my defense, you had that whole Portuguese Water Dog thing going on the first two years I knew you. How was I supposed to know there was a person under there?"

"I'm not sure you're in any position to pass judgment right now." He tugged at my ponytail, then paused. "How come you keep avoiding my question, Sully?"

I looked Pete squarely in the eye. "Because you already know the answer. I've got two syllables for you, sir. *Ver-tismes*. You read my tweets. Only one thing provokes that level of insanity."

Pete smiled. "Too much coffee?"

"Try again."

Pete looked up at the sky and scratched his invisible beard. "I mean, this is just a theory, but you think I'm hot?"

"Don't be smug," I said, shoving him gently in the stomach. "The fact is, you gave me Paris. I figure the least I can do is let you take me out to dinner a couple of nights a week. Just don't make me wear that poodle perfume. I might vomit."

Pete's eyes went soft as he brushed my cheek with his thumb. "Sully, you've broken my heart every day for the past three years, under every condition possible. So go ahead. Insult me all you want. My heart will always be yours."

Major swoon, *avec* sigh.

fifty-five

What college student dreads the end of school? This one. On the first Friday in June, we took a three-hour exam in the morning, then spent most of the afternoon in the courtyard of the Centre Lafayette. All of our fellow students and most of the staff were there. Even Meg, who brought her new French boyfriend. Turns out strep throat was actually good for Meg's health, because while we were in the south of France, she became better acquainted with her friend Corinne's older brother, the *très beau* Thierry.

After the official end-of-school party, our little group of six had an early dinner *chez* Marie-France for the last time. She busted out the best champagne from the wine cellar. And we finally got to meet her Venetian Scotsman – the very ginger, very gorgeous, very *ten years her junior* Angus Fitzgibbons.

Later that night, we walked together as far as the Pont des Arts, where the six of us lined up, arms around waists, and watched the sun setting over the Seine. I tried to memorize every second, but that pesky melancholy that had been chasing me down all week kept spoiling the moment. Who knew if we would ever be together like this again, here, in this place? I couldn't see how we would. And even if we all managed to return again, it could never be the same. We would eventually move on with our lives, always sharing these memories, but we'd never recapture this moment, when we were happy together and in love with Paris.

When the sun finally set in the distance, Harper and Kelly headed home and Dan asked Anne to take a walk by the river.

And then there were two, standing on the exact spot where Gigi and Pops had gotten engaged fifty years earlier.

Pete slipped his jacket around me, guiding my arms into the sleeves. I loved wearing Pete's jacket. It smelled like him. And tonight I had to laugh because it smelled of the scent I'd made him at the perfume factory.

"Nice cologne, Russell," I said, snuggling against his chest.

"Thanks. Some chick made it. I think she has a thing for me."

"She just might." I *so* did.

Tonight, Pete was wearing the same shirt he'd worn the night of *La Nuit Blanche*, and I began to wonder if he'd done it on purpose. His grandmother had been right. Pete was one of the most sentimental people I'd ever known. It was probably what I loved most about him.

"Hey, Sully," he said, resting his chin on my shoulder. "Do me a favor and check the right pocket of my jacket. I think there's something in there for you."

"What? But I didn't get you anything!"

Pete sighed, and slid his hand into the pocket at my waist. "Always so concerned with the rules." He handed me a small velvet pouch. "Now stop complaining and be careful opening this, because as you can see, there are rickety slats in this bridge and they might crumble out from underneath you if you let something so important slip through your fingers."

"Not even a month in and you're mocking my metaphors." I slid my fingers carefully inside the tiny pouch to find a tiny antique silver charm. I couldn't tell how old it was, but it looked to be at least half a century old. Engraved in really small letters was the French phrase *je t'aime plus qu'hier, moins que demain* – I love you more than yesterday, less than tomorrow.

"Pops gave it to my grandmother when they were in school here. Gigi saw your charm bracelet when you came to the house to visit her. That evening, she asked me to get her jewelry box. When she took out this charm, she told me to give it to you. I tried to explain to her that you were in love with someone else, but Gigi said, "Peter, don't be a fool. Take it back with you to Paris. You never know what might happen. Besides, I've got a good feeling about that Meredith Sullivan. She sees the real you.""

"But, Pete, what if something happens? It belonged to Gigi. You should keep it."

Pete pushed the charm back into the pouch, closed my hands around it, then closed his hand around mine. "Nothing's going to happen. If Gigi said to give it to you, it's yours."

I dropped the pouch back into his pocket, then kissed Pete like this was our last chance. Every time we kissed, I still felt a little sad at all the months we'd wasted orbiting around one another when we were both feeling the same thing – heartbroken in love.

When Pete pulled away, he took my hands in his. "So, listen. I did something this week that I'm not sure you're going to like."

"You signed up for Irish step dancing classes?"

"You're not too far off there. You know how you keep saying you're nervous to meet Kate?"

For two years since our Nana died, my parents had been leasing her house to some vacation property rental company. But after my dad's surgery, Ian had convinced them that we should put it up for sale, so I was meeting him tomorrow in Ireland to do what I could to help. But much to my chagrin, Ian had also invited the mysterious Kate Maher – his new girlfriend. The one Drew claimed no one liked.

I shivered. "Did you hire a private investigator or something?"

"No," he smiled. "I called your brother to find out which flight you're taking to Shannon tomorrow. I'm coming with you to Ireland."

"Wait, what? Are you serious?"

"Yeah. I don't have to be home for a while – Gigi had all her legal stuff so organized that I don't have much to do anyway. And I don't know about you, but I don't feel like pining over you for a whole month when we've both been pining all year already."

I couldn't help myself. I hugged Pete so long that I was sure he might push me away. I knew if I said anything else, I would start crying, and there had already been too many tears this year.

"Okay, I'm a little relieved," he said quietly into my ear. "Because your mom also called and invited me to stay in Ian's old room for the rest of the summer when we get back to Oregon. They need extra help at the restaurant since your dad's on leave, so..."

Little did Pete know that ever since he'd helped me get home, my family loved him more than they loved me. And they didn't even know anything yet about the scholarship or his parents' accident. This time, I did cry. But only until Pete kissed me again.

"I guess that's another yes," he said, pulling away. "Let's see if the third time's the charm."

It always came back to three, didn't it?

Pete reached into his jeans pocket, then looked back up at me. "Before you overreact, this is not my lavaliere."

I lifted an eyebrow. Had he heard what happened with Drew last fall? Surely not.

"Here." He took my hand in his, then turned it over, palm facing up. I looked down to find a small, old-fashioned silver key no bigger than a paper clip. "Can you guess what it is?"

"Um... a metronome?"

Pete grabbed it back. "Play nice, Sully."

"Okay, it's a key, but what's it for? Please say a zeppelin. Or wait... a Zamboni?"

"Ah. So close." Pete produced a padlock from behind his back. It was larger than normal, smooth and flat, and as he handed it to me, I saw that it had two sets of initials and two dates written on it. When I looked more closely, I realized they must be his grandparents' initials and the date of their wedding around fifty years ago. And below it, also written in Pete's distinctive script, were two more sets of initials, with a date twenty-eight years ago.

His parents' anniversary.

When I looked back up, he held a Sharpie in his left hand. "I brought this padlock with me when we flew back in March. I found it at Gigi's house, in Pops's toolbox."

"But Pete, we're not allowed to..."

"Slow down, Sully. I know it's against the rules. But I'm pretty sure we've seen at least one way to sidestep the City of Paris's ordinance. Remember?"

"You mean that couple on *La Nuit Blanche*? The ones who threw the lock in the river, then kept the key for themselves? I can't believe you remember that."

"Of course I remember." Pete handed me the Sharpie. "Look, no matter what, I'm dropping this padlock in the river tonight for Gigi and Pops, and for my parents. But I was hoping we could add our names here as well. You know, to make you-plus-me official."

Pete watched me expectantly, but there was no question in my mind. I opened the pen cap and wrote *PBR + MFS, June 5th (but really a long, long, LONG time before that)*. Good thing he'd brought the fine point pen. I handed the padlock back to Pete for inspection, and he smiled so brightly that I forgot for a moment how to breathe.

After a moment, he took out the tiny old key again and handed it to me. "For safekeeping," he whispered, then kissed me for what felt like hours.

When the river below us seemed momentarily traffic-free, Pete turned me toward the Eiffel Tower, and the two of us leaned quickly over the edge and dropped the padlock to the bottom of the Seine. Then he took my hand and led me back across the bridge, then down the higgledy-piggledy streets back to my tiny *chambre de bonne* for the last time.

Well, the last time for a while anyway. I have a good feeling about this Pete Russell. He sees the real me.

acknowledgements

If the world of *The Bridge* were real, Meredith and her friends would have been born the year I lived in Paris – the same year I got the idea for this book. My original drafts read more like a memoir, but in sketching real life onto the page, I learned that my stories weren't mine alone to share.

So instead, I wrote about an Irish-American girl from a coastal town in Oregon who falls in love with Paris, with her dearest friend, and with someone who changes her life. And while I populated Meredith's story with a few scenes from my own, this novel is not an autobiography. It's my love letter to Paris, to my friends, and to a moment that forever transformed who I would become.

So thank you for reading *The Bridge*. The following people helped me put it into your hands.

First and always, I thank my Heavenly Father, Author of Life, for blessing me with the gifts of language and stories, but more importantly, with the gift of your Son's Love. *Sola gratia.*

To my parents, Richard and Mary Jane, who are living examples of what true love really means: thank you for walking this road with me, for reading every draft, for your constant encouragement, for refusing to let me quit, and for flanking me at every turn. There's no way this story could exist without your big-picture vision or the adventures we've had since you let teenage Jill take French (despite rumors that it's impractical). *I love you guys*. We had fun, didn't we?

To my Beckett/Cox/McWhinney aunts, uncles, and cousins: I love you all so much. Thank you for being my clan. (But listen, y'all, let's never talk about those kissing scenes. Like, ever.)

To Jennifer Allen, Ashley Alvarado, Angela Azevedo, Hannah Beckwith, Lori Bennett, Nancy Bennett, Tracy Bickhaus, Avery Burns, Tiffany Byrd, Katy Byrne, Stephanie Carrington, Don and Sandra Clark, Susan Cordre, Krissi Dallas, Erin Daniel, Brooke DeVore, Lauren DeVore, Megan Grace DeVore, Amy Gilman, Annette Gunter, Faith Hampton, Holly Hatton, Mary Hinson, Andi Hooker, John Huston, Martha Jordan, Amy Kitchen, Lauren Knight, Alexa Kuffel, Erin McCullough, Hannah McGinnis, Jimmy McWhinney, Haley Moore, Meredith Moore, Lynley Nall, Kerrie O'Mara, Stephanie Osborne, Becca Polk, Amanda Porter, Cindy Prudich, Dusty Rabe, Heather Reid, Eddie Renz, Rina Reynolds, Kelsea Riddick, Robin Roach, Angela Senor, Amanda Sileven, Ashley Stiernagle, Kirston Stroder, Dianah Thelen, Tarran Turner, Stacy Wells, Edna and Johnny Westmoreland, Sheri Pettit White, Meg Wilder, and Adrienne White (with her trusty pink pen!) – THANK YOU for weighing in on every page with your helpful notes in the margins and encouraging doodles. You guys are my favorites.

Huge thanks to Eddie Renz at Chemist Creative for the beautiful cover design and for my website. Shout out to Mike and ReJana Krause at BluDoor Studios (and to Macie, light-catcher extraordinaire!) for the gorgeous headshots. A gigantic *merci* to my girl Miah Oren for your generous help with all things left-brained, and to my favorite whippersnapper, Miranda Mabery, for designing my social media campaign and promotional materials. Squishy hugs to Tarran Turner for the Tower 19 Press logo and to Peggy Smolen for your insight and positivity. And a fist bump over the sea to my favorite Parisian, Florian Bartsch, for encouraging my work *always*.

Heartfelt gratitude to Ella Kennen for giving Meredith's story a clearer direction and a stronger backbone. To Sharon Duncan: it means the world to me that you would share your time and expertise to edit this story. Thank you for your wisdom, your encouragement, and for all the creative ways you've shaped Meredith's tale. I could never repay the million things you've done over the years to make this book possible. But most of all, I feel lucky to have such a friend.

The Texas bookish community is unabashedly supportive. Julie Murphy, thank you for introducing a random Twitter follower (me) to the crew. Shout out to Heather Acker, Misty Baker, Jess Capelle, China DeSpain, Caron Ervin, Rebekah Faubion, Amy Gideon, Amy Gilman, Heather Goodwin, Mary Hinson, Karen Jensen, Jenny Martin, Meredith Moore, Kayla Olson, Kristin Trevino, and Becky Wallace. Y'all are the best encouragers ever! Special thanks from the bottom of my heart to Britney Cossey, Destiny Cole, Krissi Dallas, Kari Olson, Heather Reid, Gabi Sikes, and Stacy Wells for the late-night check-ins, writing dates, and rock star support you've always given me. I'm pretty sure the pages of this book are laced with your laughter, love, several pounds of cheese fries, and *lots* of extra napkins (because laptops + coffee = frenemies).

Somewhere between the first draft and this one, I went from high school French teacher to cubicle warrior, and I owe everyone in both of those worlds a tremendous debt of gratitude. I'm sorry there's not enough space here to list all of you! To my teacher friends and former students: I miss you all every single day. Thank you for cheering me forward, always. To Matt: thank you for seeing left-brained potential in a mightily right-brained person and for adding me to your team. To my corporate colleagues: I never expected to find such kind souls in a world of spreadsheets and fiscal acronyms. You have no idea the difference your quiet encouragement has made in my life.

To the educators who influenced this story in a million ways only I can see – Norma Browning, Marie-Madeleine Charlier, Sharon Cooper, Maurice Elton, Monsieur Gutman, Catherine Healey, Judy Kencke, Jan Marston, Donna McBride, Margie McCabe, Yvonne McDonald, Nancy O'Connor, Kay Pfaltz, Isabelle Roynier, Charles Sala, and Monsieur Senninger – *merci mille fois* for pouring your souls into mine.

I dedicate Meredith & Pete's love of Big Band to the late Leon Breeden and Peanuts Hucko and to Louise Tobin Hucko and Jim Riggs. May we carry on your legacy.

To the people of Lincoln City, Oregon and the staff at the Ester Lee: for me, you are the supporting cast of Meredith's world. Thanks for your hospitality while I wrote the first draft.

To my cousin, Jimmy McWhinney: you will never know how much your consistent, intentional check-ins have spurred me forward. Thank you for saying what I need to hear without reproach. I'm so proud of who you are. Sorry I bossed you around when we were little.

To Susan Cordre: I may be an only child, but you are my sister in every way that counts. Thank you not only for listening but for *hearing* me. You slogged through my wonkiest draft and still insisted I write a sequel. Bless you for making me laugh, and for always being my bulldog cheerleader.

And finally – to Kelly Barnes, Meg Frost, Maury Hebert, Robin Hutson, Catherine Jones, Nathalie Lonsdale, Nikki Lowrey, Kerrie O'Mara, Julie Pham, and also to Jack Aalborg, April Beauboeuf, Emily Bentzen, Bruce Ford, Andrew Gillies, Heather Hartley, Todd Howard, Meredith Hubble, Greg Leidner, Tomàs Martin, Karen Prezioso Marx, Jenn Merritt, Amy O'Neil, Josh Saunders, Matthew Chandler Slack, Jennifer Spaulding, Raymond Truong and Katie Wood: I could have written this book a hundred thousand different ways, and it would *never* have captured our time accurately. So I left in the magical coffee machine, but deliberately left out so much more.

No doubt you are the only people in the world who understand why those days across the Atlantic changed all the days afterward.

In the Paris of my mind, you are always there, eating lunch with me in the Jardin de Luxembourg, walking uphill both ways in the snow during the month-long Métro strike, or sitting beside me on the middle bench of the Pont des Arts, watching the sun set over the Seine.

You, *chers amis,* are <u>my</u> bridge.

about the author

Jill Cox pursued a Bachelor's and then a Master's degree in French Language and Literature so she could study abroad in Paris (twice), then taught high school French so she could convince others to join in the fun. A native Texan, Jill spends her days drinking more coffee than necessary and her free time writing stories about the people and places she loves best. Read more at jillcoxbooks.com, or follow Jill on social media @jillcoxbooks.

Made in the USA
Lexington, KY
27 March 2017